STRUTTIN' HOME

autobiography of a blues singin' stray cat

I0552946

Lisa Annette Powell

ISBN: 978-0-9906428-9-3

Cover photo by Jennifer Sanders of her kitty, Hannah, (retouched) struttin' in for Strut; graphics by Brian Busse

Dedicated to friends

Frede, a true Renaissance lady. Musician and music lover, avid book reader, animal lover, and an inspiration to all.

I greatly miss your cheerleading, "When is your next story coming out?" and "What is it about?"

Matt, fun-loving, creative, eager to learn, innovative and a super vocalist. Strut would love to duet with you.

The talented musicians I was privileged to jam with: Danny Paul, Don Bussel, and Mr. K.

The heavenly band is angelically enhanced by all your presence!

But we miss you here.

Frede and her horse, Destiny

Engineer Matt working his farm with his dog, Henry

Other stories by author:

CatSkill Trilogy consisting of: CATSKILL, First of CatSkill Trilogy- recipient of Certificate of Excellence

CATSKILL'S LIONESS

CATSKILLS TANGO

ROAD TO FEARLESS- Winner of World's Best Cat Litterary Award

IOU A HORSE

SOUL SEARCH

CATCH

To all music lovers- please refer to the eclectic list of songs (located at the end of the story) the well-traveled Strut hints at one way or another.

Oops, there's another one!

For those needing a challenge, try and list the songs as you read the chapters.

Interested in learning more of certain characters portrayed in the story? Please check out the CATSKILL Trilogy and CATCH.

When you reach a place where everything 'feels' right, you are home!

1

"Shaaadd up, cat!" A nasal twang fit to make my tail kink inside out singes the airwaves. It dares to call itself a singer? Insensitive-to-ears-head-case is wringin' my last nerve. B.B. save me!

"*rrrraaaaaaaaRRRRRRR,*" I yowl a long, sweet cool-daddy note just to up the ante. Ain't nobody spittin' bars better than this here cat. 'S how it rolls. Anything the chick thinks she can sing I know I can sing better. My voice is tight- no imperfections- if I do say so myself.

"Get your song list ready. New lead guitar's coming tonight." This news flash broadcasts from drummer boy, sittin', smokin' out the side of his mouth, and twirlin' one drumstick at a time- not the edible kind. Unfortunate for my achin' guts.

Nose mutters a few choice words I recognize. Most begin with 'f'.

"Another one? How many this month?" The bass guitar twig snorts. Between belchin' and hackin' and snortin' he's one bone shy of a noisy, messed-up skeleton. Got hair to match, what's left of it. Strings-are-us, but hey, he never complains 'bout me pimpin' the goods.

And when twig hits those movin' bass riffs you hear only the phat notes. Provided the nose shuts up. Bass and drummer can lay out a beat that near broke the collar and is off the chain. Why nose ain't gone is beyond my smarts.

Drummer is a homeboy- it's his crib, see. The physical opposite of the bass player he's one heavy-duty, but cool. Don't mind me hangin' out on his window groupie-shelf durin' their practice sessions- such as they are.

Quick rap rap on the door. I hear you knockin' flits through my head. "Rowoooorowww!" On the low-down I offer a fittin' bar of welcome notes.

"Pizza delivery," drills back.

"Must be the lead guitar," bass man shivers a gigglin' fit.

Drummer throws back his fat hairy head and crows. Must be an inside joke is all I can figure. The chick don't seem to get the punch line either, but on that score, I'm not surprised. A pint shy of a forty describes her lack of gray matter.

Nose snakes to the door, shakin' dat thang, on too-tall shoes, careful of the mic cords, monitor cords, mixer cords, instrument cables. Opens the door with a 'what am I, the maid?' roll of the eyes.

Johnny B Good light me up- if it ain't a reg'lar homeboy! My puss is plastered in the open window- diggin' what's makin' the scene.

Lookin' rather spry with cool chimin' hair I've never seen the likes of before (little balls swing on his locks as he walks), clean clothes- no patches, odoriferous flat box in one hand, guitar in the other. A long carton hangs from his shoulder and strapped to his substantial, but not fat, back is a thick box I detect is an amp.

"Hey, Rom, got a light?" Bass spits out, snickers like he's the only joker in town.

Bang-'em boy's mouth releases a smoke stick which hits the floor, guffaws- he's one happy chimney- twirls both drumsticks and hits the high hat.

I unnerstan' the jist of a body within seconds- a nat'ral lifesavin' inclination I developed early on. Dis here tomcat got skills. Ya wanna live? Best learn from the first step, one step at a time and don't stop, says this here king of the road.

I dig this homeboy ain't a player to mess wit- no Cathy's clown here. An overall sense of 'treat me fair and we'll get along' is proper evident. Pity the fool who crosses this'n. One straight-up G recognizes another- that ol' black magic edge.

Potential new homey scans the surround. Flashy drum set, multiple amps, monitors, a mic stand the nose sucks up to like it's her last supper. When she lets loose on it my hair stands up like a shock of weeds- electrified to hell and gone.

I abandon my shelf when she thinks she's hittin' the right high notes. Janis Joplin'd tear her hair out and Aretha'd run for the hills. Save me, Ella!

Rest of the room is carpet-full of smoke stick burn holes, crazy walls made of egg cartons, and my window- open to freshen the smoke-fogged air.

I watch him casin' the joint. Until he gigs my way.

"Rrrrrowwwww," I trill by way of 'whass up?'

He's got my fly vote, and whatever's cruisin' in that flat box smells worth investigatin'. A helluva lot better scented than the stinkin' garbage cast-offs I'm usually stuck with, or the rare mouse sportin' more than bones. This mornin' I took down a bird hunkerin' on a French fry- more feathers than meat. French fry wasn't too bad, but I'm grubbin' 24/7. Always hungry- jonesin' for groceries. Smart cat don't let no opportunity pass him by.

Homeboy's luggage slips from hand, shoulder, back. He trips my way with the aroma box that grips my guts.

"This the lead singer?"

Damn straight! I'm dead to rights 'bout this brotha!

Nose rattles off her snide limited vocab. Glad she didn't wibble-warble right off and send him packin'. This is one acquaintance I'm of a mind to acquaint.

10

He grins. Brotha knows what's up in dis here crib.

"Whose cat?" I let him give me the once over- with eyes, no touch. The limit of my 'I can be polite'.

"Some stray. Hangs around on Mondays and Thursdays—
"

"Gets in the way of my vocaaals," nose smites the air and is ignored by all.

"Can't seem to drive it away. Guess it's got a thing for live music," drummer hitches a roll-of-fat shoulder.

Yeah, I got a thing alright- cravin' a phat tune. Ain't heard a record-worthy song yet, but hey, a cat can hope. I figure to give my new homeboy a taste of my fave blues expertise later. Right now, my stomach thinks my mouth went out for smokes.

"Hey, Cool Cat, music lover, huh?"

"Rrrrr," I rumble as he lifts the window higher.

"Don't let that aaanimal in heeere," nose whines.

"I let him hang 'round, toss him a little something now and again, figure he'll keep vermin away," hefty shrugs both chunky shoulders into a non-existent neck. He is so full of sh...poop- exaggeratin' his propensity to provide me with anythin' resemblin' somethin' worth eatin'. Drummer boy don't let no leftovers be- means nuthin' left for me.

"It's worse than *** vermiiiin," potty-mouth nasally pouts and sticks out her tongue at me. What am I, two years old?

Hacker hawks, spits a human hairball into a cup, swigs his beer, tunes his bass. I know when the tuning is proper- I've perfect pitch. Just ask me.

"Ya gonna talk to the cat or play music?"

"I have to finish my supper. Show me the song list while I eat," homey addresses the room, and to me, "Join me, Cool Cat?"

My shocked eyes swell in sweet emotion and I chirrup like a baby, "rrrrrrrrrrrrrrr."

"This here," he fingers the box with its mouth-tantalizing scent burstin' out and he piles an ample servin' on my ledge, "is the best pepperoni pizza in town. Let me know what you think, okay?"

"Here's my list of soooongs," nose's shufflin' as…butt cuts in. I'd hiss, 'cept I'm too busy dyin' and goin' to rock-n-roll heaven with angel food blessin' my tastebuds.

"Good, huh?" My favorite homeboy winks at me. He taps a long, calloused finger on a piece of paper nose presents to him. "What key do you do these in?"

Nose tosses her hair with a blank look, then huffs, "The usual."

Bass man snorts, "She gets close to key of G for most of the lot."

My homey winks at me again, balances his dinner box on his half of the ledge and indulges in a primo pizza slice of his own.

Now I don't claim to be no saint. My paw scoots out and cadges claws full of…

"All you had to do was ask," he kindly smiles at me, unsticking my stickers from the goods by pullin' back on the pizza, stretchin' the melty goods. "Tell you what, Cool Cat, I'll split the rest with you." He rolls his share up and devours it like a smoke stick without smoke, wipes his lips and readies his gear. Waits for the count while I devour slices of cat nirvana. But I keep an eye on the latest performer, claws crossed.

Can't believe my gustatorial luck wit the grub. Hope to the Blues Brothers he stays and can make his guitar strut its thang like SRV. Like no tomorrow, I'm diggin' in, continue to savor my extravagant windfall. 'Cept when I'm protectin' my hearin' from the nose.

Finally, she shuts up her honker and gives my homey the chance to rip it up on the rhythm laid down by bass and drums. Sweet sounds of my youngest days! Brotha got it goin' on- makin' dat ol' scarred axe wail dem me and the devil blues! Ol' school!

Pizza forgotten, I sit up, wait for my chance. There! Got my mojo workin'! I belt out how the damned 12-bar blues was written to be sung. I harmonize with his licks, chill when he softens quiet and low, and lay on the "*ROWWWWWWWWRRRR*" when he pours it on.

Maaaaaan, Bro gets into the tunes! He's away in blues dreamland, head thrown back, eyes closed, lips pursed, chimin' hair hangin' down behind as his fingers love all over dem strings. Seems like da fret board ain't long enough for dem big ol' fingers to catwalk on. But I can hang- no contest.

When he returns to the here and now, he applauds my skill with the warmest eyes and smile- homey 'preciates real talent! Pretty soon it's just me and my homeboy, call and response. Cuttin' heads. Bass and drummer set it out and savor. Amp volume's loud enough nose stomps off to another room wit yuck plastered on her face.

His fingers flash down the neck, bendin' strings, tappin' fit to create soft echoes, hushes, and he nods to me. I can dig dis game!

But nose returns and spoils it- the never was, let alone wannabe. "Heyyyy you, I got more verrrrses!" What a screech!

My homeboy is too off-the-charts genteel. He discontinues the lead, quiets the rhythm, and nose twangs/destroys what she dares call 'verrrrses'.

"You're off key," he gently critiques, 'stead of really tellin' it like it is- which is what I been doin' since I come up in dis here joint.

Bass man gurgles. Bang 'em finds an invisible bug to peer at far from the direction of nose.

"You thiiink you can commmme in heeerrra and make fun of meeee?"

What a monstrous puss! Oops, bad taste to use puss. B word more appropriate.

"Tell hiiiimmm to hit the rooooad," nose pouts.

Drummer and bass exchange bets on who's gonna call the shots.

"RRRRRRRRAAAERRRR," I give 'em the 411 on how to take care of bidness.

Nose stomps her foot, nearly falls off her high heels. Nobody's beggin' her to stay and nobody's gonna give her one reason to stay here. Bless my homey!

"Well, I neeeeverrr," she wobbles to the door and slams it hard enough to thrum the drums as she exits.

"That's for sure," bass snorts. "Chick's a brick wall short of a brick house."

I figure this relates to smarts, but I don't pretend to comprehend everythin' I hear.

"Damn fine guitar playing. Can you sing?"

"Some, but I won't last all night," my homey sips at a jug of- can you dig it?- water!

14

"Give us one of your songs," bang-'em puffs on a smoke, idly taps both drumsticks.

"Pride and Joy?"

"Stevie Ray, cool!" Glowin' smoke stick hits the carpet and drummer taps one, two, three, four.

And for the third time tonight, I'm rollin' phat! It started with groceries to die for, courtesy of a true blues man, and now I get to flaunt my pipes again.

My homey ain't like some players that believe they're the only stars shinin' and consequently hog all the spotlight. Once he's gone through a round of singin' and lead, his chin gives me the 'get ready' signal. The volume descends and I...I'm in the band!

"*ARRRRowwwwrRRRRR!*"

Lucked 'cross one phat thang. But I'm gettin' ahead of myself.

2

Gotta smooth my thoughts to the beginnin' of my blues hit parade. Arch my back, give the ol' stickers a proper sharpenin', curl up and...here goes.

I was born under a bad sign. No shi... My bad. CatSkill (more on the coolest cat of all time further on up the road of my autobio, unless you already read *CATCH* or *CATSKILL*) is a shaman with superb cat skills and at an opportune moment he put this advice to me:

'You might try recounting your own travails- think of it as your blues diary. Be cathartic—'

'Cath what?' I mind-speak to his voice inside my head. A totally private confab with THE Head Cat, pretty sweet, huh?

'Balance, my friend. Think bridge over troubled waters,' he tilts his head with a peaceful gleam in his powerful eyes.

'Gotcha! Jose liked that tune after a big meal,' I recall.

'Digestive material, eh?'

'I've had a helluva ride—'

His scan pierces me- a sourpuss quirk tweaks a corner of his mouth. 'Learning and using a new language is a brain kicker.'

I amend my hood talk, 'I've had an eventful life.'

Fair easy to indulge in proper English skills after listenin' nightly to all Sky's stories. Oops- you'll get to know her, too. Soon.

'Tell it like it is,' CatSkill croons fit to stir one's heart. Cat can sing!

'You do know your tunes- soundin' tight, m'man!'

'We'll certainly jam on the flipside,' he chuffs/chants, and that's what got me started on this blues diary bidness.

When I was a little bitty baby, only thing rockin' was over my head- but not for long.

See, I was born under Bad Sign. Name of the ramshackle juke joint leanin' in the wind atop mother's choice of delivery room.

The sign itself was so off kilter, hangin' on hope, you expected it to hit some unsuspectin' head any moment on its way down. Anybody with a lick of sense gave it a wide berth upon enterin' the hallowed premises.

Paint chips dust in the wind. A new set of threads (paint job) must've escaped the budget. Holes aplenty in all the timber walls. Scatter-brain lights barely cast shadows- when they condescended to work at all. But the entire place existed, and must've been held upright, by the good vibrations inside. Tunes so far off the hook- I'm talkin' outta sight!

In the dirt under the mis-matched planks lyin' in for a floor, me and my two brothers were born to be wild. Lanky, scarred Moms chose a fairly dry spot in a corner to drop us.

She nourished us all she could, but one bro didn't make it. I watched her totin' his tiny body off one night when she went huntin'. Nobody explained the facts of that's life and death to me- learned 'em on my own.

We hunkered in together when stinky drip drops rained down from our noisy, buckin' roof. Ooooee, the smells we endured- mis-placed pi...urine, smoke sticks a'huffin', hawkin' spit, old and new sweat- humans don't see clean like us cats- and some other stink on the ladies and gents. Learned to get out of the way wit da quickness when any liquid drizzled down.

At first the stuff fallin' begged my curiosity- soons as I was big enough to explore the outskirts of our makin'-do den. M'Moms quickly caught me out and rolled my ass as I licked up a very strange, pungent fluid drainin' from a toppled bottle above. Boom, boom- my lights nearly went out between the as...butt whoopin' and the weirdness punchin' my tongue!

Shakin' my head tryin' to rinse out my mouth while she went off like Mike Tyson and the preacher man all in one. Screechin' and battin'. Sumpin' about rottin' the guts of humans. O-o-h child, she hustled me away with my head spinnin', my ears burnin', and my tongue tryin' to figure the taste out- like it or not.

As she hustled me back to our side of the crib hood, Moms happened to spy a wannabe rat lookin' for love in all the wrong places- dinner on a dirt plank! Appeasement in lieu of rotgut. But her snarl of 'don't do it again', is permanently engraved in my brain. I'm minded of her much later learnin' more of whiskey and beer blues.

The hood, or poor side of town, gen'rally ain't kind to the hungry of any species- ain't speakin' solely 'bout grub. Somethin' is always poppin' off. Rackets r us. But over the reg'lar clamor of hood scroungin', where Bad Sign was happenin', came the finest sounds imaginable.

Blues. Old blues makers like Jimmy Reed, Robert Johnson, Muddy Waters, Blind Lemon Jefferson and more. Sweet guitar Lucille when B.B. King played the lady- layin' out his heart and soul. Songs that could never die.

And the divas steppin' up to pipe the standards of the blues ladies Etta James, Ella, Aretha, Bessie Smith and more. And the wannabees who probably would have been just as famous if given

18

a shot at fortune. Man, I heard women "*rrrowwwll*" fit to make your skin jump, jive and wail.

Lots of names. Lots of phat tunes bandied over our heads. Puttin' up wid hardship come easier with heaven singin' every night.

Me, I was hooked from early on. I like to say I'm birth-of-the-blues-born. I inherited, memorized those sounds and made 'em mine. Practiced adjustin' my voice to fit in and be heard. Pitch, correct key, scattin', vibrato- you name it, I'm game.

"RRRRrrrrr," I explored octaves. Ain't no singer got stronger vocal apparatus than mine, I betcha! Trainin' from the get-go.

Hood equals blues. Shattered bottles, bad tastes, thick foggy air fit to make you hack, out and out fights, blood. If trouble stumbled into Bad Sign though, old gent tendin' bar hollered, "TAKE IT OUTSIDE," and the blues-lovers backed him up- escorted the bad boys out, none too gently. Upright joint dedicated to real music.

Most folks attendin' were older, peaceable. Few young bloods got deep into the sound- prob'ly changed/saved their lives.

All but the smokin' seemed to shut up when the band idly sauntered to the stage- the only section of the joint that regularly received shorin' up. This is why the peeps came to Bad Sign- for the blues. Get away from life to listen to life.

Soon as I could crawl out of dirt city without Moms pitchin' a hissy fit, I'd find a safe ledge or peep hole, peer inside and ogle the players tunin' instruments, countin' down and layin' out a dope ride. Singers testin' mics and warblin' to warm up the vocals. The sounds wrapped me up and wouldn't let go- SWEET!

I seen humans swayin' with glazed eyes, movin' close together- fightin' without fightin'- in time to the beat. The drinkin' slowed, too, as the joint put a spell on yous. Hoodoo lives.

Didn't make no never minds how many musicians crowded stage-side at one time, or the number of different groups takin' turns, or how long a particlar number ran on- Bad Sign brung down the roof with 'preciation. Audience packed in tight- no room for a mouse to squeak between bodies.

I'd commit the 8-bar or 12-bar blues to memory and practice once Bad Sign closed for the short time between night and day- talk about rock around the clock. Got cursed for my efforts by my sib and Moms, but I'd bring it on home anyway, til I wore myself out.

Wasn't long before my siren of a mother had no interest in me or bro. Tomcats come callin'. Time to blow that pop stand. Either that or get my ass kicked. No sweet good-byes. Not in the hood. Not with the blues. Only thing sweet 'bout the blues is the sound.

Quarter to 3, not much activity in the joint, I hit the road, Jack. Kinda sorry to see the last of the old place, but figured it was soon to cave in. Music can't prop up the impossible forever. Roof had as many missing parts as the floor and the walls. The few un-boarded-up windows were nothin' but broken panes. Took a short peek behind me as my one for the road. Time to put my talent to the test and take my show elsewhere.

Lost sight of my bro- we headed in different directions. Heard the queen caterwaul to the strongest players midst the fightin' tomcats. Birth of the blues startin' all over again.

Had to be right careful headin' out. Turf wars and a bad 'un or two aimin' to start a little sumpin' sumpin' on the side make for dangerous travelin'. Four leggeds- cats and dogs- vyin' for space or grub. Humans and roosters, the same. Learnin' the blues, baby, learnin' the blues.

Growin' up, I figured wit da quickness when to just watch-keepin' it on the down-lo, hidin' to get the best views of the hissin' screamin' blood-battles, po-po activity- any unrest. When to take charge, when to move on- doin' da gambler.

Honed my voice long side my growin' list a gangsta skills. Within a year, hood was far, far in my past. Only music memories worth accompanyin' me.

As particular parts of me developed, I'd try an opponent on for size. Every win expanded my expertise and earned a little somethin' in the way of female company for the effort.

Every loss learned me more. One lean, mean, fightin' machine. Nobody's baby, not me. 'Black and orange cat with attitude,' I'd hear murmurs from other players. 'R E S P E C T,' I'd trill.

Walkin' after midnight's the best time to avoid most humans. I deal with other animals by stayin' aware, spyin' ahead and always have a back door handy.

Movin' on, listenin' in at nooks that might offer bare necessities. Searchin' for the vibes that move me. If the music's right I hang 'round til I'm run-off. Or strut on my way if I get ticked-off at the lack of real talent.

Some young players call the screamin', cussin', boppin' car bidness music. Got news for 'em- that ain't the real deal. Wanna know music head for Bad Sign, if it's still there. I hear it's a generation thang, but I don't buy it. Sweet tunes is sweet tunes. Word.

Had a cool gig goin' on for too short a time. A high covered roost harbored me from rain and stingin' wind. Crib ranked midst a stretch of huge old buildings- factories, they call 'em. I'd seen many cats creepin' in shadows, huntin', makin' out and makin' do. That's cool, I'm down with live and let live.

One night under a bad moon risin', I'm rollin' phat, workin' my total range- which is considerable, just ask me. Beltin' the blues fit to make the old souls sigh at the crossroads once more. One talented devil of a cat- me!

Surprise, surprise! A coven of chorus-ready queens drifted out of nooks and crannies and started singin' back-up! On point, I got my mojo workin'. Whoooeee- listenin' to the lady cats wailin' to my song!

Ranged far below me in an arc of moonlight, the queens and their kits sat with tails idly swayin' to this magic moment beat. Their tremolo "*aaarrrrrr's*" echoed-ringin' in the alley followin' my lead "rrrRRRrrrr".

Call and response feline style. It was 13 women and me the only cool mac daddy around! The greatest night of my life to date- me with my own band! Man, we crushed it!

Til some tone-deaf, hyped-up, security guard had the gall to take a shot at me. Whizzed right past my ear, struck a piercing note on a metal stack and pinged into a wood beam. Never seen cats scatter so fast. Ruined a da...dang fine thang! Straight-up thug's number one on my shi...poop list. Oh, to catch the s.o.b. nappin'!

Instead, I hit the road. Again. Just call me the wanderer.

Late night near mornin' I ended up in a dark alley some distance from desperate-ville. Decided to check out a place called Red's, cuz of the familiar scents. Grizzled dude takin' out the garbage eyed me with a less-than-friendly sneer. I felt the same way 'bout him, but shoot, one dead rat later we got to seein' eye to eye.

Guy tossed me the dregs of a hamburger. Better than rat, but not by much- a crazy sauce on it deadened my taste buds for hours.

Red's sported live music once in a blue moon. Heard some chick do a Janis Joplin number. Now there's a blisterin' piece of my heart sound I relish. Chick had it goin' on! Too bad she didn't stay- crowd seemed to agree with me. Unfortunately, the rest of the crap passin' their fried brains for tunes is the cry-in-your beer twang that curdles my gut.

Those nights I'd go trollin'.

What is it about a certain sound that drives me? Blues don't take no shi...poop from nobody. The sound, the words, cut straight to the meat. Blues is all kinds of livin' I reckon. And I'm kickin' it to be livin' large.

Like I always say, the smart cat never stops learnin'. One step at a time. Me, I'm king of the road. Call me the breeze, blowin' wherever I wanta go and whenever. Only thing got a hold on me is blues. Rock's doable if done right. Oh, and grub. Lots of grub. And maybe a little sumpin sumpin in the way of female company...

3

Knockin'. Zat you, Homey? While I warm up my vocals my feets be dancin' on the window sill. Anticipation. What's grubbin' on the menu tonight?

"Somebody shut that damned cat up! Please, I can't find the right key."

The latest, less-than-worthy, diva lead singer couldn't find a key if it lodged in her ear along with the numerous other glinting objects stuck there. I'm serious. Wannabe singers trip through here like yesterday's smoke. Save me, Ella!

Chicks can't remember lyrics, when to come in and with the correct pitch. Think all they gotta do is flash a lotta skin. What cat wants scourged ears while watchin' naked flab?

Now me- I got perfect pitch, never miss the cue to come in, but I do 'preciate a little warm-up. "RRRrrrrRRRrrrr." Can't help it the chick be trippin' on a player. Mind yer own pipes, trash-wipe!

"I think he's cool- a musical cat." My fave homeboy spots me with a delighted grin ridin' his puss, wanders to my ledge, high fives me to which I offer my usual "rrrr" by way of 'hey good lookin', whatcha got cookin'?'

He unwraps the bologna sandwich he brought just for me. Man alive, I'm eatin' high! The slightest movement of his head sends his mane chimin' with a singin' swish, and he smilingly digs into his own extra-thick sandwich.

"How many bands have a mascot?" Amused, Jess, the new bass, swigs the hard-core stuff from a bottle. Swiggin' hooch, interestin' taste if ya can stand it, but I've decided it's not my bag. Or M'Moms decided for me under the bad sign.

"We're Cur and the Dogs, dumbass," the bitch pouts.

"Look, you wanta start name callin—" Jess unstraps his bass, unplugs, grabs his amp handle and plunges for the door.

"Jess, don't go," diva wilts, begs. That she does quite well. At least she ain't spoutin' no huge nasal whine. Chick's act includes battin' weird overlong eyelashes as if she's got a bug in her eye, and she thrusts her ample chest at Jess.

Bass dude eyes her wrigglin', rethinks his options, stalls.

"Jesse's girl," the lead guitar, m'boy, mumbles between bites.

The drummer tosses his drum sticks, catches 'em on the fly. Must have cat in him in spite of over-doin' the groceries. Whereas his fingers are nimble, his butt is crashed- too heavy to move from the way-too-tiny seat back of his glittery drums.

"If we're gonna rehearse, let's do it," twiddle thumbs pounds the bass drum foot pedal.

This is the usual fractiousness of musical wannabees, 'cept for my fave. Haven't a clue why he puts up with this lack-of-talent lot.

Course, the drummer knows his bidness, and it is his crib. But the band's been through 7 singers in less than 7 weeks. I hear him layin' down the complaints once the others leave, which is my cue to bounce. Ain't runnin' no confessional outlet- got better thangs to do.

Two bass players- Boneyard got sick the last time he played with us. Bad news. Despite his rackin' cough, he was easy to get along with and he could play his simple-style bass. Jess found us right after; he's less-than-satisfactory and on the sensitive side of the fence. Needs coddlin'- misses the least notion of walk like a man. Save me!

Grub greedily partaken of, I impatiently pace and chitter-chatter, observin' the group's ill-gotten attempts to put together sumpin' worth hearin'.

No agreement on a song list or order of go, and nobody comes together on how to play a song- fast, slow, 2-count, 4-count, which key. The latest bass swigger and the drummer can't keep a beat on track. Miss the twig- he had accurate sense of rhythm.

For the umpteenth time, I wonder why my goin'-on homey sticks around. He's in a different world from this lot of wannabe noise-makers. Talent and respect and not strung-out on any rotgut or other brain-rot substance. Why are you here, Bro?

The thought of him bouncin' (leavin'- I'll interpret some, but can't be raisin' ya all your life) stickers my craw. The grub he brings me isn't my first consideration, though it is definitely topnotch. I do love bologna sandwiches and pepperoni pizza. Homey treats me right and he knows blues like they's in his blood.

If I had my druthers and another shape, I'd be a lead guitar player and lead singer. My claws could strum the strings, but hell, the damn guitar weighs more than I do!

So, I'm perfectin' my range of octaves without a complaint I can hear- drown 'em out. "*rrrowwwLLLRRRR*," I caterwaul away. I'm rollin' phat again, 'specially when my homeboy gives me the eye and lets me strut my thang.

I take a breather.

"I swear, if…" a string of the worst rap pops out of her mouth- how does she eat with that thing?

"Aw, leave him alone. You got the opening riff? One, two, three, four," drummer counts off. My homey's fingers slide down the guitar neck with awesome precision and a sound to make you sit up and slap yo'self silly sizzles.

But it's the same-ol', same-ol'. The rest can't seem to start the same time. Drummer's on it, bass is behind the count, and the diva- instead of comin' in with the first verse runs to what humans call the bathroom or chooses to dive for a drink. Maybe rotgut might help? Nah, she hacks it like always, no matter what's in her bottle.

I'm sick to my sanity of hearin' her pitiful excuses for 'singin''. Git it on or git gone, for the love of a minor note!

How long, how long? Past time to offer more of my musical expertise. "Mrowwww, rrrowww, Mrowww."

"Shut up, you****** cat!" She be player-hatin', the skank.

Wanna trash-talk? I'm game, "*RRRROWRRRRRRRRRR!*"

"Hey, the cat's got the right pitch," drummer smirks.

That's cuz practice makes perfect when you practice perfect- a concept that seems totally beyond the chick and her Jesse. They be frontin'. Save me, B.B!

My homey drowns out the ensuin' argument with an agile 8 bars of lightning-fast licks in the highest register, bendin' strings and givin' 'em the ol' vibrato with a kickin' dose of harmonics thrown in for good measure. And when the background hoopla begins to die, he turns down the volume and I sing the blues the way they's born to be sung.

I can dig this life. Grub and blues comin' my way compliments of my homey. Now if we could find a 'preciative audience and an Etta sound alike, resurrect Boneyard, dis Jesse...

4

"Yo, Cool Cat, get in a tight spot with your latest lady love?"

Talkin' bout this little ol' swat on my cheek and neck? Sissy sashayin' sis took exception to my serenadin' foreplay. Ain't nothin' but a thang, homey- chill out!

Homeboy studies my wounded puss with the concern I recall mother used to have when I was too new to do for myself. Frownin', he unwraps and shares a ham and cheese sandwich bigger than me. And that's sayin' somethin'!

Ain't much to the outside of a sandwich, but the inner stuff- *mmmmm*, right proper. I lick an escaped spit of mustard off the ledge, pin down a slice of ham melted to cheese and tear in.

Homey cocks his head side to side, sendin' his hair beads softly whisperin'. His half of supper lies forgotten atop his guitar case. No need for me to steal another bite for he's more-n-fair divyin' out the goods.

I reckon he's admirin' my trophy smarts. Chick decided to play hard to get 'stead of turnin' on the love light. Shoot, when you got the toughest tom in town callin' to get his mac on what's your problem? Dizzy diva. Few scratches and a rapprochement later, we went our separate ways.

"You know, when I scratch-up my arm, I use this ointment," he pulls out a little jar, opens it, sits it next to my dinner. Ignorin' the scentless stuff, I continue relishin' the warm ham and cheese. Figure he otta to do the same.

"If you give a bro a chance, buddy, this'll make it heal quick."

Heal? Ain't that what spit is for?

Now, we been on eye to eye speakin' terms for a goodly 'mount of time. But speakin' ain't interferin' with a brotha's personal space. I ain't a touchy/feely kinda cat. Don't need no nursemaid, neither. Keep yer hands to yerself.

Stare-down impasse. Amazingly, Bro's nearly as adept at the game as I am. Matter of trust? It's a mutual break-off- my supper's callin', and he acts like he's gonna get his grub on.

"Leave that stinking, fleabag alone. I want to try out this new song," the latest chick ticks on the mic with curved nails longer than her fingers. Painted up in weird shiny colors to boot.

Got a lot a nerve callin' me names. Ain't no fleas or stink on me. I'm mighty scrupulous with my superfly coat.

Wanta try yer claws against mine? I give her a nasty grunt, fittin' to dance. R E S P E C T- sumpin' she otta know 'bout.

Group's counted off singers like bug zappers zippin' skeeters. Ol' Jesse lost his girl- couldn't make the cut with him or the band. This one won't last long, I'm bettin'. Thinks singin' blues is wailin' a death knell in the night. Makes me wanta cough up a hairball in her direction.

A couple of interims were a stretch of the imagination. One black magic woman with a better attitude and possibilities sang a different style than the boys play. She graciously offered me a small hunk of roast beef out of her swag bag. Almost wished I understood her kind of music, cuz she wasn't frontin'. Definite talent. Sad to say, she bowed out with, "Sorry boys, blues aren't what I sing." Serious? Blues is where it's at, woman!

An eye-rollin' jail bait lasted the count of an open door. The homeys got some smarts. Next, a wannabe showed up to practice higher than air. If he had two feet on the ground might've fit in. Can't figure how he managed to duck inside the door- he was that far gone.

Old wheezin' dude couldn't make it through one set without needin' a seat- a huge seat. Brotha was bigger than the drummer! Any smart cat'll tell you, too much weight ain't poindexter. Gotta suck in air to sing- ask the scat queen, Ella. Lady could roll out them syllable sounds fit to bring down the house!

Clean-cut player did somethin' cool with a small thin box in his mouth. I got some vocal ideas from his mouth moochin'. But a singer he was not. Good-bye!

Broad- go a deuce or a deuce and a half- (one huge chick) was allergic to and afraid of cats. Potential there considering the range of notes she shrieked at sight of me. For the love of a bass note! Atchoo to you, too! Baby got back, but no smack. Big as…butt, but nuttin' else worth nuttin'.

What's up with humans eating so much they grow umpteen sizes beyond their bones?

Wish my fave would just play and sing the whole night, but he begs off and drummer says bands with a girl seem to get more gigs. Hard to figure. Chicks seem like more trouble than they're worth.

This latest nut case proves my point. Can't finish a number without a hell-on-heels, drama queen uproar. Ain't a single ounce of musical brains, but she's advisin' and snipin' 'stead of takin' care of bidness.

"C'mon, leave the *** cat," she screeches over the mic.

Hold yer ears or lose 'em, brothas!

My homey pins her with a face devoid of expression. Too much to hope he'll send her packin'?

"What do you say, Cool Cat?" He dabs a finger in the jelly goo, holds it up for my inspection and--

Damn, if he ain't quick! I barely feel the slight swipe 'longside my neck.

"Try this," and he distracts my abruptly growin' disgruntlement with a top-shelf surprise. "Saved this just for you, friend- salmon."

I gulp like hellzapoppin', and I'm here to tell you I'm down with salmon! Off the hook! My tongue flicks out to five-finger the last tidbit.

Fast on my mark cuz one eye's always on alert, I duck at somethin' flyin' through the air in my direction- an empty can. Homey grabs it before it hits my sill.

That stinkin' bitch dips her chin, hides a smirk behind weird colored hair, acts all innocent, checks a chart. But my fave unfolds from sittin' beside me, strolls like death walkin' towards her. One big G with the edge firin' up. Chick betta think.

Mix it up, Bro, I hiss.

"Don't ever do that again- do you understand?" His tone is mighty low and full of ol' school gangsta comeuppance.

"He's right, don't be throwin' shit in my house—"

"***cat gets more respect than I do! Filthy creature could have the plague!"

Dig it, the chick wants to talk respect- bet she can't spell it. For damned sure, she can't sing it. Player-hater. The only plague here is—

"You hear me? I won't warn you again." My homeboy towers over the witch. Causes her to drop all her song sheets. Papers flit-scatter everywhere. Good luck pickin' 'em up with dem useless appendages.

"Okaaay," she grits, tries a flirty smile, but homey ain't havin' it.

Beat 'em counts off and lead guitar strums the walk down til bass finds the correct riff rhythm in time. Chick stutters gettin' her act together. No Etta or Aretha, but it does a passin' Bring it on Home.

I settle in, wait for my cue to sing, or protect my hearin'-dependin' on what's ridin' on the list.

Three songs later, the wannabe pitcher is snipin' 'bout my fave hoggin' the spotlight. Sends my ears sideways. I'm itchin' to jump in the mix and shut her up- messed up skank! Give her a taste of what true claws be designed for.

"Look, you don't need 32 bars of lead," she tosses her hair and flags the chart. Diva knows what a bar is? Well, dust my broom!

"You want to turn a 4-minute song into a 2-minute song?"

"Uh—" she stumbles.

"Let him do his thing," bass man shrugs, finishes off his drink of choice. By the scent, I do b'lieve it's sumpin' flammable. The longer the session, the fuzzier his talk. And the worse behind he falls. Reckon if he drank enough, he might git around to bein' on time.

"Gotta gig lined up next Thursday if we can pull this off without all the bitchin'," twiddle thumbs drops a bomb.

So-called singer's the only one never played to a live audience, but she thinks she can call the shots. Like I say, chicks is more trouble...

"Fine by me. I've got lots of—"

"Lead guitar's up—"

"Wait a minute," she flaunts her ill-concealed chest to no avail.

Totally ignored by the boys, she huffs and puffs, and my homey smiles my way. "Stray Cat Strut- for you, my friend," he winks. "Get ready, Cool Cat."

A slice of music heaven leads into a goin'-on walk down. My homey has my full attention. I sizzle watchin' his fingers dance on that old guitar neck.

"Anytime, Cool Cat."

"RRROWWerrr, RRRROWWerrr, RRROWW, RROW," I'm the star blues singer!

Homeboy saunters my way, lovin' on his guitar like I'm all that and then some. We're in perfect sync.

"Too right, buddy," he murmurs compliments.

I shut up after 4 go rounds. I ain't no hog- figure it's his turn to shine.

"Black and orange—"

Oooh, is the diva dawg ticked! What an ugly pooch muzzle!

At the close of what I consider my theme song, drummer tosses his sticks, "Awesome!"

Bass man tips his head, lights up a stinkin' stick, and spews stinkin' smoke. She lights up one, too, and eyes blazin' gives me a crapload of what-for while flushin' circles of smoke. Chick got a lot of nerve remarkin' on my aroma.

"What the ** am I supposed to do while he's *** with the damn cat?"

"If you can't get with the beat, get out of the heat," bass snorts and sniggers.

"AAArrrrrrrr," I present my 2-cents worth and the rest of the homeys laugh and laugh.

She flounces off to the john, swings her bony butt close to my ledge. My stickers are en pointe. Come a little bit closer, I trill.

A coupla things I really dig. Dry warm crib for coppin' some z's ranks mighty high. Red- he beds down atop his bar business. Drags his weary ass up a wood stairway every night. That same set of steps comes in handy for the daily sharpenin' of my stickers.

Once Red hits the head and then the bed, I sneak out of the shadows, vault onto the rail, meander on up with perfect balance. Another fancy leap puts me ledge-wise to a high roost window half my size. I nudge the rotted frame, and poooh yeah- got my own pad. Evicted the resident mice wit da quickness. One oddball chipmunk gave me the runaround, but I run it down and had a midnight snack.

The buildin' sharin' Red's alley is a warehouse. Lights out before dark in that shindig. Once Red shuts off the neon and locks his swingin' door, a modicum of quiet actually exists- if you ignore the sparse traffic. Easy to see I ain't zactly in the hood no mo.

Up in my bird's nest rest, I'm rollin' large. Take my nightly bath, curl up and dream, undisturbed. How a brotha outta live.

Outsides my crib, I'm doin' it old school when trespassers cross my path. I intend to stay top tom. Some trash-talkin' player cattin' into my realm- I send him down the road talkin' to hisself. Wit da quickness.

Female is a different game. Gettin' my mac on wid da ladies has got me some kits somewhere- you betcha. Just don't get up in my grill for child support- ain't no welfare 'round here. Don't wanna hear 'baby need shoes'. Or anythin' else!

My homeboy, we're two of a kind, I figure. Our own selves. Don't cotton to what the other hoodbillies are up to so long as it's not on our turf.

He don't puff on stinkin' sticks, no sippin' on a forty- beer they call it. Temporarily forgettin' my first go-round with the stuff, I tried lappin' up one of Twig's spills. Even without M'Moms's swats, I can tell ya, I ain't feelin' it- as in, why would you put dat in yo mouth? Tongue done gone walkabout, word.

Homey's got a clean mouth on him. No constant droppin' f-words like no other words ever been said. He listens to others' opinions when they are delivered respectfully. I'm workin' on that particlar skill, but my heart ain't buyin' it.

He shrugs off the snipey-butt wannabe singer. Keeps an even keel attitude. 'Cept, he did call her out when she took after me.

What does that mean? Only one ever stood up for me was M'Moms and that was only when I was a tiny kit. After a certain age, it's 'you are on your own, see ya later alligator.'

A weird, off-the-hook sensation digs into me. Homey...cares 'bout me? The thinkin' end of things ain't my strong suit less'n I need it to get out of a scrape. Can't shake it, though. Homey and me?

Wonder where he goes after rehearsin'? Seems to live on the fly is all I gather.

Got me a bird's eye view from atop his hood, peekin' in the glass of the big box on wheels he rides roads with. When he wasn't about, I slipped through his open window to get a better whiff.

Homey's crib is alright- simple, clean and tight. Box of clothes, bedroll, a few books, and a crate bearin' bottles of water- orderly as my threads (my coat, for the offside folks). No distractin' odors- must keep 'the facilities' elsewhere. No mess where ya dress. Smart cat!

What if I hide in those folded clothes and sneak off with him? Be cool to have longer one-on-one, steppin-out-wit-my-homey time. But maybe he won't cotton to my interceptin' his personal space. Reckon I wouldn't, either. Hate to waste the good thang we got goin' on.

Tried to follow him once, 'cept I ain't fast enough to head out on the highway- there be dangers beyond my skill set.

Pointless cogitatin'. Born to be wild- that's me. Figure Homey's the same, hence his livin' on wheels.

Ain't I tough enough to go it alone? Don't need no sidekick...no entanglements, I tell myself. Yeah, yeah, it ain't me babe...

Top cat status didn't come overnight. First scraps were with my bro, but I was bigger, so no contest. But bigger ain't always the winner. Gotta know when to hold 'em, gotta know when to head the other way. But if I'm feelin' it, I shuck up my ample coat, let my tail grow four sizes and hiss, 'wanna break it down?'

Guess if you're lucky enough to grow up, you stand a chance to get smart. If not, you get dead.

My screamin' vocals have sent more'n a few uptown hustlers scattin' on their way. I'm bad to the bone, see- don't mess wid me.

To the few that stick around to mix it up, I hunker in, lash out, screech, show fangs and calc'late when to move in for the takedown.

Cat fights ain't for the weak of heart. Me, I figure what's worth fightin' for and scheme accordingly. M'Moms didn't raise no fool. Females are plentiful- don't need to go to war- what is it good for? On to the next chick.

Less I'm out cruisin' to admin' a bruisin' and rake some hide. Save my soul, New Orleans, ain't no saint here. Times I gotta let loose like a hell hound's on my trail. Seems like I can't help myself.

Relations with humans- no close quarters. Red and I keep our distance, with respect.

No girly-girl sweet nothin's talk, "Here kitty, kitty," to me. Go away little girl. Get back, Jack- don't do it again-words to live by.

So, what is this…thing giggin' my craw? What draws me to the lead guitar? Why's *he* my homeboy? Conundrum, ho hum.

Been a few blue moons' worth of days since look who done come up in here. The night don't begin til Homey makes the scene.

Tonight's grub is bologna- hold the pickles. I can smell it as he drops his gear and grins my way.

"Got something for you to try out, Cool Cat," he murmurs while we dine, semi al fresco, window wide open.

The skank wears her usual smirk and snidely nags, "Eat on your own time." Repeatedly.

I hear ya knockin', but ya can't come in, I muse. Man, is that appropriate- chick's always late, if she remembers the words!

I turn a deaf ear as she continues to yakety yak, but I finally condescend to give her the benefit of my outstandin' vocal expertise, "*RRRRRRROWWWWWRRRRRR!*" I lose count of the bars, but they is powerful!

Drummer and bass chuckle and high five drinks of choice. "Peace, for once, will you, girly?" They start talkin' smack in the corner, stealin' her center stage.

Chick hates to be ignored, "Can we get started?"

"Can you chill?" Homey quietly asks.

"I thought we had a gig coming up?"

"You're the one needs rehearsin'. We got our parts down tight," bass optimistically spouts, beer foam spews out his mouth, drips on his raggedy shirt.

"Then what the hell am I doing here?"

Bass man slaps his guitar strings, creates a deep rumblin' sound wid his effects pedal workin' double time. Drummer twirls his sticks, shifts his bulk and grins.

"Hey, cat lover!" she fumes over the mic.

Homey and me are mindin' our own bidness, quietly finishin' our groceries, savorin' the flavor and our acquaintance.

"Get off it, will ya? Look, we can do this without you, but we can't play without him," bang 'em states the truth.

She flips her favorite finger- chick needs to chew off that overgrown, useless nail. Be glad to help her out- dispense wid da finger, too. Just sayin'.

Homey winks at me, offers a fragrant fish smellin' treat. He picks up his ol' guitar, switches a few levers, eyes me diggin' on the goods.

"Listen, Cool Cat," and his fingers tackle the strings- bright lights, big city!

Bass throws back his head in the throes of purest delight, "Sweet Child of Mine, sweet!"

Now there's a lick I can do.

"Aaheee, Aaheee, aaheee," he sings and glances at me.

"AAAHEEEAAAHEEE," I respond. Back and forth. Homey and me. The window rattles gleefully over my head. Where do we go now? Don't get no better than this! We be boogie chillen!

Homey sings 'bout a smilin' chick, then segues into one of the diva's numbers. He might be playin' her chords, but he's talkin' to me.

"AAHEEE, AEEE…" I trill, my tail keeping the beat on the window ledge.

"Cool Cat, you the man!"

I'll hear those words the rest of my life from somewhere deep inside. And feel…can't put words or music to whatever it is I feel.

Cuz that's the last time I see my homey.

6

When my homey ain't playin', I go trollin'- takin' a different path every evenin'. Luck across a familiar tune- cool Jimmy Reed's Got Me Runnin'. That cat knew the score. I stick around listenin' to blues in the night done right.

"Got me runnin', got me hidin'"- perfect philosophy for a streetwise cat. The glory don't last but a few numbers- what's wrong wid yous? Some wannabe player on the far, far side of Jimmy Reed takes the stage, singin' (if you can call it that) 'bout a sexy tractor- whatever the hell a tractor is!

I split. No crossin' roads if a culvert is handy. If no other recourse, look both ways and high tail it for all I'm worth. Skirt groups of more than one and try to give a wide berth to the one, too.

Avoid the scent of dog. Cat/dog is a 50/50 shot at winnin' and not one I'm usually up to bettin' on. Hang in the weeds and shadows. All senses on prowl alert to stay safe from sneaky predators on high, as well as the ground-bound. Never can tell where or when the shit's gonna hit the fan.

All the while I'm walkin', I'm keen to hear the proper notes. I'm jonesin' for the blues- kinda my natural state- blues born and bred and no friends in low places or anywhere else.

But blues ain't happenin', tonight- more's the pity.

Let's see what Hook's (my fave stop for fish) is tossin' out the back door.

Passin' up the roach coaches and motels, my nose scents the requisite goods nearin', and somethin' not so good.

'This is my turf,' hisses a stringy tom with the scars to back him up.

My muscles automatically ripple, and I'm gleanin' onto whatever's simmerin' in my blood, cuz it just won't shut up. Maybe I'm over-hungry- gut is railin', or maybe I'm simply ticked-off cuz they evicted the Jimmy Reed player from the stage for some tractor-lovin' twanger.

Either way, I dig in, claws unsheathin', ears flattenin'. 'For another minute, if you're lucky,' I screech my acceptance of the duel.

'You best pack a lunch, baby boy,' sneers the striped tom, flashin' his tail in bits of strewn glass, and layin' mutilated ears against his scrawny, wiry neck.

'Only M'Moms calls me baby boy,' I hit him with my best shot of bluesy stridency- all 4 bars 'companied wid a howl fit to wake the dead.

Alley seems to breed cats like roaches. Both species peek from out of the woodwork, eyes alight. Free entertainment tonight!

Got no time for small talk. Hook's fish is just a gander up the street. And my gut is grumblin' wid gusto.

So, without further ado, I pounce. Ol' tom's not suspectin' a full out frontal attack. He's used to talkin' smack. Notice his scars ain't fresh ones.

"*rrroOOWRRRrrrrrrrrrWW*," my vocals loudly ascend the scale and dip deep to further split what's left of his ears, before I latch on with fangs and claws sunderin' his hide. Sing my song and spit out fur, rollin' in street stench reminiscent of the hood. Down and dirty. Ol' school.

Ol' tom frees hisself. I actually give him an out. He slinks low, lookin' for a sweet hook-up.

"OWWERRRR!" 'Wanna dance again, ol' man?' I don't mind sweepin' the street with him, cept I'm hungry as hell's fire lookin' for timber.

We circle each other with half-hearted swipes. His breathin' is wheezy. Don't wanta catch anythin' from this snot-nose.

I challenge an Aretha-beltin' R E S P E C T roar- hopin' he just runs off like rocks are peltin' him.

Our tournament must draw more than the shadow creepers. All scuttle into hidin' as the f-word cannons, along with breakin' rotgut bottles tossed our way. I barely escape the deluge thrown from above. Ol' tom gets hit in the side. Stunned, he rocks, catches his balance for a sec and then, scats.

Me, I'm feelin' the mac daddy, until I cadge a splinter of glass in one of my footpads. Slinkin' behind an overflowin' garbage bin, I extract it, apply healin' spit and strut to Hook's. Gotta satisfy at least one of my cravin's tonight.

Part of me feels sorry for the ol' gangsta. Betcha he wasn't that old, just looked the part. Street livin's hard livin'. Welcome to the blues I trill as Hook's peers into view.

7

"Why didn't you answer your phone?"

"Had to get out of hearing range. You got it?"

"Lost the bugger right off. Up and disappeared on me, but I got my eyes out long as you're willing to pay."

"Yeah, but I'm not made of money."

Much later the same night.

"Guess what?"

"It's 2 a.m.," whines the female.

"Remember Jackie?"

"You're calling to tell me about some bimbo?"

"Nah, me and Jackie had a few drinks at Red's. Told her about your mission. Dig this- she's seen the damn cat. Black and orange stray lives at the bar. Red brags on it all the time!"

Been keepin' it on the down-low since the last band rehearsal. Some shadow watcher trailin' my tail. Easy to lose the hoodbilly, but it got me to thinkin'. Ain't nobody bothered my whereabouts before. What's up with dis bs?

Sensin' a change of wind beyond the natural change of seasons. One thing to count on- change. Blues was born on account of change.

Down on the corner, I garner a nice chunk of fish with hot sauce- come to love that stingin'-the-tongue sensation. Figure to hole up for a while, til it's time to see my homey again. Maybe I'll steal inside of his van (whatcha call a box on wheels).

Nah, best not, can't be trippin' on a brotha!

But hangin' out day and night in the crib ain't cuttin' it for free and easy me. A little honey's soundin' the siren and it's hard to ignore. Somethin' poppin' off. Hmmm...little action is just what I need.

Easier than slingin' Homey's grub, I run off a couple players nosin' 'round the goods, and I cozy up to Miss Willin' Calico with my dope old fashioned love song. Livin' in the moment. Slow ride 'n satisfaction.

My own damn fault. Sated with my vigorous outpourin' of the night, I kinda check the coast- much less en pointe than usual. Seems clear. I tend to my reg'lar sharpenin' on the wood stair post before high-tailin' it up the steps. Stop for a lengthy yawn at the stars and a good night stretch. I'm lookin' forward to nappin' directly, yes indeedy.

Vault up to the top of the rail, puss extends out to nudge my crooked door, hear its grudgin' complaint, slither in and...WHAT THE—

I'm slidin' down fast- shootin' off like the hood in full Saturday night swing, all fours scramblin', can't get a grip...

"J.C., J.C, what am I doing? Oh god, I never heard crying like this! Not even in the horror movies. What has that ditzy girl got me into? J.C., J.C., what would J.C. do?

I'll go crazy many more miles of this. Radio won't drown out the sound. Damn broad didn't pay me near enough!"

I'll J.C. your ass! I'm one pissed-off mother! Wannabe chick skank singer paid some ***so-n-so to take me…where?

Gonna shoot my ass?

Well, baby cakes, you ain't dealin' with a full deck if you think this cat's gonna roll over. I will survive!

I pound the airwaves with all my considerable vocal power- deafen your enemy's a decent beginnin' battle plan- rattle their nerves. My fully awakened brain's workin' overtime. Damned good thing I sharpened my stickers. Got this box shreddin' like peelin' paint at Bad Sign.

Hell's comin' your way, you J.C. spoutin' s o b! Highway to hell it is- can't stop me!

Feels like sun-up is close; been travelin' way too long at a fast pace. I've derailed the trap quite substantial-like while drownin' out the whiny J.C.'s- whoever he is- by near squanderin' my vocal chords.

Vehicle's pullin' off. Rocks skitterin'. Stoppin' off kilter. My trap slides right. The screechin' door opens. I bide my time, notice the scents are different. Not hood, not alley, no warehouse district… Don't reckon I'm comin' home, Bill Bailey.

46

"J.C., so sorry, so sorry. You'll do all right here, kitty. Red's gonna kill me, and I deserve it. J.C., J.C...."

Shakin' hands fumblin' wit da big house (prison, case y'all checked out). All the encouragement I need. I bust up and through, spit in his eye, sideswipe his mouth mid J.C., kick-n-claw for all I'm worth (which is considerable) and tear his hair out as I rip/scoot across the top of his head. Won't be needin' a barber any time soon. If ever!

Who's sorry now, ya honky-tonk-hatin' catnapper?

I catapult to the road, don't stop to check my artwork on his liquid face. Leave the sniveler behind wit da quickness. 'Cept there ain't no roads like I know 'em. Grass- more grass than I ever believed existed. And look at all the trees- *daaaaammn!* This ain't Kansas, Dorothy. Or is it?

Gettin' a might slap-happy here. Throat's so dry I'm spittin' dust. Sun on my back and it ain't no sunny side of the street. Shade ahead. Darker gen'rally means little critters hangin' round, poss'bil puddle. Drink and a meal, here I come.

Far to my tail-side the fool is still blubberin'. My mama didn't raise no fool, I roar- more like a crackle. Have to take five on my singin', but hey, I'm livin'. I'll get along; I will! Bet yer J.C. spoutin' fool's hide on it!

Wonder what Homey'll think when I don't show up for practice. Him, I'll miss. First thing in my life I can say that about. Will he care I'm gone? Who's gonna sing back-up? If I could only get my hooks on that...

Thirsty blues. Hmmm, maybe I'll write a worthy tune, waitin' for my pipes to recover. Sure could use a pizza and some of Homey's spring water 'bout now.

8

"There you are," the lead singer giggles, flings her blue-green dyed hair, flaunts her tightly up-thrust chest and checks her good-for-nothing, matching nails.

A change in the air. I felt it walking up the drive. All too quiet at the window. Cool Cat always beats me here...

"Where's the cat?" I pointedly ignore the flighty diva.

"Hell, if I know. Kinda surprised he's not here. Never misses band rehearsal," the drummer is innocently confused. I can read him.

I pin the bass guitar. "You?"

"Stray cat, your guess is as good as mine. Maybe he's makin' out, maybe he's met..." he abruptly clams up and shrugs. His eyes aren't a clear agenda, but he's intuiting other than what he's saying. The tuner occupies his full attention. The flat E-string steals his aplomb.

I unload my gear, stride to the window, sandwich bag gripped in my hand. Flinging up the peeling frame of glass, I stick my head out, check both directions. Right, left, no sign. The sensation in my heart is more unpleasant than I've encountered in a very, very, long time. Tried to stay away from such.

"Let's get started. I mean, after you eat," she puts on a false courtesy act not inherent in her repertoire. The bitching is overtly missing tonight.

If I were a dog my hackles would be up and I'd be snarling.

"It's just a cat, for crying out loud! Let's go over the set," she fans the chart in coquette fashion. The others are silent, wondering.

My lip curls, my gut enflames, and I'm on the witch thicker than the mustard on my share of supper. CC isn't over-fond of the condiment on his bologna sandwich, I reflect with a twinge.

I've one hand on her throat, calloused fingers dig into soft tissue and I savor the fright in her ridiculous, copper-contact-lens eyes. Her lips flutter to speak as her face make-up surrenders to an ashen pallet.

"Easy man, easy," the drummer murmurs, hesitant to lift his bulk from the drum stool. Bass sets aside his guitar to come to the rescue, thinks better of it with my single swift glance of warning. No one here is fit to take me on.

I'll ease off after I allow some of the uncaged anger to deflate. After I get an answer.

If they were apprised of my volatility, they'd not have let me in no matter how freaking skilled I am with a guitar.

I exert the requisite force to further whiten the… Bitch is too good a term for this female. Pathogenic pangolin (a ripe colorful descriptive I latched onto in my youth) suits, but she'd fail to understand the rodent reference. Too stupid to remember the lyrics of a song let alone have an inkling of simple etiquette.

"Where's… the… cat?" Each word carries a razor-sharp threat couched in a low bass pitch.

Rarely do I meet a like-minded soul, don't want to. The cat wouldn't believe his effect on me- he's too cool for cogitating on those lines. CC is special- he knows he is. Was? I refuse to think along those lines.

"Easy, man, how could she know?"

"But you do know, don't you?" I lean in to scent the fear.

"I...I didn't..."

Snarling in her face, I bare my teeth- every one. Let her think what she will.

"Look..."

But I quell any further interference from the drummer and bass guitar.

"Don't even reach for a phone," I sneer.

"C'mon, tell him if you know anything. We've got to practi--" dies on the drummer's lips.

A feral gleam sparks in my eyes; it reflects in hers. "Don't lie. I'll know if you do," I whisper caution.

"I...p...paid a guy to g...get rid of it. It's just a cat. C...can't hear myself through the monitors when it—"

"And you are just a piece of worthless, no-talent flesh. Is he alive?"

Murder one would be a new one for my record. Hell, I've been everywhere else. IF they could take me alive.

"Well, I...d...didn't kill him!"

"Where's the fool doing your dirty work? Give me his number."

She blurts a cell phone number which promptly registers in my head. I toss her into the egg-crate plastered wall and turn to gather my gear.

"Hey, where you going? We got a gig tomorrow!"

I scan the hopeless room, devoid of the only worthwhile aspect. I include myself.

"You know what you can do with the gig," and I mentally curse the course of events. Curse the female, curse myself. But I don't curse the cat.

I'd been half a mind to invite CC to come with me. Rolling stone that I am. Isn't any life for a cat, though. Little to recommend itself to a guitar player, either. Welcome to the blues, my life's motto.

Turns out the guy got $50 to drive CC out to the country and dump him. Hard to understand much of what he said. Seems CC tore his mouth severely enough to warrant 25 stitches and 35 more atop his head.

Couldn't recall where he stopped. Kept repeating, "Sheshus shise, sheshus shise."

CC. I took every highway out of town. Reminiscent of Kentucky Rain, I spent days tracking, calling, stopping and asking, "Seen a big black and orange stray cat?"

No success. Success is for dreamers, and I gave up on it lifetimes ago.

The hammering in my chest... Thought that life was over. Feelings- lived through all the phases of hell life shat at me. No complaints. No bragging. Just fact. As a young teenager, trust only existed as a 5-letter word in somebody else's dictionary. Never mine.

My mother passed on early- lucky, I guess. Papa was a rolling stone before marrying. Man grew up in the worst dregs of the world, but never a bad word for anyone. Believed in the good book and the blues.

He loved on the strings of an old battered electric guitar. With the utmost loaded emotion erupting, he told all life's stories in his music. The birds stopped their chirping when my daddy played outside, sitting and rocking on the porch of our farm.

"That's the blues, son. Blues is real life. Take a punch, give a punch, but get up on your feet, take one step at a time, boy, learn and live," he'd advise in his raspy, cigarette-despoiled voice.

Can't deal with thinking back on the last day of...us.

Did fair keeping women from the hard knot standing in for a heart. Slipped a couple times, but learned from the experiences. Plenty of material, along with Daddy's, to write and sing about.

'Don't go there,' I cut myself off. A body should only have to bear a single circle of hell once. Dante be hanged!

Occasionally I strayed into rock, more so for the arrangements than the lyrics- but there were a few I'd gather into my song list. Throwing down on a set of expressive licks is my high. Cheaper than the other scapegoats readily available, and healthier, too.

Stayed mostly to myself. I didn't take any bull from anybody. Got the mindset and bulk to back me up. The scars are hidden.

My response to it all?

Well, I evicted the f-word from my vocabulary, but it's on the tip of my tongue right now.

CC sang under the wire. Only a survivor could belt the blues like that enormous cat. Sharing my supper...

A survivor. I ought to recognize one. Survive is what I do.

"CC, my friend, we'll meet again where the great blues artists go to jam- rock and roll heaven. Stay well."

The last highway out of town after the umpteenth stop, I salute perhaps the best friend I ever had- certainly the most entertaining one- as I peer across a pasture. I swipe at my eyes. Pizza and bologna sandwiches won't ever taste the same.

Hope is for dreamers, too.

Got to keep moving. Blues don't wait around for anybody and nobody knows you when you're down and out.

9

Scootchin' under a wood rail, I roll my bad-to-the-bone-ass tumblin' dice ways over deep grass. No stones, no glass. Just thick, sweet-scented, soft growth. A dip in the ground provides a much-needed sippity-sip. My tongue's busier than Bad Sign in the un-still of the night. Unpolluted rain leftovers salve my irritated throat.

Alert and starvin', I head for a stand of brush, check my pace, don't wanna freakout the breakfast menu. I'm a little on the late side of the plate, critters already gone to their day burrows, but I catch a whiff of somethin' curious.

Hug the shadows. Different kinda buildin's up ahead. Big- I do mean BIG- critters tied to a post. A fluff ball of a dog lazes nearby. Few feline players. Some guy dispensin' grub to the writhin'-round-about pusses. I wait til he heads opposite the roach coach and move in. Gut's bellyachin' like a bad (ain't talkin' good here, folks) bass riff, what with all that clawin'-my-way-out bidness.

'Whass up, my peoples?' Huh, these domestics ain't scatterin' when I make the scene! Givin' me the look-whats-done-crawled-up-in-here eye as I strut to the groceries. Prob'ly ain't seen the likes of me. More's the pity.

Fluff ball prances up, got a high-pitched "arf, arf, arf." Grates on the ears.

I bat him aside and hiss, 'player.'

But instead of pushin' my heft into the feline chowin'-down ring and grabbin' a mouthful, a heavy-set tabby queen sprints near and spits at me, 'mind your manners!'

'I know you ain't talkin' to me, baby girl! Hunger ain't got no manners, what you on about?'

'We might share, but you can't have it all,' miss-ain't-missin'-no-groceries-uppity-up huffs, and her kin flank her, cuttin' off a brotha's access.

Fluff yaps and bounces behind her. 'Yeah, hide behind a cat, pissant.'

'Y'all 'bout to get on my last nerve. I been through a night of hellzapoppin' and I'm so hungry my gut thinks it's moved outta town and left my mouth behind. You don't even want to mess with me!'

"What's this? Another damned stray? Get outta here!"

I've taken on Mama Fat Cakes and Arf, the fluff, but a rock-tossin' honky is not in the script. Voice ain't yet up-n-runnin' to curse with; I race for cover, tuckin' my tail out of firin' range.

But I got skills. Bide my time, opportunity knocks. Hidden in the depths of overgrown shrubbery near one humongous vat of water, I wait and watch.

The rock-pitcher perceives my surrender, smirks, and fills the cat bowls more'n a meal's worth. Somethin's up.

"Get the horses loaded. We'll be late," he shouts to what I assume are his daughters carryin' armfuls out to a long, long trailer. Small as they are, the youngsters then lead the beasts off like they own the monsters. And the beasts follow like they don't know no better. Hmmm. Big dumb…

Tuck away info- dogs towerin' over humans are horses.

Suddenly, my view is rudely interrupted. *"Ha onk, ha onnkk!"*

My ears flatten and I issue a short warnin' which ain't zactly soundin' up to snuff. "Rrrrowww!"

55

I swat to maintain personal space. 'You ain't got what it takes to mess with me, honky!'

Hey, is that a pun? Flippin' thing waddles honkin' on big funky feet, flappin' wings bigger than any birds I ever seen. Crazy critter.

Demon thing snaps its long neck at my tail fast as a homeboy fleein' from the po-po in their siren-blastin' cars.

I calc'late I can run faster than any honky, but I'm standin' my ground- got

my dander up. 'Bout to git dealt wit,' I snarl and whip out claws, sideswipe its little beady-eyed face. Bat, bat, bat.

"Aaa onk, ha onk, ha onnk!" Honky waddles off to the huge water pot, singin' the blues. Won't bother me no more, 'cept for my hearin'. Aretha, save me! Thing needs some voice lessons.

With honky sunk in the puddle-to-beat-all-puddles, I lap up some more juice, feel my voice fixin' to come to papa. I continue casin' the joint. Horses are led into that long vehicle, tied inside, and dust spews storms as it rolls out the drive.

All's good in the hood- not that this joint resembles my birth place in any way, shape or form. Time to make my move.

Fluff went with his peeps- fair quiet, now. Fat mama and her crumb-snatchers are done grubbin' and gone to tuck-in for cat naps inside a fragrant buildin' loaded with dead grass. Top cat, me, digs in to soothe my achin' gut. Dry cat food is better than nothin', but boy I'm jonesin' for a pizza!

Ain't lookin' for a home like I heard somethin' called a boll weevil singin' 'bout from a house I cruised past- wrong kinda music. Hard to figure the stuff folks listen to. I'd grow dead with some of them noises repeatin' in my head.

If I were bent on a full-time crib this might suffice. But the cool grass for rollin' in is mixed up with a po-duck scent- reckon it has to do with the heaps of shite left by the horses. Give them babies a wide berth- hate to bathe off any of that stink.

Nap's a decent notion before checkin' out. Give the old stickers a sharpenin' on the wood wall, climb makeshift steps inside the fragrant joint, curl up in a thick bed of dry grass. Quiet in the middle of the day, proper.

Right before I close my eyes, I wonder what Homey's up to. Did he really give a rat's ass when I didn't show? Only reason I stuck around long as I did was... Oh well, guess it was just one of those things.

10

Best cat nap I ever had, but I hear the horses callin' the horse version of 'I'm home!' I'm blues hoofin' it. No honky rock-tossin' for me.

Cover some interestin' territory. Land, lots of land, and trees and available water and burrows to nap in. My super-sleuth huntin' skills are scarcely tested. If you can hunt in the hood and survive you can make it anywhere. Lots of tasty critters beggin' to be my lunch. Scarce few buildin's, few humans. S'good. Too many 2-leggeds together is gen'rally not conducive to cat safety. Loud, hurryin', cursin', trappin', throwin', shootin'- you name it, 2-leggeds be doin' it.

Now, I gotta give credit where credit's due. Sometime afore Red and I reached our unnerstandin', I strolled a gravel path leadin' to mighty fine vibes whifflin' from a small, old but kept-up crib. Kinda set off from a line of similar, but unkempt shacks.

A coupla kids rousted in front of the weedy, less-colorful digs- talkin' smack and smokin' stinkin' sticks. Gotta watch out for them likes. Crumb-snatchers known to throw sh…stuff now and agin like it's a sport- hoop optional. Bowl-the-cat's their game. Playin' dodge ball don't cut it for me.

To gain a better listen in safe quarters, I snuck under the sparklin' musical brotha's porch. Draggin' my butt from continual walkabout, dumpster-divin', belly a tad off from gulpin' a too-slow-on-the-gone side mouse, I temporarily shut down the movin' is provin' philosophy.

Takin' a load off, I figured to wait for the night shades to condone a silhouette. Rockabye baby lullaby of smooth notes agreed with my 40 winks.

Woke to the sound of silence, or as near as one hears in parts of this here ol' world. I cautiously poked my nose out. Coast was clear, so I slipped on through the break in the flowers, checked right, left and up, and stretched out the kinks til all were smooth and ready to move. Feelin' all right, I proceeded...

"Lookee here, Mama, got us a bona fide guest!"

Uh oh, immediate full alert, prepared to dive...

"Don't be scared, Bud. Been there myself a time or two. Brother gotta watch out for his brother, like the good book says. Don't always happen sich-like, but I reckon to do my part. Mama, any leftovers for our visitor?"

Ol' guy ain't fixed to bust off his porch rocker, but I'm fixin' to make a quick getaway when one heck of a bowl sets down for my 'spection. I give it a lengthy check-it whiff. Can't be too careful- ain't unknown for bad substances to be included. But seemed this homey was legit.

"S'okay, Bud? Y'all cotton to pork chops and sweet taters? Say, you like the blues harp?"

Didn't 'pear to mind my lack of manners. Caught him grinnin' at Mama.

While I dug into the first decent grub since M'Mom's teats, (remember this was some time afore I met Red and my homeboy) a glorious melody- blues, mind you- what I heard that caused me to stop in the first place- saturated the night.

A low and slow tempo. Cries of life's hit-em-when-they're-down and a jump-up to jubilation. All hung on like no wayward wind tomorrow. Night birds didn't bother to compete-they jist shut up their beaks. And he played it with his mouth!

Top it off- Mama picked strings and sung a mournful mouthful! The two traded off and his stripped vocal chords told the story of his mis-adventures in someplace called the risin' sun.

Hearkened to the Bad Sign musicians' sound. Half wondered if he might have played there.

Between a mess of fine grub and off-the-hook music, I stayed longer than I expected to- put a spell on me? Maybe. Did some more growin' while studyin' the surrounds. Mama and her 2-legged hep cat mostly kept to themselves and stayed home. Evenin's spent on the porch. And no 2-legged or4-legged competition put a puss in to challenge me for my rights. Cat mighta got a little too complaisant…

Until damned if a relative didn't drop off a big, hairy barkin' mutt. "Just watch him for a couple days, okay?"

Much more'n a couple days later I'm thoroughly ticked. "Ruff, ruff, ruff." No rhythm to the cuss, no 'preciation, no manners, either. Dog be player-hatin'- grousin' over the landlords' fine music talent.

Managed to clock its nose with a double swipe of claws. Didn't shut the beast up. Figured war was fixin' to impede on my horizon any day.

Ol' guy and Mama had the too-good-to-say-no, good book blues and could play my blue heaven out of the sky, but for the life of a blues' riff, they could not control the damned, never-leavin' dog!

On the road again.

11

Don't cotton to music out of a box. Hear it blastin' outta cars fittin' to shake your booty- not mine, but ya feelin' me? Box tunes holler from houses, and amidst groups of folks settin' out in nature.

If the noise level ain't off-the-charts enough, ya can't unnerstan' the story cuz the words are all fuzzed-over. Can't nobody speak the speak clear? Or it's all screamin' f-words. Then to top it off there's too much talkin' in-between them uncool wannabe tunes 'bout stuff ain't nobody wantin'. Save me, B.B.!

Is it possible I might encounter a box playin' nothin' but blues? And playin' 'em right? Wit no talkin' inbetween?

Don't make no never minds, I got my ears perked for the real deal- live and phat.

After days of walk on in decent terrain, a wood-workin' man trips my curiosity. I settle in the shade and watch him use his hands and gadgets and make nest boxes for birds. Birdy cribs are hangin' from every limb and hook available. He's perched them just out of my reach. On thin limbs not conducive to support my grand girth. But I ain't hungerin' jist yet, so I'll hang 'round for a spell.

Later, he switches to constructin' matchin' chairs- all the while hummin' tunes I'm unfamiliar with, but they don't hurt my ears. Possibil'ties?

A break in my road relations won't upset my non-existent itinerary. I'm a freebird- you get my drift by now. And the mound of shavin's pilin' up outside his workplace is callin' my name.

He don't pay me no 'tention, so I steal round the hummin' chipper to investigate a roll spot.

Like nothin' I ever caught a whiff of! If they was edible, I'd be rollin' phat. Literal and figurative! Best of all, consequent to bathin' in 'em like a bird in the dust, all the nasty crawlin' critters squattin' out in my fur and bitin' the hell outta my a..., oops butt, are gone!

Itchin's a... Switch off the itchin', hipdipdadowop! I'm scattin' too fine!

Minds me of the cat (2-legged player) doin' Cab Calloway's Minnie the Moocher once at Bad Sign. He had the flow goin' in a language all his own! Wish I could hear ol' Cab and Ella scat it out together and live- talk about cuttin' heads!

A sweet last roll and sneeze- did woodworker hear me? I peer over to the busy brotha, blink dust from my eyes. Don't seem like he notices, or he's playin' it real cool. I b'lieve I'll chillax for a bit, take a cat nap- be made in the shade. A day dreamin' boy.

Stickin' 'round on the lo-lo earns me a double bonus. Guy's 24-carat in the kitchen and a musician to boot- guitar man! He sets a plate on the ground outside of his wood crib, with a "Here, Gato."

Givin' me a peaceful easy feelin' once-over, he returns to his chair, settin' in the last of the sunshine, inhales a scentful dish of his own, and takes to grubbin'.

Nuttin' reg'lar 'bout dis here grub, but hey, I'm game. Hunger makes interestin' friends. Off THE hook and then some- applies to the dinner. Weird combo of chicken and little white pieces in a tangy sauce.

I'm garbagin' like a fat man at a hamburger eatin' contest, remainin' on guard, but woodman stays put and minds his own bidness. We finish up 'bout the same time, and I tend to washin' up. Right partic'lar Mr. Clean, that's me. Meantime, homey digs up an instrument for dessert, and in an instant I'm all ears. His guitar trills sweet notes that linger, knockin' at my repertoire, and light my fire. Like the meal, hits crazy new feelin's, but I'm cravin' to...

"Rrrrrowrrrrrrowwrrr," purrs out like a forty on payday. I saunter into the dim, moth-burdened light, closer and closer. Can't help myself- gotta sing. *"Rowwrrrrrowrrr."*

Homey nods amiably, without droppin' a note. Got his number- he's straight-up, and I ain't shy. Skip toe-steppin', I launch up onto his deck, don't miss a beat. Sit at his bare feet and we jam. I'm in the house!

"Like Santana, my friend? SMOOTH is one fine vibe." He feathers a string better than any bird on the wing. And the note flies, vibrato style.

Santana and smooth- more news to me, but it's dope. My paws are punchin' the deck for more.

"Here's another," he strokes his guitar neck, adjusts a string's tunin', and hoo-yeah, I got my mojo workin' with a bona-fide player.

Good on you, man! Keep breakin' it down! My voice is ready to spit some bars. *"Rrrrrrrrrrrrrrrrr,"* I throw down, tryin' to gauge the meter. Nice to give the ol' pipes a real workout, been too long.

Takes me a few strides to come in proper, but like all the best players (of music, mind you) he presents me with every chance to mix-it up.

Why, homey's singin' bout a woman with evil ways! Readin' my mind? You had doin's wit that... But I shut up the past and sing the present. I'm feelin' it for the entire set.

Gotta tune 'bout a long tall woman in a black dress which minds me of a partic'lar queen I partied wit one amorous night.

"Could we have a confabulation? My fingers need a timeout." He leans the non-electric guitar against the wall, relaxes back, glances at his fingertips and pins me with a friendly 'whass up?' grin.

Confab...what? I cock my confused head, give him the 'what language you speakin', man?'

"Confabulate- a heart to heart."

Beats me. I yawn, maybe we're done for the night?

"Hmmm...chat, talk?"

Talk. Got it. "Rrrrr."

"Sorry if my English might be a little different than what you're used to," he kindly remarks.

Ya think? Ain't jist the language, but s'okay, you be cool.

He's soft-speakin', shades of education. Definitely not from the hood- not a single f-word. Got a built-in musical tone. Reminds me of chimin'... But I ain't fixin' to go there.

Talk I can do anytime, but I'd rather sing. Listen up, bro, *"rrrrRRRRrrrrowww."* Ya feel me?

"I see. I believe the expression is, 'you're the man'."

Damn straight!

"My name is Jose, by the way. I'm glad you liked supper. May I call you Gato?"

Gato? I mull it over. Ain't Cool Cat, but...that's all done wit. Jose is just in time.

"Means cat in my first language," he explains. "Or Musico, if you'd rather?"

I turn my head, flip my tail, "rrrrr." Call me whatever, just don't call me late to the grub or the tunes, how's that?

"Eh, bien, Gato. Shall we continue?"

That's what I'm talkin' 'bout, and you know dis, man!

"I hope you like this one. I'm feeling a little Malaguena."

And his fingers love the strings in a different, spell-bindin' siren. Slow, emotional. I'm so enchanted by this fresh, yet ancient soundin' music, it takes me a minute to unnerstan' the vibe. It hits me full force- this is music Jose grew up with! Like me and blues-which can be slow and full of power, too.

His eyes gone all dreamy-like while his fingers stroll memory lane on the fat guitar neck. I'm down wit it, Jose. I got a past, too, Bro.

I decide to join in with this number. Brotha's eyes stay closed- thinkin' and playin' on his roots. But I hit the right key, come in on the one, and his dark eyes swing wide open, his nostrils flare. Knock me over if his eyes ain't beginnin' to rain into smilin' lips. We ain't so different- blues is universal. Our jammin' is long into the night.

Durin' the day, I hang out to roll in the shavin's and nap in the shade after a spicy lunch provided by my host. What a crib! After our nightly jam sessions, I explore the area. There's a hood of tin cans with folks livin' in 'em down the way. Nothin' worth singin' 'bout. Some folks do the most un-explicable stuff. Imagine, livin' in a can, for the love of tomorrow!

If I watch Jose work, he talks to me like I'm his reg'lar homeboy. His speech appeals to me. Been away from the hood for quite a while now. Maybe I'll change it up- kinda like a speakin' upgrade.

After supper, as day prepares for bed, our jammin' pops off wit an out-of-my-box song list. I'm learnin' all kinds of stuff- too cool for school.

"Check this out, Gato. It's called La Bamba." Another kickin' number. I find a spot to fit in. Too phat!

And Jose's got plenty more. His fingers slide and jump and race. Feel like jumpin' myself- Jumpin' Jack Flash style. Got the bars of a blues tune, but that's it. Here I go, "*RRRRR, erRRRRR., RRRRR erRRRRR.*" Livin' large!

"Go, Gato, go! Johnny be good--" Jose calls this style classic rock- go figure. All I know, is I'm on board. This rock, I can dig.

With each new song, Jose gives me time to groove. Gotta love a true-blue musician. Though he does bring to mind…

But dis homeboy don't seem hip to the blues. Ain't included in his panoply (see, I'm learnin') of en pointe tunes. But I endeavor to steer him to 'turn on your love light' with my highly-trained vocals. And ooh yeah, does he deliver!

"I'm not much of a singer, but I will try something for you, Gato," he winks and pulls out a smokin' BB King sound.

His singin' is a mite too clean for Every Day I've Got the Blues, but his guitar ain't missin' the pathos.

S'okay, homey, my voice has natural blues rasp. I give him a few pointers on the up and up. Good turn deserves a good turn, right? Maybe some of the ol' guy and Mama's good book is hitchin' a ride inside of me? Somethin's got a hold of me.

Admire Jose's courage, but The Thrill is Gone is definitely out of that boy's park. Ah well, everybody can't be the big dog, or cat, but s'okay- it's all right now.

One sun-down, he lays it out. Life's like that- think you got it made in the shade, think again. Change- ain't nothin' but a thang.

"Friend, I'll be leaving soon. My place will be empty for many months." He scans his property like he's memorizin' the layout.

"You're welcome to the cedar shed, or if you'd like to come with me, we can continue our friendship. I've many deliveries and shows to make the rounds of..." he trails off as I turn away and sniff the air.

To make good on his offer, he opens his door and settles his kind dark eyes on me.

But I back off wit da quickness. Being a house cat ain't my style. No way, Jose.

"I understand," he murmurs low and...sad. "It's been an honor and a privilege to jam with you, Gato. You are one cool cat!"

As he says my old moniker, I stop dead.

"Ah, someone somewhere has remarked on your amazing talent. Perhaps that someone is missing you?"

Wouldn't bet on it. If you missed a body, you'd go find him, right?

I meow my thanks and hit the blues highway. Just one of those things might become my mantra.

His, "take care and good luck," sighs behind me.

12

Find…me. The whole concept rankles me. I don't want nobody findin' me. Ain't got nobody, but I ain't lost. Got it jist like I like it. Footloose and free- no chains on dis cat.

See, the blues trail don't worry none 'bout nothin' 'cept right now. Folks'd do well to think more 'bout right now than all the hasslin' of tomorrow. Tomorrow, I love ya, but I ain't frettin' over ya.

Pick yoself up and get back in the game. Move it- that's life! Singin' 'bout happenin's is better than cryin', dyin' or imbibin'. To survive, you mind the here and now- s'all that's pertinent.

Stalkin' the next meal, roostin' or ruckusin' fills up most of the day. Wit a little cozyin' up thrown in here and dere when the right chick's at paw.

I'm scentin' weather fixin' on changin' up. Smart cat is watchin' the trees shuckin' their phat threads. Means cold's knockin' on the door. Gotta find a dry crib for one, with nearby groceries.

Further on up the road an abandoned, sizeable shack presents possibil'ties. No comin' and goin' of 2-leggeds. Or so I 'riginally thought.

Use all my senses to check the coast's clear. Use only one and it's like to backfire. Cat can get dead real fast. And I ain't 'bout to step into no trap. Got too much livin' to do.

I traipse across a rickety porch deck, mindin' the holes, slink through a jagged openin' with the loose shoulders my breed specializes in. Among other skills.

On the lookout for competition. So far so good. Locate a ratty-ass chair in a dry location. Do a little grub shoppin'- lotsa mice. B'lieve I hit it big.

After a snack, I realign the remnant stuffin' in the 2-legged sit-down, curl up for an overdue nap and digestion of the day's doin's.

Five winks in I jump up, electrified. Every hair I lay claim to is standin' on end, whiskers and tail atwitch.

What the...!

Bulgin' eyes peer into the black shadows. They say seein' is b'lievin', but I'm here to state ain't seein' is b'lievin'!

Been privy to many a wang-dang-doodle in the hood, and out of the old neighborhood I started quite a few. Rolled in mud, guts and beer and glass- can't begin to compare with what confronts me now.

Ain't never seen/not seen this kinda goin's on in any of my surrounds.

Loose stuff skitters like 'what's poppin' off in the hood tonight?'. Wisps of carpet bat me upside the head three times. Bits bouncin' and flyin' about like a ghost baseball team without bases. Or maybe I'm home plate?

No players. No batters. No seen ones, anyhoo.

"RRRRR," I umpire into the melee only to feel my catnap chair rattle like somethin' fat slid into it, hard. Now a cat is known for pretty decent night vision, but I ain't seein' nothin'!

Small stones, papers and sticks skitter cross the floor like livin' creatures, click-clackin' when bustin' against each other. Overhead, the leftovers of a light fixture swing to and fro- groanin' in its beat-the-band off kilter rhythm. A flat spoof on the wall spins- reminds me of the Bad Sign sign in a storm. Best take cover? From what?

Silence takes a turn, but in the far room…

Curiosity didn't kill the cat, stupidity did. Me, I ain't afraid of nothin'. Like the tune says, 'I don't worry 'bout nothin' cuz I know nothin' gonna be alright.' I'm down wit da idiosyncrasies of life. Cool word, eh?

I abdicate my roost. Like the new lingo? Thought I'd broaden my horizons after listenin' to Jose. He was quite voluble in my presence- reckon I filled in for a listenin' post. I bet my homey and Jose'd confabulate like brothas from different mothas.

Why am I givin' a rat's ass second thinkin' bout Homey?

Shake it off. Takin' my sweet time, I stalk the source of the shifted racket. Did the players fall outta the joint? Place got more holes than Bad Sign.

I'd never have crept into this decrepit ol' house if it didn't have so many escape routes, ya dig? Usin' the ol' smarts.

Commotion lambasts the cookin' room. Scents of grub still cling to crazily canted chairs, bloated counters, stained walls, shreds of curtains and shucked-up floors.

If the house is rockin'… Chairs tilt back and forth without any breeze. Sounds like a game of tag goin' down- racin' cross the top of the table, vaultin' onto the counter, up into open-door cabinet shelves, swing them doors and shuffle off.

Plop! I swear a fat cat hit the ground, hoists itself up and bounds in front of me as fast as a fat cat might. I feel the slightest of draughts by heavy duty's passin' by.

Bang, bang! Dented pots clatter. The shred of curtain shreds further from its rod above the window. Somethin' clamorin' clanks in the sink. Cupboard doors (the ones which still hang on hinges) whop-whop, but don't open. Half expectin' to hear, 'pizza delivery', I'm wishin' strong.

I hunker into a prime-view seat and take stock of the free-for-all ghost baseball team. Ghost cats?

A thin stream of mis-guided moon shine (not the drinkin' shine) struggles to breach the filthy glass, cast a glow on...

Serious as a knife fight on a hot Saturday night in the hood- I blink multiple times to be sure- the outline of a large tom cat sittin' up on the edge of the sink paws at the moonbeam!

Fly me to the moon if it ain't the coolest sight I ever did kinda see! Spooky!

"Rowwww?" I'm itchin' to join in. Imagine a cat fight without physical repercussions!

I ain't braggin' on war wounds, but the opposite, see? I am the champeen of...

'Yo haints,' but these homeboys ain't down wit hospitality. No response.

Best of my seein'/countin' seems to be three of 'em. Sink cat flies over my head, followed by another fleein' the window sill, and an enormous blob stuck on the floor immediately chases after.

Hot on their tails, I race the ghost cats into the hall- I'm a player. But they've disappeared. Did I jist say that? Ghosts disappeared, right. Reckon they done fled up the stairs. Have to take the second innin' upstairs. I'm on it.

Now the jist of it is, ghost cats is silent. It's only the objects of their interest or impact soundin' the pandemonium. Gotta wonder what dem players was like when livin' in real live zoot suits.

"Oh, about the same," I hear an amused rejoinder.

"Rrrrrr!" There's fightin' grit in my growl. Would startle the norm, but nothin' here approaches normal. And how did this newcomer sneak in here?

"I see," an ol' woman haint sidles out of a cupboard like smoke driftin' at Bad Sign, titters like a gigglin' chick makin' over the star B-ball man. "I see you've met my boys, Cahoots, King and Fat Frank." I see right through her motherly smile. And the rest of her, too.

Her boys, hmmm. Fat Frank- that explains a lot of the slippin' and bashin' into solids. Kinda funny, a hefty ghost cat. So, weight follows ya wherever, huh. Am I trippin'?

"Oh, don't mind me, I only live here. As do my boys. Never turn away a stray, never did. There's a mite of a little female around here somewhere, but she keeps to herself- a very sad case." The regret in this admission is a blues song all by itself. Wonder if it sings?

"Sing? I used to...long ago, but only to my kitties. Perhaps I'll try again," the shade reminisces. "Thank you for the suggestion."

I'm sorta seein' the original homegal, I b'lieve, in threads no gal would want to be caught dead in- oops! 'Meanin' no disrespect, lady.'

"That's all right, dear. Make yourself at home, you are most welcome here. Good night." Wisp of an elderly woman whisks up the stairway.

And shake it up, baby, if I ain't hearin' the dregs of Mack the Knife layin' it on the line wit a kick in it! Lady ghost with pizazzz- I'm feelin' it! In a spooky kinda way.

Some house, word (means seriously).

13

You can be damned sure soon as you think you got it all figured out some s.o.b. yanks yer chain. My winter crib notion went down like a warm 40 on a hot day. And not due to the ghosts.

Gotta write my own blues beats. False Hope Blues, I'll call 'em. Homeboy and the band. Jose and the sweet-scent shavin's. Now the woodpile I still venture out to, and dig a superb roll in cuz they ain't too far a jaunt from the house of haunts. Jose, he was cool, but I get the whole movin' on bidness. Maybe I'll see him later, alligator.

Best thang 'bout a ramshackle house full of ghosts? No competition for food or a place to sleep, and when the lady of the manor ain't croonin', I provide the musical interlude- once the ruckus entertainment settles. Some crazy far side kinda thang, but I'm down wit it.

Third sun here, a babe in the woods wandered in. Prob'ly the sad case the ol' gal mentioned. I figure s'all good in the hood. Big house- what's left of it. I ain't gonna chase no kit away. I'm down wit a live warm body to curl up and nap with durin' the comin' cold.

She fearfully crawled in like a half-dead bug, tiny head craned right and left, and afore I could make intros, the kit scampered out wit da quickness when fat cat rolled/fell off a chair and sent a tin can on a merry bounce.

That's life, I felt like callin' after her, but kinda sounded awful mean so I kept it to myself. Kit's got her own problems and good luck to her. Didn't say it out loud, not my style.

Third night here, chill and wet as wet can get, I'm fixin' to turn in when…CRASH!!

I jump up, fired up. For a second, I think I'm still in the hood. Glass sprayin' from rocks bustin' in what remains of windows. There's skitterin' 'cross the floor. Curses, challenges smack-shoutin' from outside. Rain promptly blowin' in the new entry ways. Damn humans can't leave a body peaceable-like.

Lots of skedaddlin' ensues, and a pitiful cry shrieks escalatin' octaves from upstairs afore abruptly dyin'. What a voice! Why ain't I made the acquaintance of that diva? And just how did she sneak in without my catchin' on? Slip, slidin' away, am I?

Sudden silence sweats the house. Anybody left? Ghosts gone to ground? What with all the trash-talkin' and rock tossin' I ain't figurin' on stickin' round either- hoodbillies might decide to bring their party inside.

Fixin' to git soaked, I up and head out for the shavin' shed- take a safe, pre-planned exit. Come back when the storm's blown out. Maybe.

Lurkin' in the dark thick brush past the wannabe thinks-he's-all-that pitcher, I keep my wary head down, spy a huge tree. Spread-out, ragged roots host a den underneath. Get a whiff of the scared-to-death kit. Prob'ly tremblin' in the depths, fixin' to have a heart attack. Should offer a 'buck-up, you're safe from Godzilla', only protectin' and encouragin' ain't my style. Ever body's 'sponsible for its own self. Carin' is sharin' and I don't do either one.

Before I quit the scene, the giant thug hoists some daredevil chick up by her hair. Can't have too much sense hangin' wit da likes of that walkin' trash, baby girl.

She's boxin' like Ali on speed and I 'spect prayin', 'I need a hero.'

I almost check my course. Ain't nothin' fair in life, but...

Hell, I decide I will put my 2-cents in. Bugger ruined a phat layout for me. And that chick's got guts. Not smarts, but guts.

Off to the side is a crude dude dressed like an industrial-size garbage bag, and two huddled, sodden female 2-leggeds- hangin' chick's friends? Whatever their story, they are worthless at takin' sides.

"Stop it! Come on, let's go. It's cold and we're soaked." Whinin' audience, what a waste.

Not me. I stand for my rights. 'Specially as I was here first- you *********!

Ante up, big bad Leroy Brown, I fume, this junkyard cat is gonna...

Afore I can unsheathe my claws and lay out my finest fightin' vocal challenge, an OG (old gangster=somebody you DON'T wanna mess wid. Can't be teachin' my lingo all your life) steps out of a fog like a dream come true.

"CatSkill at your service," OG touts, and the girl is immediately released as the wannabe tough swings to meet TROUBLE he never dreamed existed.

The tall, mysterious CatSkill (livin', not a ghost) stranger serves up an ass-whuppin' I thrill to spectate. Top cat puts the hurt on the smack-spoutin' hoodbilly so fast he don't know what hit him.

Agile 'n quick, rather like a cat. Altogether admirable old school tactics. Laid out thug bum faster than a hound dog on a trail.

CatSkill momentarily surveys the result of his handiwork splayed out in a cold puddle, shakes his head. Thick mane of hair on the OG needs a better tendin' to, but who am I to fault this manly perfection at work?

Hoodbilly manages to stumble to his feet, splashes a sick rain dance, and like a weekend drunk staggers off in the wake of the long-gone whiners.

The rain stalls out; the girl's okay. The ghost cats and whoever else is in residence are safe. I shelve my 2-cents. Shavin's are callin' my name.

But I catch the final spooksville act. After CatSkill converses wit the chick, he up and vanishes!

I don't pay no more 'tention to the girl. She's inspectin' the ghost cat cavin'-in abode- more power to her. Seems a cat I ain't made da acquaintance of (prob'ly the diva I heard earlier) is talkin' to the chick. I'll leave the gutsy girl to all the resident entertainment. Obviously, she ain't got no fears, either.

Now, I bet you're wonderin' how this here cat is so very hip to ghosts.

Old gent runnin' Bad Sign (looked as old as the juke joint) set up a shot every night for the resident ghost, and one for himself, right before lockin' up and headin' out back to bed.

"One for you, Champ, and one more for the road," bartender toasted in his smoke-stick, grungy whisper. He'd eye a signed picture hangin' pride-of-place behind the bar, salute with his shot glass and down the contents.

Story was a pitcher born next door made a name for himself in major league baseball. Got famous in days when he was a stand-out anomaly. When his arm finally failed, he returned to the old neighborhood, bought Bad Sign and died soon after.

I mean, how do you live without your passion?

Anyhow, once the shot was set out and the bartender raised his glass, the ghost's shot disappeared- the whiskey, not the glass. The small glass simply tipped as if appreciatin' the remembrance.

Now and again, when least expected durin' a quiet night (very rare), a baseball would roll cross the bar- takin' out an empty bottle, or ringin' a shot glass. Folks'd peer 'round, bug-eyed and tremblin'. Some took fingers and crossed themselves. Most smiled erratically when the bartender yelled, "Play ball!"

Hey bartender then poured drinks fast as he could and the customers made sure they disappeared faster- equalin' the ghost star pitcher.

I was privy a time or two. There were more holes in that ate-up wood floor than a rat has exit routes- plenty to hide and see from. Curiosity don't have to kill nobody. Listen and learn.

So, I ain't met nothin' yet to put the fear in me. I got da blues for company, and if a ghost wants to revisit the home turf who am I to bum a brotha out?

Bathin' off the ghost spider webs acquired from slippin' into my fave shavin' shed, I paw dust over some excess baggage in a far corner, slow ride in gangsta cologne, prepare myself an insulated curl-up zone and grab a quiet cat nap.

Time spent huntin' the surrounds provides me breakfast. Miss Hook's fish leftovers, but that's how it rolls.

With dusk on my tail, I strut into the nearby tin can hood. Got my pre-casin' in, of course. Humans livin' in long tin cans! Sumpin' wrong wit dat scene. I skirt the noisy kids-r-us section, ignore the hood hoopla minus the cappin' blasts, turn up my nose at the box 'tunes'. Save me, Santana! No true players of the musical variety strummin' in this joint? Reckon that's what livin' in tin cans does. Get a real crib, ya bunch of losers.

Near the wooded end of Tincanville some young queen is holdin' court. The wannabe lovers wrastle over who gits the prize. Could've busted right in 'cept she don't stir my mac. Queen looks down right peaked. Pity the kits. But not my problem.

Ain't got no problems, no hidden agendas, no baby-need-shoes to add to my hit parade.

In the underside of a stand of bushes crouch humans with covered traps. Cadge a whiff of somethin' smellin' tasty- they be settin' bait.   Bein' from the hood, and the smarter of feline specimens, I have 'caution' for a middle name.

Damned good thing, too. Scrawny youngster noses in and wham bang, thank you, ma'am- the door to the cage shuts wit da finality. Homey got played!

Further strollin' showcases more of the same trappers. Took a bit for the caterwaulin' to raise the roof, but not the door. Homeboys prob'bly stuffed themselves wit the bait first, 'stead of takin' care of bidness.

No still of the night happenin' here, I'm steppin' out. Further on up the road, I catch the scent of another tomcat. Maybe somethin' interestin' might develop? Ain't had a good scrap lately, and I do have to keep in prime shape.

Paddin' stealthily out from a run-down shed…

'Yo, champ!' I hiss at one grizzled tonnage. Ol' gangsta (fighter with a record, in this case) been around the block more scars than I can reliably count. Misshapen face, torn ears, one glarin' eye, the other half-closed, missin' most of his whiskers, most of his hair, too. But a lean, mean fightin' machine, not fixin' to retire anytime soon.

Now it's a fact of nature a stray tom on walkabout is bound to cross into contentious territory- no way 'round it. Word. (Means serious in hood talk.)

'My turf, boy,' he instructs with mangled ears laid back and a throaty growl and one and a half eyes flared.

Sounds familiar.

Hastily, I re-think my inclination. Got a long record of wins endorsed in his bearin'. And so I'm figurin' he's earned the right to the rest of his life, and poo yeah, nothin' here's worth testin' my mettle for anyway.

'Got no beef wit you, OG. I'm steppin' out.' I arc to the left, give plenty of room, not from fear, simply respect. He's got mine. Few OGs make it to his age. What I reckon is his age. Can't never be too sure...

"RRRRRR!!" He spits and I catch the gleam of a few teeth still in residence. 'Think I can't take you on?' OG is layin' down wit the challenge.

Ain't proper for me to back out now. Be a walk-off of shame. Ain't happenin'. Unless...

Figure I got a mite better than even shot considerin' my skills- fight record, weight, attitude, age, and all the strong teeth in my head. Versus his experience. I could take it or leave it. Don't need to prove anythin'. I decide to give him an out. Or at least give it my best shot of smarts-atude.

'Don't make no damn difference to me. Both of us can live on.' I sound like I'm makin' sense

'Livin'? Call this livin'?'

'Livin's better than dyin',' I equably respond though my tail is mirrorin' his- lashin' side to side.

This confab ain't lookin' too promisin'. I hunker down...

'One more for the road,' he snarls and lays into me quicker than white lightnin' goin' down on a Saturday night tear-all.

Claws unsheathed, paws bat like bloods bearin' knives in a turf war. Teeth seekin' to find grab-holds. Ol' tom still got da skills- he writhes away like snakes from a fire and bounds on for more.

I ain't lost a fight in some time, and don't 'spect to start tonight, but I gotta admit my paws are up 'n full.

"RRROWWWW!" My high-pitched scream ends in his throat.

He wrangles my ears, but I roll him. Wait for my stranglehold to drain the life from Mr. No-Quitter.

There is tearin' at my face, ears, but I'm busy dishin' out. I spit out blood, give him a second's respite- a chance to step off.

OG must have a death wish ridin' his train. He don't hesitate at all- givin' it every trick he's ever picked up. Reckon I'll oblige with my youthful vigor. I rake at his guts til he loses his grit. We disengage, snarlin'. He totters to his feet. I hold my peace, but my tail is not happy with my head.

I rail notes off the scale- my respect hail to the OG as he 3-legged limps into the deepest shadows.

Thrill is gone, OG, thrill is gone. Go on, sing your blues in the night.

14

"Were you lucky enough to get that old tomcat?"

Can't a body sally forth victorious without some trapper disruptin' the party?

"No, but there's been one monumental cat fight. Whole neighborhood heard it. Saw the old tomcat hobbling away- badly injured, I'll bet. Let's see if we can entice that noisy black and orange beast."

Beast, me? Betcher ass you ain't catchin' this homeboy. I'm outta here. A song seems appropriate, cuz those po-po trappers don't know just who they fixin' to mess wid.

Got my blues boogie shoes on. Struttin' like a flash, damn the road. Yeah, baby, got my blues shoes on, you wannabees. I'm struttin' on down the road. Blues come knockin', I'm ditchin' this here load.

One, two, three, four, five, step six. Y'all ain't catchin' me, cuz baby, I'm major slick!

I leave 'em with an ear-splittin' ascent of my octave powers.

A fair distance from tin can cat carnival, I slow. Nobody on my tail. Dark, quiet. Slowly discoverin' the extent of my wounds. Stiffness settin' in, too. Injuries need lickin' and a rest-up.

Draggin' butt, I'm on the lookout for a place to lay low. Shoulda went back to the shavins, but didn't want to chance runnin' the gauntlet of trappers.

Hear a rockin' beat, sumpin' bout a high steppin' daddy, exudin' from a dimly lit house beyond a fence just ahead.

Phat phrase. I might consider myself a high stepper, once I take care of bidness.

Back of the music house is a suitable lights-out shed. Place to lay low and recoup? Like the preacher man roars, 'Praise be!'

Wit the state of me, I'm reckonin' against boundin' up and fence walkin'. Best I check for easy access. Find a loose plank, nudge it aside, head for the shed after assurin' myself no hostiles are nosin' 'round. Like some of my new vocab? What a body kin learn!

Crib's lackin' a fair number of its coverin's, makes it simple to slip in. Boxes upon boxes means plenty to explore later when grub time sounds off. Man, what I'd give for a plate of Jose's tight specialty or a Hook's toss out! Wishin' ain't eatin', on to the necessaries.

Traipsin' and scoutin', I locate a comfy size space for the likes of me to tuck in. Groomin' occupies me seemingly forever. Blood and dirt and skin and hair between my toes, grimy coat, sore ears, muzzle and neck scraped aplenty, and what d'ya know? My one eye is havin' a hard time stayin' open!

OG got his licks in. Good on you, champ! I ain't vengeful. Brotha's got to make do best he can.

Cat nap here I come. I'm flat out...

Senses all-out alert. Someone's sneakin' round the corner and for damned sure it ain't Mack the Knife! My homegal, Ella, wailed about that cat. Billie and Etta was also ladies sang blues like blues meant to be sung. Koko and Moms had it in 'em, too.

Lotsa great musical arteests. No time to digress- back to what's on the menu right now.

Stealthy, these players ain't.

I stretch the kinks away, preparin'. Whooeee- the stiff done set in. OG sure let me have it. Faster than lines formin' at Bad Sign for drinks, I bathe my injured eye open. Better to see y'all wit!

Move it, quick, but silent. Wake up skills, I silently scream. Ain't no time for pussy-footin'! Figures, too, I'm workin' shy of grub.

Think you got me, suckers? You got another thing comin'!

If a cat ain't hoistin' better sense than the average rat in plannin' escape routes ain't got the gall to call itself a cat.

Quieter than a wary mouse, I slink, a second shadow to the multiple boxes stacked up tight in this here maze. Trespassers to the left of me, exit to the right...

Can't keep a smart cat down. Yeah, been down so long, down don't bother me. No time to sing my praises. Stay primed. Height is out of the question. Don't stand a silent chance of vaultin' to the top- the boxes reach pert to the ceilin', and if they wobble and my stiff bod chances to fall- here I am, stuck in the middle of one nasty trip.

In my favor there's no light penetratin' from outside. Kudos to the boxes, for that slight toss-a-bone to the cat.

Down this away, cross, slim-up enough to stretch between a box and a wall. There's my opening- salvation, here I come.

Damn! Plank stickin' it closed.

"There, hear him over by the door?" Trappers, two of 'em. Shoulda known. Who else goes through this much trouble for a cat? Leave out poison, sic the dog on 'em, or shoot 'em and leave 'em is the usual in other hoods.

Scout another route. Climbin's a waste. Even if I manage to get myself up, ain't no openin's out among the rafters, no shelves to hide or fight from. Think, I badger my brains.

Trappers are movin' the boxes about- hmmm... What's yer game?

I flatten, streak further along the wall. Keep movin', keep on movin'. Shades of Jimmy Reed- you got me runnin'...

It's finally near total dark; I ain't had a mouthful of nuttin' since the day before. That mouse squeakin' is one lucky so-and-so. Word. Somebody gonna pay for this predicament!

My gut thinks my mouth gone walkabout, or got wiped out in the fight. As for singin' my frustrations, throat's dry as the damned boxes. If the things weren't sealed up, I'd consider tuckin' in.

Hate to say it, but movin' on is gittin' some impossible. All exit routes bein' blocked up by these street ballers shufflin' box walls into a new puzzle.

B'lieve half my life's wastin' away playin' keep away in cat hell. Man, I'm in deep- these straight trippin' trappers...

Finally, I'm 'boxed' in, confronted with a single open avenue.

"Rrrrrr," my lowest register vents my extreme displeasure in its limited capacity.

"Do you have enough energy to sing to it?" A male grumbles. "I'm starving and seriously considering eating the cat snacks, myself."

I ignore the 'it', but not the, 'sing'? Snacks?

The scent of some grub is waftin' my way from, you guessed it- a ***trap.

Why don't they hit the road, Jack, and we'll all go party our separate ways? And then it happens- an unbelievable surprise in this nightmare!

"Mooooon river…"

Save me, Ella! A crooner with the phat sound of the first lady! Every hair on my body stands attention. The sweetness rolls on.

Sing to me, baby girl! Am I dreamin', thinkin' this bona fide singer could give Ella or Etta or Billie or Lena a run for the money?

Whooeeee! Exhausted, yet entranced, I'm fools-rush-in unaware I'm struttin' to a you-put-a-spell-on-me sound pipin' me…

Into a gapin' door. Into the realm of a waftin' scent beat-to-the-band better than dumpster divin' at Hook's. Well, beat me, daddy, eight to the bar!

Dinner and a concert- I can dig it. My tail hastens to join me as the trap door springs shut. Too bad, so sad, but hell, I fought the law before and won. No worries. Leastways, ain't no J.C. spoutin', just pure vibes warblin'.

The sweet music continues as I'm escorted to wherever. A little time to make some plans. Maybe sing along?

Moon river, eh?

15

Short bookin' stint. I down the grub wit da quickness, jonesin' for more. Caught off guard by a sudden stop, I rail to myself- get yer game face on homey cuz don't know what's poppin' off next.

Fantasizin' 'bout the chick's vocal skills- which stimulated my crazy feelin' response of steppin' in the jailhouse now- got me all twisted up. Intent on the keepin' on croonin' of the diva and the potentiality of our music-makin' future, I forget to plan. Chick certainly needs new material to go wit her phat pipes. Gotta include real blues and that's where I come in. Become her manager and…

My throat is somewhat soothed and stompin' to show her the birth of the blues. Done right proper.

"rrrrowwwwwrrrrrROWWRRR."

Instead of takin' the hint and doin' the rightful harmonic call and response, she stops altogether. I have that effect on chicks.

But the car ain't movin' no more. Forgot to plan my attack once the jail releases this phat cat- you upside down G!

"Here we go, buddy," she murmurs wit da sweetness of pour a little sugar on me.

I ain't nobody's buddy. Can't fool me fakin' sweet talk, sista. Singin' is a whole nutha ball game. What the…

Cage opens. I'm slip/dumped into a thick wrap-up. St. James infirmary- this ain't! Smells tasty, but what's thug boy up to?

"What have we here?"

Trappers done brung me to Mr. Smiley. I'll give him somethin' to smile about. Let me at yer puss! Learn ya a whole new religion, I will!

"I'm Dr. Xavier. Nice size kitty. You'll be fine, I'm sure. Let's get a good look at you, shall we?"

Kitty? Who, me?

I'm wrestlin' to get out of mummy-ville, but the male trapper is got a hold on me. The chick dares to hum as if that'll wipe away the transgressions! Too late, baby cakes, you done lost your appeal.

My display of teeth ain't convincin' 'em to get back, Jack. Claws is wrapped up tight, no use. I feel an unfair prick. Boy is there gonna be a shit storm…

Joint closin' time, I reckon. Head's as fuzzy as a 3-day drunk lyin' in a putrid alley.

Force an eye open. Too quiet. Two senses seem to work- most of my sight and all my hearin'. Dark. Dim light in the distance. A darker shadow saunters by…wherever the hell I am!

I'm too bamboozled to rise and check out the furtive one. It's all I can manage with the one eye slitted. Why am I as tired as a newborn kit after suckin' M'Moms' milk?

Who's dat sneakin? Somethin' vaguely familiar… Sniffer's way off base- scent of cat and human- mixed?

"It'll get better. Trust me," the shadow stops and speaks to me.

Better? You playin' me, right? I don't trust nobody. I think I emit a pitiful growl.

"I know," he congenially offers.

What the hell do you know? Who are you? Open dis here up and we'll both know a little sumpin' sumpin'! I guarantee it!

A chuckle with the vocal depth and vibrato worthy of a fly (top-notch) musician accompanies him as he departs.

Wait a confounded minute! I can't fight the go-back-to-sleeps. Nobody knows you when yer down and out, right?

"CatSkill, til we meet again." I think I hear.

Sometime later- much later by the sound of my grumblin' gut- I wake to sound and light. Still a bit foggy in the brain.

Stretchin' stimulates the ol' mojo workin' despite a little residual ache from battlin' the OG.

I case the entire of this jail cell. Slick walls. No window. Nothin' to climb up and get my ass outta here. Pro side, it's warm, but cold don't confront me none. Faint hint of other cats.

Maaan, am I righteously pi…ticked off!

My initial trumpet hits the air waves with the longest, drawn-out, high-pitched, turn-me-loose shriek I can muster. Lappin' at the dish of water, I prepare for war- we'll see what it's good for. Ears are gonna pay, if nothin' else is available.

"Somebody's feeling better, I see." This from a fat broad who stops and gives me the once over.

Though sore, my hindered eye joins the uninjured one and I glare a response fittin' to equal my next oral diatribe (lingo compliments of the educated Jose). I unsheathe my stickers, ready to break it down. Bring it on home, deuce'-n-a-half. My rebound is windin' up to have a go!

"This darn latch always sticks," she fiddles with the door. Legs spread for added oomph, she puts her whole self into it- and that's sayin sumpin'!

Door unleashes and I'm on opportunity like stink and fleas on a junkyard dog.

Bowlin' into the gate with my own considerable heft, I knock her askew. No panty-waist cat here- I got you, babe! I bolt through fatty legs. The cat is IN the house- let the jailhouse rock begin!

Shootin' down the hall, I skid through an open door. Hear her none-too-fast-to-catch-me jostlin' rearward. Chair to table to cabinet I bound, and free everythin' not tied down, includin' the junk inside the cabinet with its lousy excuse for a lock.

Ding! Ding! I hit the jackpot as items clatter to the floor and into each other- breakin' more'n a few glass bottles in their descent. Music to my ears.

I scramble out as another openin' presents itself, leavin' heavy-duty to flounder in my upended wake.

"What the…"

War- this is what it's good for, hooorah! Yo, bud, stick around cuz you asked for it.

"Dr. X, I'm so sorry. The brute caught me off guard--"

"Bound to happen at some point, Stella. Don't worry…"

I hear Mr. Smiley doc as I move it on up.

I don't delay my position in order to give a point-to-point on the finer points of gettin' the hell outta this joint. Another door pops open, I slither in. No time to freebird the cabinets, but I send all else on a free ride in all directions.

Skim by a flailin' wannabe trapper. The "here, kitty, kitty," call receives an appropriate multi-curse rejoinder.

Too many of these small rooms loaded with dislodge-ables. I divest every shelf of its shi…stuff. Love the cheer of breakage and the plaintive scramblin' of 2-leggeds behind me. Got my game on, come play!

The more mayhem, the better I like it. Told y'all- paybacks are hell! I'll give 'em a run for the money that'll go down in jail history. Breathless broads look like nerds jackassin' it on a basketball court. Jumpin', runnin', but nuttin' poppin' off. No score for y'all.

Can I get a jump, jive, wail to accompany my singin' my own 'Who da man?' blues?

Flyin' over the top of fatty's head- she ass-over-teakettled and is tryin' to dodge fallout- I race on. The only way to go is ahead through the hall. My bulk kicks open an unlocked door which kindly swings wide for me. Aha, now here's a room large enough to play keep-away in! Can you dig it?

Mr. Smiley bozo has entered the fray. Come one, come all- I'm pitchin' the biggest wang dang doodle this joint ever seen! Come fly with me…

"Our newest…guest is on the loose," the pinch-hitter calmly states the obvious.

Guest, my a…butt! The voice is rather familiar, but no time to waste on polite introductions.

"Stella, make sure the front door is locked."

I see light outside, but no way to get there. Reckon we'll continue the shake, rattle and roll. Up on a chunk of wood, I rabbit

kick a stack of papers. Sailin' city. Topple a can of thin sticks-
they fall, roll, ping. Bingo! A big bag goes dumps-ville- look at
all the junk!

"My purse—" fatty Stella wails.

Too bad, so sad- what ya carryin' all that for anyhow? And
not a single thing to eat, what's wrong wit you? I give 'em a
strident ululation, "*RRRrrrAAAAARRRR.*" Top that, Stella, I dare
ya.

I paddy-cake on tiny black trays and see odd happenin's on
a flat screen. Shuck off a skatin', corded sumpin' or other.

"Oh, no, the computer!"

Bang- there goes a tickin' box and a ringin' somethin' to
boot. If I had the time I'd chew that coil, but high stakes plants are
callin' my name. Up the ante!

Atop a high shelf, I bulldoze all the containers of greens.
Plants and dirt shimmy on down. Shame, shame, I miss a curious
head, but get a load of the new yard!

"I want a raise," some chick cries.

"Sky should be the one heading off World War III. Look at
this mess! And who's going to clean it all up?"

"We need Garrett- nothing is out of his realm," calm
advises.

"I can't get to the clinic phone through this sh…storm, and
my cell was in my purse the whirlwind Tasmanian devil just
upended! Hey, don't step on my new lipstick!"

Tasmanian devil? New one on me.

"I'll call him," calm states. Ah yeah, recall hits me- the
smiley thug from last night- the one who stuck me with lights out.

I'd surely like to return the favor. Give 'im the ol' one, two and wipe that smile to the backside of over the rainbow. Word.

"I quit," fatty huffs.

Can't handle old school, huh? What d'ya think was gonna happen? Truss up a homeboy, lock me in a cage. Yo, I'm from the hood. Ain't got no house manners- not that I'd use 'em on the likes of youse.

Now ain't this some crazy… What kind of a crack-pot crib is dis joint? Rockwall wit water runnin' down it- bless my bluesy butt! No perchin' goin' down on that slipperoo. Why ain't y'all got windows to open? Never heard of air? Ain't no tunes up in here, either. Y'all is wasted space.

Best move it. Keep trappers outta tail range and off balance.

Another shelf. Special delivery! I send all plants south to the ground where plants belong. Broken pots, more free dirt showers for everyone!

Runnin' out of runway, I soar onto the top of a pond.

"Oh hell, the new fish tank…"

Hell aint' got nothin' on a ticked-off cat!

My landin' spot atop the pond slips from under me, skitters the opposite way of my tail. Plop! I'm in deep, but don't confront me none cuz I'm cool wit water. Touchin' bottom I vault up. Surprise, surprise I got a doggone fish on my kisser and soggy greens, too.

"Hang on, Sally, I'm coming," calm wit da sticker whispers.

Fish goes flyin' when I catch the pond rim wit my front paws and bust out, shakin' like a wet dog and rarin' to rip it up and ball some more! Too bad the pond weighs more'n me- can't even tilt the sucker- cuz addin' water to the dirt below makes mud, more fun!

Yo, nice catch! I roll off three bars accolade as calm softly lands the out-of-its-element in his hands. Watchin' its tail flip, I'm thinkin': got dat special sauce, slices of bread? I be ready for a fish sandwich here. I'll share. Ha! Not wit da likes of y'all.

But fisherman ignores me, dares my battlefield, replaces the fat fish in the pond and stands guard, darin' me to try it again.

"Guess my aquarium will be better off at home," he asides to the audience of two.

No fish for breakfast, okay. I ain't done pitchin' this wang dang doodle. Less somebody sees clearly now and sets me free! It ain't over til the fat lady sings and ol' fatty standin' by wouldn't know a blues note on a bet. Save me, I can see the outside callin' me, just open the damn door!

Managin' to claw my way to the top of a wall of pictures I check my future roost. Light fixture, here I come.

Lights swing like a pendulum do. Climbin' the fixture's pole, the ceilin' is solid- no way up to get out. A rock ledge provides me another venture. Too bad nothin's sittin' on it cuz I'm rarin' to wreak all possible havoc. And then some.

Now, all this time I been singin' my hit parade with a vocal range no band can match. Talk about match- just put me some grub in a matchbox- gonna forget 'bout you. If I could only step out of this joint! Unappreciative bunch of losers.

"I can't stand it anymore. I need ear plugs," a disheveled chick snivels, drops the trap to use her hands to plaster her ears.

That ain't all you need, babe, I'd like to tell her, but I got to plan my next move.

Amid the awe-struck chain of fools, I bound like a red rubber ball, ignore the box trap settin' in my path, race through the dirt to a tree(?) in the corner. Lame-ass wannabe tree, no heft. Down we tumble, tree and me, onto a slick surface. Gotta git further along, if I can make it...

Claws no use in this stretch. I'm outta ammo, surrounded by frustrated, box-clad trappers. Time to ramp up the rant ante. Didn't think I had anythin' left in the ol' voice box, did ya?

"Loose cat, huh?" Recognize this guy, too. The male trapper from last night.

Why didn't you bring singer, dipshit? I'm gonna tear...

But I'm way low on the energy scale and trapper knows the score. He grimaces through my shrieks, and a huge cloth- I hate to say it- defeats me. I fight with the last of my strength, but my stickers ain't stickin'.

"Give us a chance, Mr. Highway to Hell. Oh, excuse me, Strut."

I feel that slight prickin' again and I'm ou...

Jailed again. With a loaded plate of groceries sittin' by. Small compensation, but I'm gonna rip into it like a Christmas present- sumpin' I heard 'bout once. And then they are gonna hear about it. Get ready, get ready- cuz the bell will ring for the next round.

Eat with intermittent snarls just to show I ain't down yet. Tend to a bath- fighters of all sizes keep a clean coat if they want to stay in the game. Besides my fightin' prowess, I'm a rico suave specimen and courtin' the ladies is my middle name.

What did homeboy call me? Strut? Gotta think on that.

Carefully check my victory trophies- torn ear and the other is missin' its point, bruised and clawed areas, puncture wounds. Eye's doin' good. Get the dirt out of my toes, belly hair, under my tail... Takes two licks to register the soreness- where are my...?

Hell no! Take a brotha's goods! Seriously? How did I wake up missin' a few doggone, er catgone parts? How low can anybody sink- pullin' some shi...poop thataway? How come ya do me like dat? I rail til my voice is nearly lame.

I tend to...me, best I can. Too draggin' ass to speculate on what the hell I've got myself into.

16

A nap or two later I'm deadly lookin' for round two. I raise the stakes on my disgruntlements. *"rrrRRRRRRRROWRRRR!!!"*

"Hello, Strut."

A melodic tone stymies my scalar ascent.

"I'm sorry you're not happy here," she closely minds the door as she enters my pokey (jail), scootin' a large bag in with her. "I heard you created quite a furor."

That's what you call it, eh? My ears flatten, tail slowly lashes right and left.

"Soon you'll be free, I promise. Until then, I've got something for you."

A key or a crowbar, maybe? The chick makes herself at home, fear absent. And she's hummin'. Sounds like that moon tune. I'll make a deal with you, fine mama- I'll teach you the blues and you spring me, what d'ya say?

Baby girl ain't frontin', she got possibilities- I kin hear 'em. Just needs someone to show her how to break it down. I got all the skills and ain't too proud to work with a grasshopper.

This jail cell ain't no bicycle built for two. She's in and I'm backed to the wall, crouchin'. I decide to ignore her. Like she's forgotten me all freakin' day. Drop a brotha off to suffer indignities-does she know 'bout my predicament?- and then make scarce.

I box the wall, leavin' my claw prints for posterity and give her a dose of what she's been missin'. "RRROWWrrrowwwRRRRR."

"You certainly like to sing, Strut. I like that very much. We just need a better venue for your voice."

Ain't that what I been sayin'? Somebody finally catchin' my drift?

She breaks into a tune 'bout strangers in the night, and I shut up my scramblin's long enough to judge her notes. Pure and sweet, on key and proper pitch. Baby girl's got better pipes than I've heard since bouncin' from Bad Sign.

In quietin' my rant, somethin' familiar trips my sniffer. Knock me for a blues loop- it's my favorite scent from Jose's shed! She unleashes a stock of rollin' material between me and her.

Who is this chick? Etta come to visit at last? Might know for sure if she'd pick proper singin' material.

For the love of a phat bass riff, she's dolin' out edibles too good to resist. She dribbles a mite as far as her arm reaches, waitin' for me to...

I give her a steady gaze. With patient eyes oddly reminiscent of my homeboy she sits, smiles, sings. If only she'd brought a pizza- extra pepperoni!

Never let it be said I forsake a meal from a true diva. *Maaan*, I'm a believer! Who'd believe pokey munchies'd smell this side of phat? My paw slips out, sidles the groceries closer, but my eyes pin her, dare her to interfere. I ain't so dazzled I won't wreak havoc on her, singer or no.

"GRRROWWW!" Repeat. "*rrrRRRRR!!*" Repeat. Change up the tempo. Change the pitch, the key. House is rockin', courtesy of yours truly, and I got the brawn to back up every note.

Let me the hell outta here!

One of the hired flunkies shoves my breakfast in with heavy gloves on and door held close. I shoot forward, almost catch her hand, but she manages to retreat in time.

Claws on the warpath, I shriek and tear at the bare skin walls. Others run by my cage with fingers in ears.

RESPECT, I bellow. Aretha don't have nothin' on me.

"RRRRrrrrRRRRrrrrRRRR." I prepare the repetition, but I cut it off mid-aria. Finally, somethin' worth my interest.

"Hello, Strut," singer harmonically greets me. The young diva unhooks the gate and slips in enveloped in cedar scent. My nose twitches, 'preciatively.

"You are a saucy villain, as my Grand would say," she singsongs, catlike, respectful.

Huh, saucy villain, hmmm. I been called an S.O.B., a noisy so-and-so and quite a few terms CatSkill would not consider print-worthy. I mull the moniker over. Saucy villain. Cool, but I glare the 'this is my house' stare.

Don't confront her one bit. Unconvinced, she sinks onto her haunches, hums and turns out a refill mound of shavin's which sends me itchin' to roll like a crumb-snatcher pooch in fresh mud.

"You're looking pretty good, Strut."

And why not, I snort? I got a reputation to uphold- I yammer my side of things.

Singer cocks her head, listens with sincere interest, reaches inside her coat and presents me with my just due- fish! And chicken!

I strut right up, one eye pealed on her, cuz you never know it all. The foolishness untrustworthy humans are liable to get up to is beyond reckonin'. I larned a thing or two on my travels on the blues highway.

"Sorry, I didn't introduce myself yesterday. I'm Sky. I hope you like my calling you Strut- I think it suits you. And the good news is you'll be leaving today."

Stiflin' my share of the confab while I devour the offerin's, I listen while she describes the comin' agenda.

And so here I am, havin' a heart-to-heart with a dog named after what some humans do with their legs- Yogi.

Sideline here. Guess y'all might be wondrin' what a cat knows 'bout yoga. After a night of gettin' my mac on wit several squealin' queens I'se headed for a lay-up. Sun fixin' to up and at 'em. Chanced 'cross a chick makin' like a cat. Her energy seemed okay- I mean if a human can move like a cat- ya feelin' me?

Studied on her movements- a little before nap entertainment; got a little wash-up done while spyin'. Daa...darn, the li'l mama was supple! Bendin' and stretchin' in weird ways- I mean, c'mon, standin' on yer head, legs akimbo! Anyways, she offered to share her grub. Pulled containers outta a bag- 'cept the chick don't eat nothin' like a cat. All vegetables! Outta here- I trilled. Cats need meat, for the love of an 8-bar shuffle!

'Yo, homeboy!' I address the guard dog. Seems a sensible sort, but I got to get thangs straight right from the get-go.

'I'm not your homeboy.'

And I thought cats had dibs on condescending looks. Equably, I allow him his opinion- too early to jump into a fracas. Gotta get my bearin's straight first.

Our stand-off is rudely interrupted by a dancin', twirlin', yappin' sidekick mutt.

Yapper excitedly proceeds to enlighten me on the source of their handles.

'He's named after Yogi Bear and I'm—'

'Huh, let me guess, the Tasmanian pisspot?' Figure if my act in the jailhouse earned me a 'Tasmanian' moniker I'd put it to use. Whirlin' pooch's tornado act slightly stalls.

'This is a peaceful family. Sky brings newcomers to our barn once in a while and we all get along. So, watch yourself, or hit the road, Jack.'

Now there's a phat tune. Maybe there's a lick of promise in this cur?

'Chill out, big guy. I'm feelin' ya- you're the head honcho 'round this here crib.' I figure to let it slide. For the moment.

After bein' locked up in a makeshift cage loaded with cedar shavin's by Singer Sky and her none-too-jolly, scar-faced cohort, I take my time reconnoiterin' the layout. Plenty of grub, water.

But as soon as they make themselves scarce, I poke my paws through a gate openin', get teeth and claws into action, untwist wire, un-catch hooks and hooo yeah! The big cat is off the chain!

Nosin' the door aside, I strut out. Kinda dig the new nickname.

My latest lay-up (dog only thinks it's his house) is a mixed bag. Clacker-crappers- bunch of loud-mouth, head-boppin' birds cluckin' and shi...crappin' everywhere. No shi...well, it's anywhere the dirty-butt birds shove their tail ends.

If I find the patience to orchestrate the noisemakers, perhaps they'll be suitable back-up singers. If that much patience exists in this world- I ain't holdin' out for no miracle. For the love of a Stevie Ray Vaughn lick!

I give 'em a chase to let 'em know a major player is on the scene. Not much fun in swattin' a bag of feathers that can't harmonize worth a crap. Hey, a pun?

Yogi pins me with a serious 'you're cruisin'' and I pretend to be deaf and blind until he saunters my way. Dog never runs cuz he thinks he's cock of the walk. Wit da quickness, I brashly brush amid the frickin' flock, climb up the timbers to my newfound aerial digs. Big dried grass blocks make for a sweet-scent clean nappin' spot.

Two giants below with decided potential to make the cut for a band, pay me no never-minds. Horses, I recall the term from soon after my original drop-off. The joint with a snarly queen and a goose on the loose.

At least these big boys ain't constantly cluck, cluckin'. Make soft murmurs. 'Neighs,' the biggest horse informs me. And nickers- nice tones.

Four- I refuse to call 'em relations- cats of various shades step aside as the head honcho locks up the clacker-crappers and returns to his guard duty. The pussyfooters give me a wide berth, without my havin' to prove my mettle.

'Ain't seen the likes of me, eh?' Noses in the air, they scatter. 'Pussyfooters,' I spit.

And then, there's the captive audience of one. A mite of a kitten, hunkerin' in fear, hides within a hole in the wall. Ain't yet caught the kit out of her safety zone to see what she looks like.

Now I seen fear do strange things to livin' critters, but this kit has it somethin' awful bad. Not a peep outta her. I think she's even afraid to breathe.

Me, I have no fears. Guard dog warns me to be on my best behavior with the tiny crumb-snatcher.

'Ain't into kit abuse, give me some credit,' I indignantly huff.

The terrier with his in-your-face excitability (wonder if he's on speed) is a whole other matter. I give him an ears-laid-flat growl- tired of bein' circled like the cats houndin' the dribbler on the basketball court. I lash out a final warnin' cuz dizzy can't take a hint.

Eyes rollin' with exceptional cat-like patience, Yogi spit-balls BooBoo, the pissant, out of my sphere when the whirlin' dervish continues to pester. Good thang too, cuz my patience is wearin' mighty thin.

Up on the roof of this here barn, I indulge in a suitable-length catnap. Much, much later I'll go walkin' after midnight. Night time is the right time- bein' in my element, strollin', trollin' for whatever suits my fancy. A good tune would be the thang, or a hook-up at Hook's. 'Cept I'm doubtin' on any Hook's out in this country settin'. Don't seem to be any blues clubs, neither.

Wakin' still shy of walkin' time, I meander down the wood post to the mousehole. 'Yo, kit, feel like talkin'?' I give the twitchin' ear Yogi an 'I'm cool' wink.

Expected silence from- what did Sky call the kit? Catch, yeah. 'How bout listenin'?'

I regale the kit with my wealth of experience- a tale to last the night.

My kind of peeps, no interruptin' questions. Into my third wind-up, Yogi sounds the lights-out signal. I know I ain't included in this ridiculous state of affairs as I'm a night owl, er, cat. I blithely continue my story, but the big dog fixes to push his agenda.

'I have to get up early. Hit the hay.'

'Good on you. 'Preciate you keepin' it safe.' I figure I'm unnecessarily included, yet I stick with my 'That's Life' narration as smooth as that Santana homey.

Without disturbin' the exhausted snorin' Boo, Yogi rises and gets on my case with a no-nonsense, big eye stare-down.

'You're about to wring my last nerve,' he issues. 'To bed or get out.'

Rather than slice his nose as it nears to prod my nether regions, I yawn, hoist my ass up the beam, bathe like I'm fixin' to go on a date prowl, and on-the-fly decide another nap actually sounds pretty good. There's always later.

A fair successful day. I'm freebird, and these digs present phat food, goods to roll in, place to roam without bein' hassled. Leastways, I'm believin'. We'll see.

Might stick around, might not. Let me set the record straight. I could jump-smack that dog like the roof is on fire, but he maintains. No growlin' or barin' of fangs. I figure all and sundry unnerstan' The Cat is in the house, and I ain't fixin' to abuse nobody 'cept a wanderin' varmint or three.

Sky asked me to hang tight when she put me up in the big cage- well, she didn't quite say it in my lingo. The way that baby girl sings, I might play talent scout. Got to teach her to expand her horizons, get her true groove on, for the love of Etta. Kinda at an interestin' crossroads of sorts.

Not that my ramblin' days are lightin' out on a summer wind, mind you. You don't own me, singer. Ain't no one-woman cat, not me. I'm my own cat, ya feelin' me?

17

"Strut! Struuut!"

What the...time is it? It's still dark out. Can't a brotha sleep? What is that infernal racket?

"Wheeeeeeeee!"

"Baaaak, baaaaaak, cluckkkkk!"

"Ruffff, ruff!"

"Aarkkk, ark, ark, ark, ark!"

"Mewww..." ad infinitum. Everbody's got sumpin' to noise 'bout, for the love of a decent nap!

"Darn it, Strut, please be here," singer hits a sighin' blues note- draws my attention. Reckon she's spied my last jail break and is seriously outta sorts. Fancy that!

'Cool it, pretty woman, The Cat is in the house.' I rise from my aromatic grass nest, stretch every stretchable part, give the ol' stickers a workout on a handy post, and, "RRRROWWWWW!!"

"Strut! You stayed! Oh, I'm so happy."

Damn straight, you otta be! I peer down at her as she races round the corner, very un-catlike. Are those tears in her eyes?

She claps her hands in delight. Hmm, a singer/drummer. I check out the mornin' melee. She stands amid all critters not in a huge box (stalls, they're called) with misty eyes solely on me. Singer seems oblivious to all the cuttin' loose 'feed me, feed me'. Reckon this might take some gettin' used to- bein' this noisy this darn early.

S'all right. Time to address the important matters.

Say, good lookin' what ya got cookin'?

Sad to impart, I once hung out in drys-ville while a storm was afoot. A country 'music' concert was in full swing above me, save this cat! Had to sit on my ears after a lengthy stint of that cryin'-in-your-beer noise some call music. But the saucy pork was off the hook! Sumpin' 'bout that particlar noise accompanyin' gnash-yer-teeth grub.

I add my singular incentive to the hoopla, "RRROWWWWW!" Get out in that kitchen and rattle round, woman. Tend to my breakfast, cuz I sure am a hungry cat!

"RRROWWWRRR!"

"All right gang, patience, please. I guess all of you have met our newest guest?"

I gracefully slither down the main beam- showin' off like the star I am.

'No applause, necessary,' I slowly turn my head to be admired, flash my long tail. Only muttered gripin's greetin' me. Where's a homey's props? What a bunch of losers! All eyes are fixed, expectantly, on singer 'stead of admirin' the likes of yours truly.

Sky opens cans and bags and dishes up assorted plates. I fly into the melee as she sets the various grubs on the ground.

"Rrrrrr," I warn the four shades of dirt she calls Milk, Bitter, Dark and Semi.

Meanwhile, the clacker/crappers are soundin' off like Gabriel's horn on gospel day. Hey, I been to church- mighty good grub if you catch one of them God-fearin's in a generous mood.

"Hold on, Mr. Get Smart and ladies," Sky attempts to quiet the clacker/crappers. Save your breath, singer! She catches my curious stare. "They're chickens, Strut."

Hmmm, I do like chicken, but I'm jonesin' for the savory scented grub she sets nearby. Noise-birds can wait. Have to catch one on the down low though cuz Yogi is mighty perticlar.

'Move it on over, The Big Cat's movin' in,' I brush into the pusses' midst.

Semi ain't havin' it. Showin' a spark of what-for, she spits and swats at me as the others seek shelter to her rear.

'Yo mama, you wanna step in my game?' I huff and flare my tail. Give her a chance to step off.

Instead, she advances. Prob'ly thinks Sky's got her back- she wasn't havin' nuttin' to do wit me last night.

'Don't be player-hatin',' I advise the wannabe, and un-sheath my stickers to prove I've got game. Lots of game.

'Not player-hating, hog-hating, you fat—'

'Hey, hey, I'm not your monkey! Can't a brotha—'

'You are not my brother!'

"Now listen up! None of that kind of behavior in this barn, or anywhere. Strut, you must eat your breakfast over here and leave the others alone." Singer dares to hunker too close to intervene, but Yogi's already refereein', saunterin' up to the plate.

Semi, the wanged-out bad Betty, actually spits in my eye and retreats the other side of Yogi.

'Keep it gangsta, dog,' I tout in passin' the sentry. (Stay cool, for you uneducated-in-hood lingo).

'Yo, chick, wanna try me when no one's gonna save yer a...butt?'

My challenge goes nowhere.

Sky redirects my grumblin' guts to a suitably-sized plate of groceries. "Here, you go, Strut. I promise you'll not starve, and I really am glad you stayed, though I can't imagine how you escaped Garrett's temporary lodgings."

Garrett, the male trapper. Didn't take much to outsmart that dude. I attend to the important factors while watchin' the rest of the a.m. proceedin's.

Horses have dried grass dropped into their quarters and a small smatter of grain. Yogi and the already-at-it yappin' Boo indulge in dry food. And the clacker/crappers are finally turned loose to find bugs and scattered leftovers and bits of clacker food. Ah, the sounds of silence, or as close as it might get in this barnyard hood.

As for the hidden little mite scaredy cat, Catch, fat chance the 2-leggeds'll catch that one. Probably die of a heart attack first. Never seen anyone afraid of absolutely everythin'. Kit don't even know how to walk on her own legs. Practically crawls like a damned caterpillar. Walk like a man, with four legs, is my advice. For the love of blue heaven, you're safe in these digs! Guard dog'll see to it.

The only way Sky can feed the kit is to push, with Yogi's help, a dish of smash-up close to the kit's hideout. The kit 'minds me of the scared one at the ghosts' crib. Could be her, but I got other thangs to tend to- grub, bath, nap, walkabout.

Couple days a week, Sky and her elder, Grand, climb atop the horses and head out to the woods. Get this- the dogs and pusses, minus Catch and yours truly, trail along! Hard to believe how low some felines sink. Ain't so hard up for a snack or humans, I need to follow the yellow brick road. Not this cat!

Sky and her grand toss treats as the 'follow your leader' horses walk on. And the pusses dive for the tidbits. No way, Jose,

I'm troopin' along like a wind-up toy! Instead, got my own walkabout. Lookin' for a rumble, or a snack on the run, is more in key with the likes of me. I'm feelin' pumped, all healed. Ear's a mite cockeyed, but hey, let's roll!

'Get ready, I'm comin!' Casin' the joint is only appropriate for the smart cat. Get the lay of the land, right off.

I cadge an aerial view from up in a thick oak tree- plenty of big branches to lounge on, and in no time I'm a pro of my new digs. Trees galore. Lazily slip slidin' away stream for a drink or fishin'. Pond off in the distance for catchin' hoppers. No pavin' paradise like bright lights, big city. I can explore to my heart's content- little critters beware, your days are numbered!

Boundin' through the clacker/crappers, playin' grab a…butt is poppin'. My, those fat chicks can wobble/run and rant! Til the guard dog, pins me with them there eyes.

I swat a clacker butt, just to show I ain't nobody's bitch. Yogi simply stares as if to say he's got my number. S'ok, I can live wit dat- long as it don't confront me none.

Wind kicks it, plasters my whiskers to my face. I turn into its hurrah and scent the cold a-comin'. Soon. Change-up. like always. Yeah, soon I'll need to figure out where to wait out the winter. Should I stay or should I go now?

18

Disdainful, I watch the three-ring circus act on their way early one mornin', and am abruptly surprised to hear a meek question.

Seems it took the scaredy-cat kit a few days to get my drift. Figures I'm not about to attack, her anyway, or else curiosity is trippin' worse than fear. There's a draggin', creepin', stallin' outta-da-box a short distance from the kit's hidey-hole. No way she'll dare enter my personal space.

'S...Strut, where do the big dogs go?'

Two-way confabs are lower than low on my list- 'specially this early in the day. 'Ceptin' they be blues as subject material. I toss a terse response, 'Horses, not big dogs.'

'But where d...do they g...go? And why?'

Now I prefer to be the one doin' the talkin' if talkin' gotta be done. Rather be singin'. Wit all the kit's stutterin' reckon singin' ain't jumpin' outta her pipes. But I can bide my time, maybe teach her a little sumpin' sumpin'.

Unused to twenty questions, 'specially before breakfast, I snap, 'Why don't you go and find out?'

The little squirt cringes, and I feel an odd tweak in my gut. What's up wit dat?

'I'm not a mornin' kinda cat,' I venture by way of...apology. And why the hell am I apologizin'? Straight trippin' outta my nat'ral inclination.

'Why d...do they go so f...far away?'

I harrumph with stingin' velocity.

'Why d…don't you go with them? Are you g…going to stay here? Are you ever a…afraid?'

'Hell, no!'

'Why n…not?'

What am I, questions R us? My eyes roll of their own annoyed accord.

'See, kit, it's like dis. You're pretty new here, right? Fairly new to this ol' world, too. Give it time to fit yerself in. Me, I been around, seen some stuff, done some stuff. A cat of my stature joinin' a dog, pony and puss show ain't happenin'.'

'W…why, Strut?'

'Hear me out for the love of… Never mind! People like to pet, hold and cuddle with cats…' For some reason that promptly shuts me up, til Catch flounders in with—

'You d…don't let her p…pet y…you.'

Jury's out on that prospect, and so am I. I stretch and stalk off, but the pitiful kit plunders me with eyes cryin'-in-the-rain pathos.

'Look, s'far as humans go, I b'lieve you'll be okay with Sky,' I offer my placatin', worldly advice. 'Yogi looks after you better'n a bro. Ain't nobody shi…poopin' on your parade. So, chill out!'

Da…darn it, if she ain't one exasperatin'… Dust kicks inside on a wayward wind and the kit scoots back into her hole, huddles up. How can a kit be afraid of absolutely everythin'? What started it? Maybe I should ask, but I ain't no head doctor. Reckon if you live in fear and silence maybe it's only nature to bank queries that spew forth like the 40's on payday? Otta be bankin' blues!

111

'You s...sure?' The kit partially sidles out, but continues to quiver.

'Hell, kit, is anybody ever sure of anybody or anythin'?'

'Y...you are.'

'Yeah, well, you gotta have guts to exist. Can't live on dreams. Me, I'm sure of me. Peace out.' Give me one reason to stay here ain't gonna fly, so by-by!

And I Sweet Home Chicago hidey-ho before query avalanche part two falls. Ain't used to this mentorin' business. Loner, that's my style. I rock the joint when I'm fishin' for proper company- be it fight or foolin' around. Otherwise, give me room, lots of room. No ties... A certain guitar man creeps into my head and I growl the memory away, hustlin' off.

Yogi's on point, protectin' the kit is his top priority. Pop, friend, mentor, security guard. Pretty amazin' to watch the patience of that dog. Must have a cat far back in his ancestral woodpile, s'all I can figure.

At times I wonder what it must feel like to have a body care that much about you. Had an inklin' once- or I thought I had. But if it's got to end, I don't ever want to feel that way again. I don't wanta talk about it.

How can I get across to Sky a bologna sandwich or a pepperoni pizza would be great late-night snacks? Even if the memories flare up and bust a gut.

Sky's in the habit of tellin' stories before she passes out snacks. Be better if she'd improve her singin' repertoire. Instead, she tries her best to dredge Catch out of hidin', and that kit will try the patience of the dead.

Too bad the ghost cats ain't around to test my theory. Maybe I'll go visit and ask 'em to... Can ghosts travel? Might just go and find out one night.

Singer Sky has the entire barn for an audience when she begins a story. She'll stop once and ag'in to ask the kit a question. Talk about cat-got-your-tongue in a trippin' inverse sorta way. Cuz the kit ain't talkin' to humans. Barely talks to critters.

And there, if I wanted to pursue it, lies a clue. What human done rained misery on such a babe in the woods? Like I said, I'm no head doctor, nor a detective.

Me, I'm just hangin' out for the grub. Finish up the talkin', for the love of a Stevie Ray Vaughn guitar lick! Either sing or get off the stage! Night's a callin', for the love of Howlin' Wolf!

I do my best to hurry her along. "RRROWW!" Bring on the goods, sista!

"Strut, I asked Catch," she gently rebuffs me.

"*rrrRRRRrrrrrRRRR*," let's harmonize, woman! What more does a cat have to do?

"Patience," Sky smiles and returns to her story.

Patience, my ass! Can't you take a hint? Music makes the world go round.

Yogi relinquishes his stately, sphinx-like position, climbs to all fours, ready to run interference.

"*RRRROWWRRROWWW*!" Hey, I can keep this up all night! My skills'll drown out the quietin' clacker/crappers in their nightly roosts, or while they be kickin' it outside wit da bugs in the early hours. Put 'em together wit da horses munchin' dry grass, the dancin' pipsqueak...

'Can it, big mouth, or I'll upend you like a flap-jack,' Yogi's nose closes in on my nether region.

113

What the hell's a flap-jack? But I spin and hiss, 'You and what army?'

Yogi pretends he doesn't hear my throaty defiance, and Sky slyly watches us scrimmage for yardage.

Stalemate. *"rrOWWWRRR!"* I continue to push, claws diggin' in like a loco bull. I actually outran one of them critters while stalkin' a varmint in a big field of grass.

With the gentility born of doggie ancestors, Yogi lazily tries to outflank me, shovin' his nose at my posterior. But I'm quicker, spinnin', paws flick-ready.

"Strut, another night we'll do something you like, but tonight I have a story to tell about cats as gods," Sky taps her book.

Cats as gods, well, of course! Why didn't you say so? I saunter off, tail high. Wouldn't do to make singer unhappy, and tonight's selection of snacks is smellin' phat.

"rrrr," I vault to the shelf where waits the groceries. Get first dibs on a better scent, while Yogi regains his shadowin' of Catch as the story continues. Interminably. Nothin' 'bout the story, other than the part 'bout cats as gods, can compete wit a beat, and am I missin' da beat!

Sky's a smart 'un, got my number. She gives me the eye as I practically sit atop the bag of snacks. I wave my hangin' tail, peer 'round the barn, actin' as if I have a smatterin' of patience. Less so, manners, but hey, nobody's perfect. I don't think that came out quite right...

Another night, I'm missin' tunes too much to bear. Why a singer with her skills ain't usin' them 'stead of yackin' is beyond me!

I sound off a riff. *"rrOWoo, rrOWOO, RROWOO, RRROW!"*

"Strut, that's…WOW!!"

Tell me about it! Better yet, sing to me!

"I've got to tell Garrett."

What do you have to bring up the male trapper for? Dude can't sing. It's a duet, baby-cakes, not a trio!

I rattle off another line, "rrroww, rroww, rroww, ROWW!"

Her full attention is finally where it belongs- on me, and it's like the rest of the barn critters disappear.

"Mmm, mmm, mmm, mmmmm!"

She's got it! Yeah, baby, she's got it!

Without bein' aware of proximity, I move toward her, set on a personal serenade. Two, star singers. One phat duet. My paw finds itself on her knee. Shades of Big Mama and Guitar Slim in a dream combo. 'Cept I can't play a human instrument. If only my home boy… No don't go there.

"*RROWW, RROWW, RROWW, RROW!*"

"*MMMMM, MMMMM, MMMMM, MMMM!*"

An inner sense of…joy…fires me up, and I'm on a roll, givin' it my all. We're singin' the ol' call and response! No tears in heaven tonight, sugar, sugar!

Nights ain't always cool like dis. Most times, Sky gently puts me off with, "We'll sing later, Strut. Catch needs to hear good stories."

"RRRRrrrr." Better to listen to some phat tunes, is my thinkin'. But Yogi's got her back, and part of me unnerstan's her burnin' love desire to coax Catch out of scaredy-cat-i-tis.

Here's where it gets tricky, and prob'ly why CatSkill wanted me to troll this route, tho I ain't sure 'bout gittin' no kicks off it.

Been on the road time and time again. Motto is 'I won't be hangin' around'. I ain't got nobody and that's Jim dandy with this top cat.

Learnin' the blues involves shorin' up…feelin's til you get to the point where down so long, down don't bother me.

Least ways, that's what I always tell myself.

So, why…why am I one minute tryin' to steal Catch's snack, steal Sky's attention by yammerin' my musicality and then, the next thang I'm walkin'. Takin' to my crib in the rafters, or spoilin' for a fight elsewhere- cuz I don't WANT to take out Yogi. Could, but… And what exactly does that say 'bout my state of affairs?

CatSkill, this ain't route 66 you pointed me on. Route 66 is about fun. This is a…my friend, the blues highway.

Hell, I ain't never been a get-in-my-own-head sorta cat, but somethin' 'bout watchin' those pusses and dogs and horses and even the clacker/crappers enjoyin' Sky's stories…puts me off my game.

Almost feel like I got punk'd!

Forget this shi… It's Saturday and Saturday night's alright for fightin'. Yeah! Or lovin'. See what comes first to paw.

19

Scoured the surrounds. Hoofin' it for miles. No sultry siren lookin' for love. No happy night lookin' for some tush for me.

I ain't seemin' to mind the lack of female company too awful much. What's up wit dat? Sumpin' to do with missin' parts? Ain't seen a smokin' temptin' mama layin' it down in this unhood hood. Maybe there's others missin' parts, too.

Well, I'm a big player. Been puttin' on a few pounds though, all the reg'lar phat grub. Best step up my game- stay lean and mean cuz you never know what's further on up the road. All this thinkin's givin' me a headache.

Pity the fool crosses my path on my way home. Home? Strange concept. I ain't no boll weevil. What keeps me struttin' back? The duet singer Sky and I share infrequently? Great grub you can count on served on time? The camaraderie of the others in the barn and my self-exclusion?

Any of my other 'rest stops' I'd be singin' you can't keep me hangin' on.

Cold riffles my thickened coat. At least nature provided this walk-about scamp with 'propriate threads. Mostly protects me from hard cases' claws, too.

Hear a rustle in the brush ahead. Entertainment time. Unsuspectin' youngster mouse. Nearly let him go- can you believe it? What the hell's giggin' me?

I decide to give myself a break. Bathe off mouse mousse from between my talons. Swipe my face, ears, groom my tail and the rest of my physique. Feels good, doin' what comes naturally.

Diggin' my lingo? Apparently, some of Sky's stories are seepin' in, advancin' my education.

There are times Catch obviously longs to join story time and I encourage, 'Git yer ass out here! All this is for your benefit, for the love of a fish sandwich!' Don't want any hangin' back interferin' with snacks.

Most story nights I cat nap or cock half an ear. Funny thing to say cuz one of my ears is missin' its tip. OG probably bit it off in my last fight- I was a mite busy savin' my ass to recall with complete clarity.

There's a tale 'bout Damned Cat stuck in a ship full of rats turned both my ears. I'd tag team that cat and we'd disembowel every rat ever dared to ship ahoy! After the warrior's rescue by a friendly girl who changed the dueler's name to Capable, I tuned out. Stop with all the happy-ever-after bidness! More action, blood, guts, grub and blues- what stories need to keep a listener on the edge of his seat. Apparently, not the lame homebodies in this crib; I yawn.

Story 'bout the greatest cat of all- I thought she'd be talkin' 'bout me, but it involved some cool cat called CatSkill. Hmmm, a corner of my mind be fixin' on recall, but the taste of my roast beef snack drowned any other thinkin' vibes. Phat, phat, phat!

(Course, I'm tryin' to tell my side a thangs in order, so don't get confused 'bout CatSkill, folks.)

Got a big rise out of Sky when I broke into her yackety yak tirade with, "*Rowerowerowerow*!" Handed me my props, right off!

"Strut, oh I've got to tell Garrett- that's one of his favorite rock songs. Sweet Child of Mine- do it again. I must bring my recorder with me."

Just leave the male trapper out of it, chick, I sing for you. Your turn, but she don't take no hint. Can I learn borin' ol' Moon River?

Yogi finally convinces the kit outdoors, but the crumb-snatcher hides inside the big dog's legs the entire venture walkin' through the yard. Skitter-bug kit 'bout faints when a scrap of paper takes to sailin', flappin' clacker/crappers dance a noisy hip-hop and a car pulls in the drive. Like watchin' survival of the scared to death- expectin' to call the grave diggers any second! Minds me of a sultry blues diva at Bad Sign trillin', "my man's an undertaker- he's got a coffin just your size." Lady could SING!!

'Like hangin' out with the dogs, eh kit?' I kinda diss her once she slides into home base with heart thumpin' like an out-of-sync bass player. Barkin' Yogi seein' the kit inside, races to greet trapper Garrett climbin' out of his car- he's beyond hearin' my spite.

'Y...yes, I do,' Catch boldly stutters, before slippin' into her hideout for sleepy time.

'Well, goody, goody for you!'

The stick in my craw poke, pokes, and I hightail it. Let Catch under my skin, why? I gallivant familiar trails seekin' diversions til the weather spits havoc.

'The Cat is in the house,' I trumpet into subdued ranks. It's as quiet as Bad Sign once the door was braced/locked in the wee hours.

The whole crew- horses, pusses, dogs, even the clacker/crappers got ghosted and there ain't a ghost in sight. Or out of sight, or hearin', for that matter.

Howlin' wind drives rain which alternates with ice pricklin' the barn, rattlin' rafters. Call it stormy Monday- ain't no way possible for Tuesday to be as bad. PLINK. PLINK. Constant. Sounds like a night in the hood. Or one horrid wannabe drummer practicin' til hell freezes over.

'Hey, where's the snacks?' I strut on in.

Yogi blasts me, 'We're worried about Sky out in this weather. Have you noticed she's not here? Do you ever think of anyone but yourself?'

'Why should I?' I taunt.

The kit, head timidly pokin' out of her den, stutters in an uncharacteristic sound-off tone. 'Sky is so g...good to...all of us—'

'Yeah, so nice you barely crawl out to see her,' I hiss nastily, and immediately feel a twinge of shame, shame. Boy, I got it bad and that ain't good. Whatever it is I got. I'd not purposely hurt Catch...

Wit da quickness, Yogi jumps my shi...case. 'You got it so rough hot-shot, leave. Cry your bleeding heart to some rat—'

I round on him with resurrected belligerence. 'Nothin' doin. I ain't goin' out in that poppin' ice.'

'You big bragging blowhard,' Semi, like a bat out of hell, streaks from the shadows, snarlin' what-for. 'All me, me, me. Half of your tales are probably made-up, you noisy so-and-so.'

120

What is this, pick on Strut night?

'Listen, Miss Thang, it ain't braggin' if it's facts. Don't be player-hatin'.'

'Strut, we've had enough. Shut up or get lost,' Yogi resignedly pads my way, playin' bouncer, to enforce his suggestion.

It takes two to tango, yet neither one of us wants to really engage. Mutual respect? There's somethin' inexplicable in his eyes- worry for Sky? Or does he see further into me than anyone? And what does he see?

My claws hie me up the beam to my crib, and I pretend to groom, but I'm all ears listenin' to one wise- not wise-ass- dog stem the frettin' like an ol' guitar soothin' midst the concerned kit and kaboodle.

He talks about how resourceful and smart Sky is, how she'll be here soon as she can, and we should all send her good lovin' thoughts. What a load of…!

If she's so smart why ain't she here right now, tellin' dem infernal stories and dibbin' out the groceries? What's Singer doin' out in weather not fit for any livin' critter?

I yawn, curl up in a restful fragrant nest. Don't borrow trouble, comes 'round of its own accord. Don't worry 'bout nuttin' cuz nuttin' gonna be alright. Ain't got no control over it, but an uncomfortable sticker flickers inside a me.

Sky- what happens if Sky doesn't return? I reckon I'll be on the road again. Call me the wanderer if somethin's gotta give.

Big yawn. Don't borrow trouble, ain't my problem. I got street skills- unlike the doom and gloom worry-warts below me. I can find another hangout, maybe a better one than this'n.

Nah, bein' truthful, this joint is the shi…pretty darn phat.

The intensity of stressed vibes is bummin' me out. What can I do? Hell, what any blues-singin' stud worth his salt does-sing the blues!

Til Yogi threatens to find a ladder.

20

Now I say call a trap a trap. Singer Sky may be the most melodic trapper comin' round the mountain, but she's still a trapper. Chick's at the teenage stage where she wants to save the world. Calls herself a critter rescuer. I weren't in no need of bein' rescued, ya feel me? My world was rollin' phat afore she sang me to hereabouts. Just sayin'.

Capable Sky (figured she deserved Damned Cat's new moniker- you know, the ship cat from Sky's story. Me, I'd prefer to be called Damned Cat. Just my opinion.) made it home in one piece and brought live entertainment.

First things first. The night's story revolves around her and David's (trapper in trainin') escapade- rescuin'/trappin' abandoned cats and one hulk of a clumsy pup durin' a freakin' ice storm. That ping ping on the barn roof- ice. Only those missin' a few upstairs would be out in that shi…stuff- good Samaritans or no.

Nothin' like ice skatin' on the highway while homeward bound, carryin' the rescued. And for the piece de resistance- an impromptu down-hill sled ride playin' dodge ball with trees galore. Courtesy of some drunk passed out in his car in the middle of the road. Betcha he didn't suffer more'n the usual hangover. Less scar-face Garrett beat the shi…poop out of him for puttin' Sky in danger. I'd a give him all four paws. Put extra hurtin' on that scumbag sot.

Coulda been total disaster for Sky and David and their rescuees. Bet there was some tossin' bodies in the roller coaster ride from hell.

But Singer's here, no hurts I can see. Must be one top notch driver. The barn worriers are outta worries, hallelujah! Figured I coulda sung told ya so, but I'm keepin' it cool.

I kinda wonder if Yogi, in all his wisdom, had some inklin' of what Sky went through durin' her topsy-turvy venture. Got me believin' the big dog's full a soul mate-itis. He sure knew how to shovel up the consolation and the look-on-the-bright-side of life/hope bull. Things I ain't into.

Movin' on, no lookin' back. Waste of time sittin' and worryin'. And too much thinkin' ain't uppin' my game. Ramblin' on my mind, more my style.

Cockin' half an ear (which I can do now), I tune into bits and pieces of the tale, like always. Bein' from the hood, action is what stirs my machismo and keeps me poppin' on all toes. Skip all the emotional thinkin'-on bidness- for the love of a sweet blues progression. And throw in a pizza! Extra pepperoni!

I gotta give props to scar-face Garrett for rescuin' da rescuees. R E S P E C T. Knew a guy with such a trophy posted on his puss had to have street savvy beyond trappin' cats. And his playin' in the dirt farmin' ain't cuttin' it, either.

See, my meanderin's have me spyin' on Garrett and his too-fat-and-lazy mutt, C Nova. Dog's beginnin' to lose a few since comin' into Garrett's house, but sorely needs more activity- ain't you a huntin' dog, hound dog? Anyhow, his digs are close-by in a vamped-up version of the barn I hang out in. Get dis- he sells harvested vegetables. Can't figure the likes of him so into veggies- bring on da meat!

All the growin' of goods does make for a decent place to hunt, cuz that dog ain't got it goin' on. S'all right doggie, I'm game.

I have seen scar-face lift bundles weighin' most as much as hisself! That cat knows 'bout stayin' in primo shape. Elsewise, dude lives simple-like and often has his dinners at Sky and her grand's home. S'all part of knowin' your territory and I'm a master of recon.

Anyway, it's those quiet ones you better steer clear of. They never let on they got mad skills when it comes to squarin' off an' breakin' it down. Pity the fool takin' on a true OG.

Bad Sign walkin' large (I'm talkin' so far past bad to the bone as to be on another planet) had that same do-not-cross-me presence. He sat all to his self in a corner- you could hear the chairs scrapin' the plank floor to give him proper space. Nobody sneakin' up on that cat. Nobody messin' wit his person.

Came to watch a partic'lar lady sing the blues, old school. Woman in a tight, shiny dress struttin' in shoes atop long thin sticks- dunno how she stayed upright. Foot gear clickin' in time with the bass beat. Suddenly, she be sinkin' to her knees, eyes shoved shut, grimace of pain wringin' her mouth. Voice to curdle blood right afore softenin' in a sweeeeet lilt and sendin' you to Little Wing city.

Deep in the shadows, nursin' his whiskey with a hand sportin' glowin' rings, one couldn't be sure if the OG's eyes was tearin' up, or was he fixin' to blow a hole through somethin' or someone, or maybe 'bout to smile. Coulda been all of the above.

Anyhow, Garrett sprung Sky, David, cats, and my choice of bait and box- Sparky. One humongous pup, half a sandwich shy of a sane supper.

Out for a late night stroll, ready for some action when... Lookee here, lookee here- young blood!

Gettin' closer. Clompin' round like a crack-head lost in the country. Minds me of a demented spring rabbit. Dog ain't got 'nuff sense to stick close to his calm handler, David. More fun for me.

Gotta be quick. I'm crouchin' in the leftover weedy boundary of shrubs. Haunches springy. Love the coil of energy and muscle right before I cast off flyin'.

Bam, bam, *bambambam-* a flurry of my well-placed claws on unsuspectin' nose. And I'm boot-scootin' boogyin' for cover, relishin' the squeals I leave behind.

'Hey, Sparky, maybe you'll learn not to get in my grill, but I doubt it!' I snicker and ponder the next ambush.

"*Argh, argh, argh,*" the pup deafens and floors David like a shot from a 45. Poor boy- don't stand a chance standin' when Sparky's lookin' for love in all the wrong places. But David equably laughs, calms his beast and heads on home wit, "See you, Strut."

Or not, I'm thinkin'.

Scattin' 'I'm home', to a bunch of early-nighters after I strut off my victory laps earns me no props. I snort 'nobody up in dis crib', like I give a rat's entrails. 'You gonna miss me the day I'm gone,' I trill.

Yogi peers through a half-open eye with an unappreciative warnin'. I pretend to ignore him- my reg'lar response- stretch up the barn wood wall and hone my talons as loud as I possibly can.

'Don't make me get up,' guard dog whiffles while the pissant terrier snores, dreamin' and runnin' while lyin' in place.

I arch my back, flick my tail similar to the homeboys with their errant middle fingers, prepare to vault up to my loft with the ease of the athlete I am, 'cept I hear--

'Where did you go?' Catch whispers.

'Come out with me and see.' I'm surprised to find sincerity in my invite. But Kit desperately needs some OG backbone, and this here Top Cat is the only one to help wit dat.

'I...I don't think so,' a murmur low enough to be a nightcrawler.

'Snooze ya lose,' I yawn.

'Why a...are you always leaving?'

'I say, listen to me, Catch, listen up. There's an entire world to roll around in, plenty to light my fire.'

'Ohhh.'

Silence. Other than Catch's irritatin' questions and Sky's insufficient admiration of my phat skills, nobody here gives a damn if I exist. Come spring- travelin' weather- maybe I'm out. Curlin' up, I sulk for less than a split second and get me some zzz's.

Little did I have a single clue this here homeboy was about to pitch one major wang dang doodle right up to stardom.

21

I recognize the time of year off-the-hook lights are strung on every available surface- buildin's, trees, cars, pets. Thank Stevie Ray Vaughn that Sky ain't dressin' the barn in them damned threads. I prefer darkness. Yeah, in the shag of the night, babeeee. Freaks come out at night and so does this here homey!

And the noise, noise, noise of the light season in the midst of welcome gettin'-dark-early hours! Call me Mr. Grinch, just don't fa who bore me to death. Or call me late to 'grub's on!'

Scoutin' houses 'cross the street, doin' my born-to-be-wild, first-class act. Stalkin' in the darkest nooks to gather all intel. Rather like Catch, I muse. 'Ceptin' I'm up wit da quickness when needs be.

Comin's and goin's. Parties and music everywhere. Walkabout singers grubbin' for a handout- 'cept, nary a one singin' a song to my taste. Y'all overdoin' the love 'n goodwill bidness!

Need a dose of rockin' blues no matter the season- for the love of B.B. King! Bells should be ringin' the blues. Get my drift?

I continue my shadow prowl- hopin' for...sumpin'. An early Santy visit to ol' Strut? A misplaced pizza, Hook's fish sandwich, slice of bologna? But nuttin' interestin' seems to be poppin' off, or lyin' 'round.

"Rrrrrr." In passin', I less-than-Christmasy snarl at a housecat sittin' on a step, head cocked right, gazin' curiously at...

What the blue moon! It ain't the second comin', that's for da...dang sure!

One big ass rat is hunkerin' by the basement window scratchin' at a screen which is fixin' to give way. If I ain't seen everythin'!

'You call yourself a cat,' I sneer and slink into huntin' mode. Rat thinks it's got it made in the shade, buddyin' up wit a lame-brain replica of a feline fixin' to allow vermin into his crib. Beyond belief!

One, two, three o'clock rock. My tail silently sidles to its own drummer right before my bass end propels me.

Brain-dead rat's too busy scarfin' a hole in the screen to detect its nemesis- you got another thing comin', rat! Sound of a passin' car drowns my takedown. Big bugger squeals its death knell, once.

Tis the season of givin'. I reckon Sky can have my booty as a pre-story surprise. One good snack deserves another, right?

"Merry Christmas," rings round the barn like back-up singers with enhanced reverb. Momentarily droppin' my mouthful, I take the lead. Hey, somebody's gotta step up with a phat note.

"*YOWWWWWWWRRRR*," eclipses the tame revelers, and I strut onto the scene. Any lead singer worth his props wants all eyes on him. And I am a star- just don't think yer gonna put me on top of no tree, I can get there myself. Word.

Silly dog, Boo, bounces and twirls like a whirligig- yap yappin', but can't compete with the likes of yours truly. I simply amp up my volume prior to springin' my snack surprise. Once it's all hashed-out I got the prize voice, I make a move. Wit da pride of my ancestral lineage, I drop the goods front and center.

"Oh, oh Strut!"

Yeah, she's overcome, under my thumb. I am da man!

"Why..., thank you. You are too kind. Very thoughtful."

Damn straight! There's a catch in her throat- she's so broke-up.

The other Catch- scaredy kit- has to be coaxed out of hidin' by Yogi to join the festivities. Doggone kit listens to the dog most of the time when she's not shakin' in her paws. Should be listenin' to a cat wit experience.

I scoot my present closer to Singer Sky and deign to receive my due- a scratch under the chin. First time I allow her to touch THE cat. Archin' my back to gain more satisfaction in the attention department, I condescend to peer at the audience. The groupies hush while I receive my accolades.

Time to sing my solo. I kick it up notch upon notch til I'm ringin' the starry, starry night. Or at the very least, the rafters of dis here crib.

Got my mojo workin'. Yogi begins to howl- from ear offense or joy- who cares? Boo, the whirlin' wonder, yips- hits a few true high notes. The pusses mewl, 'cept for silent night Catch who is hidin' behind Yogi's large legs. The horses softly nicker, and the clacker/crappers scuttle and cluck. Sky hums and OG Garrett chuckles, offers his arm to Sky's elder lady and they proceed to dance in soft shuffle-glidin' steps.

The only silent hold-out, the semi-hidden Catch... For some reason, this non-joinin'-in kit's hidin' suddenly jolts me like the snap of a mousetrap, and I abruptly shut-up my carolin'. Why is it Catch's reluctance gigs me?

"Ah, Strut, you're magical tonight! You are indeed a musical prodigy. Well done, and thank you," Sky applauds.

"I agree, Sky. Strut, you and I have a date with my guitar," Garrett invites.

Guitar? This OG plays? What the he...heck you been waitin' on, bro? An engraved invitation?

I brush aside whatever is curdlin' my gut concernin' Catch, let my paws- sans claws, stroll up Sky's legs, and nudge Singer for snacks right now. And this is all before the story starts.

Somehow in the musical set, my rat gift puts on the disapearin' act. No great shakes, I've been rewarded, and there's more where that sorry case came from.

I notice somethin' else- cuz not much misses these peepers- and the odd tuggin' at my heart strikes again. There's Catch sittin' in between Yogi's front legs, shyly, longingly, watchin' Sky sneakin' me a snack and another scratch prior to openin' the story book.

All of a sudden, I'm no longer in the mood. Creepin' outta the limelight, I melt into Catch's favorite shadow scenery and sorta listen to the story. Quiet house, not a creature stirrin', not even a mouse- obviously the house has a true-blue cat in residence, unlike the digs up the street.

Blah, blah, blah. I hear the words, but can't escape the dig. Somethin's got a hold on me. Searchin' my song list, I re-direct my thinkin' on Santa Baby, just slip a bologna sandwich my way. And a Hook's fish hoagy, too.

Finally, the sing-song tale ends with a Happy Christmas to all. The elder and Garrett slip out the door into a light snow shower. I'm on alert- gotta get my eats on. Seems I'm always hungry. Way I grew up, I guess.

Catch lingers rearward, feelin' safe within' Yogi's embracin' legs rather than bustlin' forth like the rest of us felines and Boo.

I'm brushin' aside all comers- top cat deserves to be first. Sky winks, rolls her eyes, "Here you go again, Strut." She's cool 'bout makin' sure everyone gets a holiday happy meal, but I'm on point countin' to make sure my groceries ain't shy.

Strange, I thought there might be sumpin' special from this 2-legged gala, stead of these ordinary tidbits. Don't stop any of us from snarkin', though.

All the while of the handouts, Yogi heartens the kit. And once the homeys are snacked, Sky entreats, "C'mon, little Catch, you've come this far."

Observin' the scene, it hits me- revelation. The kit needs Sky, no question 'bout that, but Sky needs the kit just as much, maybe more. Can see it in her eager eyes and in her hopeful leanin' toward the kit. Hmmm...interestin'.

'I can't,' Catch surrenders in defeat, tuckin' her little puss to her chest.

'Never say can't,' I yowl in disgust. 'For the love of a sweet bass riff, get yer head outta your ass!'

Yogi jumps my case, 'Watch your mouth, you're not being helpful. And it's Christmas. Can't you be nice, just once?'

I swipe my tail, cross my whiskers, 'Zipped.'

'Cept time drags on interminably, and my scenter scents there are more snacks in hidin'- the real McCoy. Ham is on the menu, for cryin' out loud! Ham is the shi...stuff!

'Good grief,' I tone it down. 'It'll be Easter before you taste Christmas!'

Yogi cocks a disgruntled ear at me and actually lifts lips, displayin' a row of fangs.

'Zipped. I'm zipped.'

Can't complain too much- after all I had extra snacks and was first on the make. But ham, I'm jonesin' for ham!

I watch the kit move, hesitantly- slower than...hell, I don't think anything's that slow!

Sky's puss lovingly, patiently awaitin'. The sound of silence, yearnin' expectation. One tiny white paw trembles, touches Sky's leg. Yogi is supportively close by the kit.

"Go ahead, Catch," she musically whispers. You can hear the prayin' in her voice, more sincere than all the Sunday church goers.

Blow the man down if the kit isn't connectin'. Big eyes poppin', meetin' Sky's over-brimmin' eyes.

Miracle in the barn- don't need no 34th street. Now, Sky's tremblin'- whole lotta shakin' goin on! Singer slowly winks at the kit, and Catch freezes- startled to find she's ventured so far outta her comfort.

"Merry Christmas, Catch. I love you," Sky smiles as tears roll over her lips. Glistenin' eyes rest with all emotion full out there on the kit who is politely, tentatively, eatin' a scentful treat off the edge of Sky's palm. Catch's tiny limbs slightly buckle, and her huge limelights sweep to and fro, on constant alert.

For some reason, I'm spellbound, watchin' this magic moment unfoldin'. Love, all good, right? Then, why do I feel like shi...poop?

Door swooshin' open, an inrush flight of snow and the miracle vanishes. Garrett inadvertently spoils somethin' I'm not sure I've ever seen in all my born days.

Catch is off faster than a hoodbilly eludin' the po-po. Yogi, like a mother hen with chicks, pads after the racin' kit, sees her safely into her mousehole den, and lies down good'n close.

"Catch, it's all right. Don't be afraid. I love you," Sky's tears flood, distortin' her mumblin' reassurance as she kneels beside Yogi.

She idly strokes his back, talkin' all the while to the kit, and Yogi, big dark kindly eyes on her, licks her cheek. The empathetic master of his domain, he doles out comfort to Catch and Singer Sky.

Easy to hear the kit's wretched little heart thumpin' up like a hard rock drummer on a high. Easy to…feel Sky's dismay after the miracle we all witnessed.

Is it Yogi's paw alone, gently stretchin' into Catch's hideyhole, that ultimately calms the fearful kit? Or is Catch listenin' and believin' Sky?

Why don't I…help the poor kit? Well, what the he…heck do I know 'bout takin' care of kits? Too busy takin' care of this here top cat. So, what do I know 'bout carin' for…anybody…sides myself? If I can't find it in me must not be second nature, huh? Maybe there's some kind of song I might sing? I dunno.

Can't imagine how awful it must be to feel like Catch.

22

After a lengthy, non-productive gallivant, I return barn-side, blind-sided by too many questions from Catch.

'Where did you go? What did you see? Did you catch any mice? Any scary things?'

'Cool it, Betty, let a bro catch his breath.' Save me, Bessie Smith! 'One of these days ya gotta get outta here; I'll take you for a real jaunt, not that hide-out under Yogi's legs doin' the stroll round the chicken field.'

The sound of silence, at last. But not a good sound... hang it!

How the kit can be afraid of her own shadow, yet spew forth queries like a street beggar on speed is beyond me. Guess if you never get around like I do, you gotta live vicariously, right?

Leastways, she joins up for story time- even if it is under Yogi's ultra-protective girth.

Here we go again, Sky's jivin' some sort of rhymin' thang called a poem. 'Bout a Pangur Ban- whatever the he...heck a Pangur Ban is!

Listen up, a little less talk and a lot more action, the musical kind, would be appreciated. For the love of Elvis!

Didn't think I knew of that cat, eh? *Maaan*, he could blister the notes of any song he wanted to sing- shoulda sung more blues, though. Had the moves, too.

I've yawned through hearin' 'bout Damned Cat (the kitnapped kit growin' up wit da quickness in the dark confines of a ship) takin' on hordes of rats- I can do that. Cats treated like gods-that'd be me. Should be me, cuz I got mass skills. The tale of the coolest cat of all, CatSkill. Like to hear more of him just to make sure he and I play in the same field, ya feel me? (Remember, I'm tryin' to tell da tale as I 'riginally recalled it.)

My fave story is about this Irishman pipin', and his dancin' yellow cat- finally sumpin' wit sound effects! Sky has to explain to the homebuds what pipin' is.

But the real live entertainment is Sky dancin' round pretendin' to pipe on the pipe and hummin' what she calls an Irish reel. Reckon it's all too true, if you're born Irish the music is born in you. Only fittin' it's in your Irish cat, too.

Overall, I'm cravin' the beat. Sky sports the talent, but she don't use it. Belt one out, Singer Sky. Forget Moon Rivers and Strangers in the Night. Choo Choo cha boogie, bring it on home, like yesterday when all my blues was right to hand and troubles was just everyday livin'!

Let's git it done right up in here- I'll show y'all the biz. Cuz I done cased the entire surrounds- talkin' miles and paw-sore miles- can't find a rockin' beat no-how, nowhere. Bunch of music-deprived wannabees! Throw out them noise boxes and learn first-hand what music can do to your soul. Hit a bass note- it'll tickle your insides right proper, 'stead a shakin' yer dang car!

Talkin' 'bout blues. This here crib ain't zactly no easy street. Catch's head-bangin' questions, the gig 'bout the Santa cat deliverin' presents to all- shoulda just dropped tunes down dem dere chimneys, the way the kit nearly made it out of catatonic-ville... What is with me lately? This place puttin' a spell on me?

Reckon if someone sang out a true tune, I mean 'sides myself, the right notes might refresh my soul. And a bro might drift away. Bars of hootchie cootchie man be downright proper and right on time. Seems wishful thinkin'.

The most recent swat-it-out with Sparky, the gallopin' goliath, ain't cuttin' it. Dog ain't singin' blues, more like whinin' further on up the road! My clobberin' his caboose is only momentary relief from what's ailin' me.

Cuttin' heads, that's what I need, but ain't no call and response blues comin' round to meet me- talk 'bout raindrops fallin' on my head.

Now, jist what's up in dis here crib, tonight? I can feel tension chompin' on the chain through the inches-open door, and it ain't stormy Monday. I slither inside, shovin' the door wider to accommodate my bulk.

'Sky's not come,' player-hater, Semi, rubs against the big-headed horse's stall. He dips his muzzle to tickle her tail, but she ain't up for it.

'What, no grub?' I stare at a ring of empty bowls. No Sky- odd... Mayhap, she's out rescuin' and we gotta wait it out? Leastaways, da weather ain't in da mix.

'Will you ever think of anything but your own stomach?' Semi hisses and spits.

Hmmmm...yeah, but they don't wanta hear what I think on. I look to the homeboy. Yogi has a head on his shoulders worthy of a tip-top cat. If answers are anywhere, Yogi will have 'em on hand, er, paw.

Homey takes his own good time, gauges me like he's scopin' the song list for the next set- makin' sure the dance numbers are correctly placed for the hour of the night and the mood of the crowd.

The whole ball game lies in his somber eyes. My hair is collectin' vibes. Ain't good ones.

'Come on, spit it out.' I ain't duckin' the shi...poop. Me, I don't worry 'bout nothin' cuz nothin' gonna be alright. Been dere, done dat. No surprises thataway.

'I'm afraid the elder's...gone.'

'Gone where?' the whirlin' dervish squeaks. 'I didn't see her come or leave.' And the dainty dancer skips to the barn door, peerin' out. Head cocks right, left, right, left, accompanied by puzzled off-key "arrrs". Whines-r-us, for the love of a non-existent and much craved sandwich- of any kind. Hey, I been out walkin', I need grub!

'Pipe down, Pipsqueak,' I growl, hunch my shoulders, figure I'm gonna go hungry or go huntin'.

I know what's intimated by the word 'gone'. Seen enough of it in the hood and out. Matter of livin', and can't do no two-steppin' 'round it.

'You gonna tell the kit?' The two of us realize what this'll mean to Sky. And to us. Trickle-down effect- shi...poop runs downhill, fo sho.

Yogi's head drops with the weight of the world. He sighs a blues riff worthy of acclaim, 'cept I ain't feelin' like givin' him no props right now. As top dog, he's got plenty to deal with aside from deliverin' what's goin' on.

I ain't nursin' a diplomatic bone in my body- can't help you, Homey. You're on your own.

Helluva way to start spring. Just when I thought 'call me the breeze' cuz I'm headin' down the road this shi...poop hits the fan. Gonna be a lot of hurtin' goin' down.

How did Jose's singin' spirit in the sky go?

23

I swear I ain't trippin'.

Could be all my ponderin' 'bout the elder goin'- she had good makin's in her. Word. Smiles for all, kind words. Thinkin' 'bout the kit and the special look Singer reserves for the crumb-snatcher- strums an 8-bar blues in my heart which is one outta here weird feelin'.

Thinkin' on Sky playin' with the kit. Hidin' and dartin' forth little bird toys the elder made and sneaked treats inside. One cool Moms, the elder. S'all I could do not to chase after those phat wingdings flappin'- they was all that.

Thinkin' 'bout the way Yogi protects the crib, and 'specially the kit. Thinkin' on the barn critters all snug abed like in the story on a silent night with here comes Santy Claus swoopin' down da chimney.

The weepin' eyes and shakin' shoulders on the now rare instance Sky comes to the barn. The commiseration in Garrett's glances when his flatulatin' sniffer, C Nova, accompanies him to feed us. At least this dog has sumpin' he can use- a trackin' sense, though I don't never see him wit a prize in his mouth.

Often David joins Garrett, and we get plenty snacks, but no stories, certainly no music, unless I carry the notes while hashin' it out with Sparky- the live entertainment section. David and Garrett do admire my gangsta skills takin' big nose down a peg or three.

But there's an air of out-go-the-lights, graveyard duty. Hard for me to figure, yet impossible to walk away from. I just know nuttin' ain't the same without Singer, happy and carin' for the lot of us.

No shi…poop, animals have mass more sense than humans. Recognize stuff that can't be helped and get on wit it.

Gotta 'mend that- Sparky ain't sparkin' a full load. Dang awkward mutt trips over his own feet- what does that say 'bout sense? Gotta watch yer step when steppin' out. And he's got a tongue longer than his legs, always droopin' goop. Even on his own self, yuck!! Gotta git David to swipe him clean- no cat'd be caught dead in his skin.

Not sure 'bout includin' the clacker/crappers in the sense department, either. I mean what does it say 'bout common sense when y'all be poopin' right where yer snoozin'? Be steppin' in and smellin' shi…poop. Save me, Aretha!

Havin' firsthand experience with ghosts, I conclude if a body enjoyed the first life why not stick around for the rest of the lives?

Like those ghost cats- Fat Frank, Cahoots and King. I hear them names shouted cuz of sumpin' the three been up to in Sky's house. Usually after a major racket soundin' off.

Now see, dem ghost cats just didn't up and bite the bullet. No way, Jose. I reg'lar case Sky's house and I see, or kinda see, those homeboys makin' theyselves to home, up to their silly games- stuff be flyin' everywhere. How them mischief makers can sail a bag of chips!

They be better off with Sky and her grand. Ain't much left of their ol' stompin' grounds. I reckon their original owner up and went on for some reason or other. Anyhow, Sky and her grandmoms welcomed the fractious haint cats same as homey guests. The elder certainly enjoyed the blighters' antics. A good laugh is good for a body, even if it's account of a mess.

But it ain't like our elder stepped out for a pack of smokes and got lost or went walkabout. Only natural for…

I ain't the first to see Sky's grandmoms hangin' round the house or visitin' us in the barn. Watch dog, Yogi, caught on wit da quickness. The cute pissant terrier (guess I'll cough up the only compliment comin' to mind) skips on Yogi's heels, delighted, and hops in circles, yappin'. The smilin' elder strolls in like always ('cept in a bit different shade and with youthful agility), pats Yogi and Boo, winks at me, kindly calls to the kit who stares at the second comin' from her hidey hole. Grandmoms lovingly strokes the horses, eyes the clacker/crappers pickin' at bugs. She calls to the pusses and they wrap round/through her, mewlin' less-than-easy-on-the-ears notes.

If we, the critters of this here crib, can see her, why can't Sky? Ain't no way to not see what the ghost cats are up to in her house. Yo, Sky, look 'round, baby girl. The spirits ain't jist in the sky, for the love of a pepperoni pizza!

I gotta hunt, even if I ain't hungry. No vermin is safe from my mood.

Night's a fallin'. This cat is bummin' to the nth degree. No awkward goofus to give what-for to. Huntin' for critters leads to zilch. Nothin' to chase- did Garrett's beagle mutt up and finally run off da goods?

Gut's acallin'. I round the corner, strut inside the barn. The hanged plates are empty! No human in sight. Too bad the elder can't open cans, or deliver a pizza or make sandwiches. Or maybe she's got off nights?

An odd whine. Is Catch…cryin'?

Yogi whiffles, nudges the kit's hidin' spot.

"Rrrrrowwwwllll!!" This house needs some good rockin' to rock all our blues away. And grub, and....

142

I figure to apply a mite of common sense which seems to be in all too short a supply in regards to the kit.

'Catch?'

There's a break in the whimperin'.

'You wanta help Sky, then buck-up! If anyone can bring her out of blues-below-zero it's you. Ya feel me?'

I tend to my pristine claws with the finesse of a top lead guitarist preppin' for a gig- gotta have da pick on point, son. Keep my insides in check from sumpin' I can't define. What this kit does to me!

'Me?' the kit squeaks. All too aware of my singular style, Yogi hovers, protectively. He's got his head cocked, ready to check me for the first word he don't cotton to.

I bite my tongue to stifle the urge to glare, curse, and slap some ass. 'You,' I growl with clipped...kindness? When have I ever indulged in kindness?

I best make myself scarce afore I overstep. Head out for the highway til I drop. Or til I can find a way to deal with the sticker probin' my guts.

Humans brag on dogs as man's best friend. Reckon Yogi is Catch's best friend, too. Ever'body's best homeboy...

Tentative steppin' into the barn. I hug shadows, make my way out.

Last I see, Sky is on her knees huggin' the guard dog with Boo dunkin' her like she's a basketball hoop. Water falls cross her cheeks. Somehow, the real deal blues singer ain't needed. I leave the friends to...friends.

I'm half-way to wherever when it hits me- Yogi did not jump my case for gettin' in Catch's grill!

24

'Yo, dawg, whass up?'

Yogi's eyes got dibs on drama. One second he's in deep, convincin' the kit out of hidin', the next he's fiercely condescendin' on this cat- wonderin' what this G (gangsta, remember?) is up to now.

'What, Strut?' Resignation magnified dumpin' on me. But I get it, dog's weighted down heavy and I'm about to hit him up more.

'Hoodbillies casin' the joint. Bad uns. Sky and David oblivious to trouble brewin'.'

If we could apprise scar-face Garrett of the sitchyation we'd meet 'em straight trippin'- one guard dog and two gangstas. Bust a few caps in... Have 'em on the run faster than po-po dogs on a take-down. Word.

'I know,' he sniffs. Interpretation- you seriously think I'm not mindin' the home turf?

I give him the benefit of his inherent ability, but I ain't the sorta cat to leave it to the dogs. Who let the dogs out don't cut it for me.

'I'm watchin', too.' My tail huffs and I head out on recon.

'Watchin' what, Strut?' Pipsqueak Boo pipes up.

'Watch yer a—'

'Strut,' Yogi snipes with less than his usual vigor.

'I'm outtey.' Though I believe in Yogi, I ain't leavin' nothin' to chance. My eyes are on like nobody's bidness. Yo, honkeys, I'll be watchin' yous, every breath you take, every step you make.

Damned good thang, too. Because the night ain't just for lovers. Come the night shakedown all my experiences'll give credence to 'Who da Man?' That'd be me.

I can hear it- crib'll be toutin' need a hero. And I'll have my game on.

Stormin' like to beat a Guns and Roses rock concert. No fit night for man or beast. Just the all-time dumbest of dumb ass thugs.

I'm up in my digs preppin' for a cat nap. Spit on a paw, swipe at an ear, when Yogi starts barkin' like hellza'poppin'. Saturday night's all right come right to life on a squirrely night at Bad Sign- before trouble-makers are bounced out the door. Good blues don't compete wit trash talkin' hoodbillies.

The puss quartet scuttles in four directions- talk about goin' to ground. The horses snort and stomp, circle in their stalls, jostle the walls- addin' to the drummer upstairs with heavy-hand on the bass drum- thunder.

Cr CRCRRRR CRASH!!

Bat them cymbals, Sticks, I silently praise the spirit in the sky. Jagged light flashes through the curtain of storm, and hang it if my hair ain't standin' on end- minus the trip to the barber shop- electrified!

The clamorin' sets off the previously nappin' clacker/crappers to do what they do best. Thankfully, not in my side of the barn or in my penthouse suite- I'm way more cool than the boy from New York City. Keep yer mess to yer own digs ya pitiful excuses for... I can imagine all the shi...poop hittin' the fan, along with mass feathers flyin'.

Boo adds his 2-cents, yippin' high register til my ears are fit to blister.

I peer over the ledge. No barn light left on, but darkness don't confront me none.

Yogi's railin' and backin' retreat. Boo dancin' against his side.

'Yo, this ain't no parade, bite some ass!' I advise. Fruitlessly.

There they be- the two, scum bag hoodbillies I seen stalkin' the woods and property borders. Waitin' for Sky to leave. Checkin' if Yogi's tied and how far from the barn he treks.

Sumbitches got sticks with traps on the end and are forcin' the guard dog back towards a stall- good thang the horse can exit out to his field or it'd be a might crowded in that joint. Yogi's strugglin' on his haunches tryin' to maintain, but the pokin' in his chest is layin' it down. Out foxed. Poor darn dog, too nice for his own good. Growlin' ain't cuttin' it, for the love of... Ah, hell!

The bigger thug- biggy drawers- directs the scene, flankin' its trap-stick so Yogi's got no escape. And his boneyard sidekick gripes how he'd rather be anywhere but here.

"I like dogs," it whines, shovin' the long, thick stick into Yogi's chest. Rain and snot run races on its face.

"I like dogs, too. Hurry up, git him in. Git both of 'em in. They'll be safe and out of our way. Ready?"

The stall door slides open just enough and Yogi's shuffled inside- flat on his a...behind. Boo is shoved sideways followin', stirrin' up dust. A losin' hand, fer sure.

That leaves the playin' field to the master martial arts cat-me, and the pitiful excuses for dance partners. 'Bout time to teach some lessons. I arch my back, wait for the opportune moment.

"We'll trap the cat and make tracks before anyone gets wise. Sell that critter come Halloween."

Trap a cat, eh? I gotta little sumpin' sumpin' to say 'bout that.

"For cryin' out loud, Halloween is months off!" Boneyard sniffles snot. "We could be makin' due with a 6-pack and a sack of White Castles."

White Castles- ah, yeah, midget burgers loaded with onions, no thanks. I'll take a pizza- call it in. I'll be needin' grub when I've finished wit da lot of yous.

"This is bizness. Black cat round Halloween brings decent dough. We'll fatten the black sucker up- get yer head straight."

Black cat? Great blues amighty! Two blind-ass rookies. Ain't no black cat in this here crib. Reckon Catch might look black when crawlin' like a bug, but the kit's got white paws and chest. And this here cat's one black and orange hellraiser. The pusses ain't black either, you dumb ***! Damn certain none of us gonna sit company with the likes of y'all. Word.

Yogi continues his fractious herald for help. Sky'll be comin'- if she can hear the barkin' over all the stormy weather blarin'. She'll call scar-face Garrett who don't take no shi... nuttin' off nobody- just look at his face.

Or will she? Hell! Best get my act together wit da quickness.

'Stay put, Catch, no matter what. It's OK,' Yogi cautions the kit, seekin' to soothe her. Poor thing's probably a joker shy of a heart attack.

Now see, a clever cat'd never be shoved into a box without recourse to an exit. This cat only got caught after a hard-won fight the night before, and bein' chased round a box convention for hours on end. Ah…I gotta call it like it is- Sky's singin' really got me.

"What if the girl comes?"

"Clip her upside her head, dipshit. We gotta git the black cat," biggy drawers sneers.

Y'all wanta hurt singer/storyteller Sky and the scared-to-death kit? Pump yer brakes, ya slime crackheads! Y'all got another thing comin'- yer in my house now!

"RRRRRAAAHHRRRRR!!" My challenge out-screams the storm, and my talons are itchin', and my tail is twitchin' better than the drummer flashin' his sticks.

"What was that?" Boneyard squeals and hunkers into biggy drawers. A flashlight swings and thuds to the ground. Dipsticks didn't even turn the thang on.

"Git off me! Just the wind, for—"

I repeat myself, "*RRRROWWERRROWERRRERRRR!!*"

Wind, my a…behind! Got 'em right where I want 'em- tremblin' in their dimwit duds.

The smart cat keeps his cool, takes stock of the low-rent G's, plans accordingly. Don't see me runnin' for the hills. Numb-nuts boneyard has a bare head- prime target for suitable anointin', and he's standin' right under my post! What a night for a daydreamin' boy!

'Kit, you do like Yogi says. I got dis. Stay hidden',' I thrum. Dog's got nerve callin' this OK. If the bugger were a cat, he'd high-tail it over the stall wall and lend a hand, for the love of-
-

'They want me, just like the trappers took my brother,' Catch cries. 'I won't let them hurt Sky--'

'Stay put, don't worry, I'm on it.' One shite of a night-hey, sounds like a song waitin' to be writ.

I extend the intro, "*ERRRRAHRRRRRERRRRAHRRR*!!!" Quake, suckers!

Suddenly, a flash of insight fired by a raggedy strip of lightnin' flips a switch inside my brain. Halloween night, ghost cats a'trollin' one misfit ramshackle house, and they are mightily pissed at the thug batterin' their territory with rocks. As if the rain and thunder peals weren't enough of a party band.

An outmatched heroine wadin' in half-cocked to tackle the huge pitcher and then...

The mother of all saviors! CatSkill was his name- Sky told us a story about dat coolest cat of all.

'Yo, CatSkill, might need a little back-up here,' I whisper to the universe right before I belt my finest Janis Joplin scream. Baby girl JJ would high-five my gusto, if I do say so myself.

One shite of a night, for sure. Cry babies- yer about to get dealt wit! But things start goin' down way too fast and all at the same time--

A drenched Sky bursts into the barn midst a rainy gust, and calls for Yogi. At first, she don't see the trespassers. The kit bounds out of hidin' to play martyr- the trap falls directly on her- right before Sky sinks to the ground.

Seconds too late...

"*RRROWRRRROWWWRRRRRRRR*!!!!" I'm airborne.

"What the—"

"It's got white feet and—"

Boneyard's pain-filled vocals can't compare with mine. All of my remarkably sharp claws pierce a crown of thorns into his scalp- my landin' zone.

"Hellll...p! Aaaah...*AAAAAAHHH!*"

"Can't see a damned thing! Where's the *** flashlight?" Biggy drawers trips, falls, comes up awkwardly swingin' and bumpin' into boneyard and the walls. Hope he don't fall on the kit, but I ain't got time to worry 'bout that.

I'm busy rainin' hell, hallelujah! My wrath descends, stickers tear and gouge, scratch, plunge deeper. All the while I string out a blues solo never recorded in the annals of Ella, JJ, or Etta, and biggy drawers humps around hittin' boneyard here and there with a shovel in the mistaken belief he might dislodge me.

Playin' dodge the tripper, I flail my tail in boneyard's eyes, further blindin' his sorry bass-end, and proceed to rip his ears off. His hands flap at me til I surgically convince them it ain't happenin'. You are on a highway to hell, and I'm drivin'!

"GET IT OFF! GET IT OFF!"

Talk about dancin' in the dark! Sway me more- I'd croon 'cept this ain't a croonin' sitchyation. Beltin' blues- my style. Two stooges and one balanced master cat at work!

Between biggy drawer's repeated f-word cussin', boneyard's wailin', clacker/crappers' cluckin' and shiten up a stinkin' hurrah, Yogi's growlin', Boo's shrieks, horses' squeals and my intermittent operatic-worthy solos you get an earful of what Judgement Day is all about.

In the midst of this particular one-cat-driven doomsday, a streak of brilliant light flushes the darkness, but I'm too busy applyin' comeuppance to really enjoy the full-out spectacle.

A chuckle resonates deep under the cacophony. "A little light on the subject, perhaps."

The single barn bulb flicks on.

"Nice hat," the deep bass voice muses. CatSkill has arrived!

As if all the spirits in the sky are in accord, they strike up a deadly beat. Thunderin' and masses of lightnin' hit it. The house is rockin'!

Don't be too late, my last nerve prays. Sky lies crumpled, and Catch, the non-listenin' kit, is an immobile spot of dark under a net. Rage flares anew deep inside of me.

Get a load of my bad boys! I roar in boneyard's ear, and tear off another slew of flesh. Cauliflower ears r us, he'll be cryin'. Nah, he won't have enough skin left to fake cauliflower ears.

"I thought I'd join this impromptu party. Thanks for the invite," CatSkill trills, winks at me. "Stick around miscreants, I must officially greet my true hosts first."

S'cool wit me, I can dance all night, if the boneyard partner don't collapse first.

I suppose it's much later that it hits me- CatSkill unnerstan's every word in my head!

25

'It's him,' Catch weeps, relieved.

Hang a bass note if it ain't! The truth of the revelation momentarily stifles my octave strut on the catwalk while my claws continue to dig in and my tail flails away on boneyard's sputterin' face- ain't gonna call it a puss.

'Wait a full-throated bar- how do you know CatSkill?' I ask Catch amidst my talon-diggin'.

'I was in a real scary place—'

'As opposed to—'

'Scary things you couldn't see half of, and Sky...Sky was there fighting with a huge—'

'Well, I'll be damned, I was there, too!' The kit must a been the one I caught a whiff of hidin' out in a tree hole.

Wit da quickest quickness, CatSkill crouches, releases Catch, and whirls upon risin' to see biggy drawers sidlin' to the exit like the fat stumble-butt he is.

I hiss, prepared to vault onto his face- I mean, I'm an equal opportunity kind of cat.

CatSkill beats me to it. He holds up a finger and volatile eyes warn the slickster, "Stay put. Strut, keep your toy occupied a bit longer. Wife, is Sky alright?" His full attention drops to--

How did I miss the angelic being kneelin' beside Singer? Did she just pop in like CatSkill? The lady scintillates (like that word? This is one learned cat even if I don't harken to all Sky's stories) with good, good, good vibrations.

Darned if she doesn't have a star twinklin' on her hand as it ministers to my girl. Sky's head is cradled in the arms of an angel-CatSkill's woman.

"Out cold, but she'll be fine soon. I'll call Dr. G—"

Once again, into the fracas from out of nowhere, pops another other-worldly with a fashion model set of threads to rival James Brown.

"You rang? Always happy to lend you my services," the newest player touts with a jaunty, cat-ate-the-cream smile. Dude thinks he's one phat sumpin'.

"Dragon, you are cruising. Your newly acquired and long overdue cat-lover status does not include my Wife."

This cat reads plainly, Dr. G would like to rival CatSkill for the lady's affection, but is totally out-classed- phat threads or no. I can feel the strength between CatSkill and his wife. Ain't no wannabe male model gonna break it.

"How did you manage to get away from your recent rescue kitty charges, anyway?"

"I left them all curled up on my bed with word I'd return soon," Dr. G informs as he gently lifts unconscious Sky and totes her to her house. And get this- no rain falls on Dr. G, the angel or Sky! A straight path of dry! Am I dreamin'?

I've continued to pull hair and other bloody stuff durin' this intermission- to the dismay of my howlin' be-boppin' culprit. Can't figure how the bugger's still standin'. What'd ya think gonna happen you go trippin' on my turf, brainless bonehead?

"Now, let's get better acquainted, shall we?" A feral-magnified gaze CatSkill tenders, full throttle, on the bug baits. "Strut, my main man, will you mind Catch's safety for me?"

The kit hasn't stirred from her jailbreak, but hunkers like road kill.

'Aye, Captain CatSkill, right on! He ain't heavy--"

"--she's my sister. I love that song! We'll talk music later."

Finally, someone with a musical bent! 'My bad, Catch,' I apologize to the kit. And to the top cat of all time, 'I'm your cat, bro. C'mon, Kit,' I launch off boneyard with extra deep-set in claws rakin' hell.

"AAAAAHHHH!!"

"Who the **** you think you are?" Biggy drawers blusters. He don't know it yet, but his a...butt is done for. Right proper dawg food!

I usher the kit up my pole, nose shovin' her tiny hind-end up, up, up. 'Gotta great view up here. Watch this baaaaad hombre strut his stuff.'

'B...b...bad?' The still shakin' kit stammers. 'CatSkill is good, i...isn't he?'

'Bad can be good. Phat's good. Gotta larn you real lingo. Let's enjoy the show. Thank the lead guitar for our super night vision cuz that bulb's seen better days.' It flicks to a dull light leftover.

The two pukes banter with mis-placed machismo. "What you think you can do to us, huh? ****"

'Talk smack, get whacked, is what I always say. Ever see such chutzpah, kiddo? Hoodbillies got another thing comin'! Gonna see a real wang dang doodle!'

Catch is silent- say it isn't so! Can't believe umpteen questions ain't rollin'. I'm honed in on the comeuppance comin', but I get it, the kit's elevator is stuck. Guess that happens when you're scared out of yer wits all the time. And then some joker drops a cage on your head.

'Check out those squirmin' thugs, Kit- worms on a hook.' I figure I'll play DJ, call out the plays.

"I'm your worst nightmare, you brain-cell, disinclined—"

'Wannabees,' I snarl my two cents, not that CatSkill needs any help from yours truly.

"Thank you, Strut," piercing, gold eyes gleam my way. Before his ultimate throwdown, "So you want to play with a black cat, eh?"

"There's two of us," spits the one with blood runnin' down his face.

Cracks me up- the ignorance on parade. I chortle when I should be composin' epitaphs- bluesy bye-byes.

A smirkin' roar accompanies an eloquent rejoinder, "Not my brain cells overtaxed. I firmly aver I'm your worst nightmare cubed to the infinite power."

'See, CatSkill's callin' 'em out, puttin' 'em on the spot. He ain't afraid of nuttin', and soon the el stupidos'll know they're in his hood!'

All the drummers outside concur. Lightnin' wraps our barn crib in a sizzle and the thunder claps cause the whole buildin' to vibrate- leadin' a body to think the roof is on fire. Every critter sounds off bedlam! Bet the clacker crap is hittin' the fan again! What a night for a shindig!

I snatch up Catch by the scruff of her neck as my roost bucks and she slithers south on loose hay.

'Hold on there, Kit! I say, I say, hold on.' I drag her to safety and keep a steady paw upon her back.

With another flash of crazed lightnin', the light bulb loses its last hurrah, and suddenly CatSkill is no longer on two legs.

'H...he's the—' Catch stutters.

'Biggest damn cat I ever saw! What an off-the-hook surprise! *Daaaaaamn!*' How in the blues' ranks did he do it?

The stench of sodden drawers has me snortin' as CatSkill, an enormous dark shadow of a cat, arches his back, and with surreal speed, swipes out a huge paw, claws long as—

'My legs,' Catch murmurs, stunned.

Me, I'm struck dumb, and I gotta tell you that don't happen much.

'Let's refrain from stinking up this lovely barn.' We listen in to CatSkill's mind-speak while he artfully, and painfully, ushers the blubberin' deadbeats out into the drivin'-beat rain.

'C'mon, Catch, show's movin'.' Gracefully, hurriedly, I shuck down the post. The kit ain't got the hang of it and lands on...

'Boo?'

Forgot all about the dang dogs!

'Yogi nosed me over the stall wall. What's going on? Who's that? Where...?' The befuddled terrier's eyes are fixin' to bust out of his skull at the sight of the enormous, all-black, mystery cat.

'Watch and learn, Tidbit.'

Poor Yogi's barkin', still stuck inside the dang stall. 'Let me see 'bout this here latch,' I call into the guard dog on lockdown. Don't want poor ol' dawg missin' out on all the fun.

'Who are you calling old?' Growls from within.

Stall door lock ain't accomodatin' this here cat's skills. 'Sorry, big boy, these stickers ain't made for this kind a work.'

Yogi repeatedly bangs full-throttle against the door. Waste of energy and time. Stall's made of sterner stuff- keeps horses in, right?

'Jailhouse rock ain't playin tonight, bro. Catch your act later.' I take my place as referee and chief cheerleader via my phat vocals just inside the barn entry. Happily, the rain drifts sideways outside. Dry front row seats for the entertainment- can't beat it!

'All we need now are some snacks,' a gruff harrumph from our rear.

'Yogi!' Boo, Catch and I chorus together.

'Cat vaulting and rabbit hopping are outside my job description. Took a lot of convincing to get Shiloh to use his big head and boost me in the... Where'd the panther come from?'

'CatSkill,' I reply without lookin' round. Too much goin' on outside. Don't wanna miss a swat.

'From the story?' Yogi's on the wonderin' side so the kit over-zealously fills in the formerly mis-placed guard dog.

'Where's Sky?'

'CatSkill's angel and some dude called dragon said she'll be fine. Carried her into the house. No worries, Yogi- now watch the real McCoy in old school action.'

I'm intent on every battin' clawed paw, the deep roarin'- great back-up bass- the agile springs as CatSkill rolls/separates his two cat toys, rabbit-kicks 'em like they're naught but big stuffed balls.

Hmmm...maybe I can learn a few new tricks? Maybe not. CatSkill moves like a basketball player on speed at the final tournament. All we need are some hoops!

'Strut, can you move like that?'

'Don't believe J.C. can move the way CatSkill does.' Fascination fills my heart.

'Who's J.C.?' Catch questions.

'Dunno. Must be one high-steppin' daddy, cuz I heard his name bandied about a lot.'

Our collective audience heads snap right and left, eager to follow every antic the shaman-shadow catwalks cross the sloppy mud-fest.

Sky's nighttime story described CatSkill's shamanic cat skills- shapeshiftin' aint' his only talent. Can't wait to see what else is up his sleeve, 'specially the music avidity.

Ah, the smell of fear, the stench of sodden drawers, the lightning-basted sky and rain-purged blood, thick mud... Minds me of a song I heard on some ol' piano some time back- boastin' of the mud, the blood and the beer. Two out of three ain't bad, I snort with gusto.

I sense the kit compilin' a shi...poop pile of questions while I hurrah. 'Too phat! Go gangsta on their as...on 'em.' I hit a few high notes for pure pleasure.

Biggy drawer's weight escalates his tumblin' dice a...butt-like slidin' home, 'cept he ain't got no home here. CatSkill's on him faster than slobber dissolvin' in the downpour. One mighty swipe of hefty black paw shoots the cucaracha straight into weepin' boneyard, who's tryin' desperately to cover his important parts, and I ain't talkin' bout his empty head atop his shrunken shoulders.

Added to the merriment, CatSkill smacks his two toys into a makeshift mudball, and proceeds to rabbit-kick more snot out of 'em.

'Let it roll!' I catcall.

Yogi howls, Boo shrieks and I step it up. I give out a long-drawn out '*RRRROOWWWWWRRRRRRRRRRRR*,' singin' a bar from Rock and Roll, Hootchicoo!

'Them two pieces of shi…poop be hummin' a mess of blues, cuz it's for damn sure, they won't be able to talk,' I inform Catch, who's invadin' my personal space to feel absolutely safe and secure. Or maybe just to get the best view.

A few, skedaddlin', bowlin' maneuvers more- them hoodbillies be resemblin' death walkin'- and the bell is rung. All points to my man, CatSkill! Champion by total devastation knockouts!

'There's one G knows how to pitch a wang dang doodle,' Yogi woofs.

I simply stare at him- I do believe my jaw has come undone. He pretends to ignore me for a loaded second before winkin' that big, dark dog eye.

'Reckon' you're having an effect on all of us, Strut. Not saying that's a good thing, mind you.'

'Why Yogi, yer my dawg!!'

26

'Party's over,' I tout, eyein' the knockouts lyin' in silent, mud-clad misery. 'Hey, Dinah, call your man, the undertaker! Mista Undertaker man got a coffin just yo size ya biggy drawers. Toss bonehead in wit ya, ha!' Got zactly what dey deserved.

"Sorry, folks, not much to work with here." CatSkill has dropped the black panther act and stands on his own two feet, head cocked askance at the slopped-up and spit-out pile of leftover rotters.

'Kinda resembles a giant hairball,' I quip, to his deep chuckling amusement. 'Shame, shame trash day is three days off,' I continue in mind-speak. 'But oh, what a night!'

Our favorite hero throws back his great-maned head and crows. "Hey, Cool Cat, I believe my friend, Dr. Gunne, can devise something much more fitting than a garbage can ride to the dump."

As if listenin' for his cue, the stranger who accompanied the angel to deliver Sky to her bed and further the healin' process, pops in. Whole lotta poppin' goin' down tonight! Literally. I'm talkin' from out of nowhere, in pimpin' style, too. Without a drop of rain fallin' on his far-out threads, can you dig it?

Yogi immediately acts the guard dog role, "Rrrrrr, woof, woof!" And stands his ground in the doorway. This Dr. Gunne ain't got no stick-wieldin' traps to prod wit.

"Thanks, Yogi, but he's with me," CatSkill grins, and fondly strokes Yogi's head.

"Did I hear 'friend' used in conjunction with my name?" Mr. James Brown lookalike's brows rise in disbelief.

"I suppose after your adopting the homeless kittens from Xavier's Rescue and Clinic, you are approximating the definition of 'friend', friend."

"CatSkill, you take the cake!" The stranger mocks and strikes a pose. Thinks he's GQ material, struttin' his mac on the catwalk.

"I am GQ material, homeboy," he swivels and smirks at me. "And I always strut my mac."

Lucille! This homey reads minds, too! I receive a star quality smile for my astute observation, or is it because of callin' him GQ on the catwalk?

"Good tune, bud. I enjoy everything Little Richard put his hand to."

And he knows music! Good golly, Miss Molly!

"Cake? Nah, not my first choice. Bonnie bring any cookies?" CatSkill exhibits anticipation with glowin' eyes- the feral look is kaput.

These two seem to have an interestin' history. I'll have to hint to Sky to read more of the CATSKILL novel and get to the bottom of their funky relationship.

"Strut, soon Sky will be able to hear everything you'd like to say to her. See, she's learning mind-speak from a lovely new cat friend- just give her a little time."

'Serious?' *Daaaam*, we'll be knockin' on heaven's door! Just think, me and Sky hittin' it!

CatSkill winks at me and turns to Dr. G.

Brushin' off invisible dust from his phat suit jacket, Gunne stands in pristine splendor. Maybe a little too admirin' of hisself? Rather like...me.

"Good thing Bonnie is handy with the weather. My silk suit hasn't suffered a lick. Unlike many of my wardrobe items in our other daring escapades together."

Ignorin' the dig, CatSkill eyes the fallen. "Dragon, I'm hoping you'll take out the trash."

"Now what in our trials and tribulations together leaves you with the slightest impression I'm ready to discard my doctoral pursuits in favor of waste disposal? Am I precipitously mistaken in thinking my sartorial elegance might escape unscathed, for once?"

Gets curiouser and curiouser these two shootin' the breeze. Don't know zactly what a dragon is, but I bet Catch'll ask and save my ignorance.

"I'll explain later, Strut," CatSkill offers.

Wow, I gotta watch my thoughts in such sublime company!

"Dragon, I'd do it myself but I have commendations to award. Let me tell you what these miscreants planned for…"

The rest is not for our ears, but whatever CatSkill says strikes Gunne like a ball bat upside the head.

The dragon thunders, "They hate cats!! They want to…harm cats? CatSkill, I tender my utmost gratitude to you for the opportunity to deal with…" In his frustration at being tongue-tied in findin' a word or two yucky enough, he actually stomps, sendin' a swathe of mud onto his catwalk-worthy slacks.

"There are no words despicable enough." In an instant, Gunne grips an inert slug in each hand and…disappears!

Jump, jive and wail- this is one night Bad Sign couldn't begin to compete with!

Hang it, we forgot to ask about Sky! But in the angel's hands she must be all right, right?

163

"Take it easy, my friends, don't worry about Sky. My Wife, Bonnie, is taking care of her and she'll be out to see you later...this morning. My, look at the time! I've accolades to bestow!"

Yogi, Boo, and I follow CatSkill into the barn. He fingers the light bulb and wit da quickness, on goes the light wit all brightness restored. From the corner of my eye, I spy the kit hunkerin' in the shadows. For the love of B.B.- ain't no more to be scared of!

'Wait, Catch,' I call, to no avail. She slinks off to her hidey hole. Not good, not good, but I bet CatSkill will get through to her.

"Boo, fetch!" CatSkill plucks somethin' from his pocket and tosses tidbits with enough velocity that they actually sound off plunks upon descent into a hay pile.

The yapper's off. He'll be busy huntin' the treats for a dog-pawin' moment or three.

Meanwhile, CatSkill flows to his haunches (what agile grace) by Yogi's side. Sincere compliments have Yogi lickin' at our savior's face. Gotta admit, dog deserves his props. Ain't his fault he ain't got it like this cat does. Maybe I kin teach him some more efficient maneuvers.

"You may be the finest dog I have ever met," CatSkill gently fondles Yogi's crown.

I gotta agree, 'That's my dawg. Word.' Yogi cocks his head my way and gives me a high five raise of paw. Can't believe the cool rollin' off him- he been hidin' out on us all this time!

But I can't help thinkin' 'bout CatSkill's accolades my way.

Yogi's grateful tongue keeps on a-lickin', saturatin' the top cat's cheek.

"Generally, only my Wife is allowed such latitude, boy," CatSkill grins. "Here, let me fix those hind quarters- a little sore, huh?"

No explainin' what Top Cat CatSkill does with his hands, but inside three bars of an 8-bar blues, Yogi is friskin' like a puppy! Don't need another Boo round here. I keep this opinion thoroughly to myself.

Really, I'm happy for Yogi- he ain't deservin' hurt. Tried to clear the damn stall wall repeatedly. Prob'ly got a hitch in his giddyup for his efforts, not bein' a cat and all. His tail's a-waggin' and CatSkill's face is lookin' rather slimed.

"Love putting my shamanic healing to good use. Yogi, you ever need anything, you call me, CatSkill. Might be the first time a cat ever came at a dog's bidding, but in your case, the honor's all mine. Here you go, Yogi," CatSkill presents a handful of tasty-scented snacks.

27

"Strut! RROWWWRRR!"

Playin' my song! "RROWWWRRR!" I can cut heads with the best of 'em.

CatSkill roars laughter. "You are one cool cat and you know it, too."

'Word on, m'man! No brag, just fact,' I wink.

"Those fools couldn't pull off cool if they landed in Antarctica," he nods his full-maned head.

Surprisingly, he's keyed into sumpin' I keep under paw, and I'm suddenly a mite unsure. But the others are busy elsewhere. Catch is as usual, hidden. Reckon it's all right…

'No-talent, wannabe band players. Your Janis Joplin scream is mind-boggling- perfect. They were jealous, you know?' CatSkill reverts to mind-speak. This confab is to be just between the two of us. I take it easy. Don't want my bidness traipsed out for all to hear.

'How did you know I wanted to be part of the band?'

'I'm privy to what makes you tick, Strut, one of my many gifts. You OK with that?'

Hesitantly, I nod. Can't go wrong wit da likes of CatSkill. Not from what I've seen.

'It takes true spirit to see real gold in front of one's face. You were tricked and left to fend for yourself- which you do so admirably, my friend. They might have got you out of their lives, but you'll haunt them til the day they die. Hey, that sounds like a song, what do you say?'

His thick mane swings right and left as if he's searchin' for the proper beat. Next thang, he's snappin' his fingers and tappin' his toes. The beat's comin' to play in my head.

'Let's write it, homeboy!' My paws are kneadin' the dirt with excitement.

His chuckle reverbs in the barn. In mind-speak for our ears only, he continues, 'I want you to consider Sky in a different light. She brought you here to her home, and she loves you.'

I'm floored. 'Loves...me?' Did my voice break? Has anyone...ever...loved...me?

'Would I lie?'

'No. I...I thank you,' I manage. What else can I say?

'Love is best when it's a two-way street. Think on it.'

CatSkill grins kindly, and I feel a wave of...a little sumpin' sumpin'... nice...wrap me up. Like bein' cared for as a kit some time ago. How long since anyone cared for me, besides Sky? My homeboy...

'I tender my whole-hearted gratitude to you for calling me and for proceeding to take matters into your very capable hands in order to protect Catch and--'

'Capable Sky.' I finish the sentiment, as he expected me to.

It flits through my head, her capably- musically- trappin' my a...butt. And her rescuin' those critters with David in tow on a stormy Monday- ain't no how Tuesday's just as bad.

'Sorry, homey, got off track,' I apologize to CatSkill.

It abruptly hits me- it's the emotional baggage the shaman wants me to study on.

CatSkill nods amiably, patiently- he's cat, after all.

167

'Strut, this cat chat is off the record. We'll conversate more at a later date. And make music, too. But there are a few things I wish you would contemplate in the meantime.' He takes a deep breath- reckon he's configurin'.

'I know very little of your birth lingo, though I am hip to the blues. Not hard for me to read your past. You're the type who'd stick til death.'

'Word up, homeboy. I...I should have been quicker on the mark. Don't ever want hurtin' on Sky or the kit, or any of these,' I peer around at my homeys. My homeys?

'My homeys ain't much in a rumble, not havin' my experience--'

'But that's cool. Differences make the world go round. You're true blue, Strut. Have you considered why you've been here longer than any of your other hangouts?'

CatSkill is pointin' to somethin'. Knows more of me than I do. Kinda digs in my gut, in a best-get-your-thinkin'-on clarion call.

'I believe you've thoroughly staked out roots, and not only in that dude's head. Boneyard, you called him?'

"Yeah, quite a contrast from biggy drawers, eh?'

An amused roar wafts a refreshin' breeze amidst all da emotion stuff.

'You think Sky loves Catch or Yogi more than you? Ain't so, homey. Love is infinite. I think you feel it, but try your hardest not to. Think on it, my friend, it'll bring a wonder into your soul you've never conceived of. Sky loves all critters, tries to understand what each one needs so she can help them feel their best.'

'I wish she'd try out lady sings the blues- what with her vocal skills,' I grumble.

'Maybe you should ask her. She's in the process of learning a whole lot about language, and undoubtedly will surprise you very soon.

Getting back to what I have to say. She brought you here because she not only loves you, but realized all a smart cat like you needed is right here. Love, home, friendship, family, folks to take care of, cedar shavings, grub.' CatSkill's brow rises as in 'get my drift?'

'I'm followin' ya,' I nod. This private confab is touchin' on stuff I'd rather stayed on the down-low, as in far, far outta sight.

'Listen, my friend—'

'Friend?' Could a cat ask for a better homey than the Top Cat of all time to be his friend?

'Oh, yes. We'll be great homeys. All these critters here will be your friends, if you let them in. Even the out-of-the-woodwork pusses. You have an overwhelming propensity for love.'

'I do?' News to me. I always been keepin' myself to myself. Mind your own bidness- a good motto.

'You jumped right in to help Catch and Sky—'

'Hey, fightin's my game and I know a little—'

'And you can guess the rest?'

"*RrrrrERRRRRRRR!*"

He echoes me perfectly- one straight-trippin' music man!

Sudden death silence. CatSkill waits me out. I'm beginnin' to feel…shy?

'Strut, why have you constantly roamed?'

'Lookin' for a phat tune,' I blurt.

CatSkill grins- waitin' for hell to freeze over or dawn to dawn?

'Music is only a start,' he trills.

For the life of me I'm missin' a clue as to where he's headin' with this downer.

'Blues entails more than vocal talent, which you certainly have. Blues are about expressing feelings, emotions. The true blues singer lays it all out, doesn't hide anything. Put all the energy of your life's learnings into the soul of the song you want to sing. For instance, take your very first victory—'

'I was blues cruisin' to the stars,' I boast.

'Life is more than surviving. Take a moment to feel every split second of the experience. What's goin' down? Make friends with new feelings. All feelings, get it? And be thankful for them.'

He wants me to get inside…my head.

'Like the lady singers you admired at Bad Sign, Strut.'

It's amazin' how he knows all about me!

'Friend, I've been around the block a long, long time. I read living things in many ways you'd not believe possible, and I have other 'gifts',' his sunlight eyes penetrate me.

'Like becomin' the great black cat?'

A slow melodic chuckle. 'That is only part of my repertoire. Let's return to you, for now. Janis Joplin's scream didn't solely erupt from her belly or throat, but her heart. You have no idea how huge your heart is. As a favor, I'd advise you to touch on all those things you'd rather not acknowledge. Do it for both of us. It'll put you on a whole new level.'

The poignancy glintin' in his golden gaze seeps inside me in a warm, yet disturbin', certainly thought-provokin' way.

'I'll catch your act later, say, Wednesday after next? And we'll do the blues justice. Right now, I need to have a word with my little lion-heart, Catch.'

'Right-o, the kit really needs you,' I'm fixin' to be let off the hook. For a bit.

But the golden stare flares an instant.

'I...guess...I do, too,' I reluctantly admit.

'Catch has always thought you're not as happy as you should be,' CatSkill strikes another chord.

'The kit thinks that? About me?' Another surprise. A real gut-wrencher, too. Happy? Well, he...heck, I'm happy. Got ever'thang I need. Don't I?

'Catch is extremely sensitive and perceptive and she cares about you. Think on it,' he winks. 'See you later, alligator.'

'Afterwhile, crocodile,' I shoot the rejoinder.

CatSkill joyously laughs. Me, I gotta bounce.

"Catch, my little lion-heart, you can't hide from me," I hear CatSkill callin' the kit as I exit the barn. Rain's called it a night, but I...I'm walkin'.

Catch, lion-heart. For a scared-to-death-of-everything kit wit'out any martial skills to slip out of safety and just give up her life to keep Sky safe...

Yeah, got a whole barn full of lions tonight, I'm surmisin'.

But I'm seein' the kit in a surprisin' new way. Word.

28

I s'pose I had intentions of startin' in on the head-speculatin' bidness right off, though it ain't never been my bag. Thinkin's good for schemin', but doin' is the thang, if ya feel me?

Struttin' along after cleanin' my claws- always keep your weapons primed- I cadge a whiff of sumpin' phat. A scent from…

Ain't into religion. I reckon I can dig what yer puttin' down- there's a spirit in the sky, or somewhere over the rainbow. Don't need no preacher man to tell me so. I mean, just look at me or CatSkill and you'll reckon there's a god, too.

Any ol' how, religious clubs aside, if you come across a church (the buildin' wit da tall stick ridin' up in the clouds) be alert for festivals, receptions, socials, picnics, etc. If there's a gatherin', be on yer toes. 'Specially if you are fittin' to get your grub on.

Now, I'll give y'all the benefit of my speriences.

Before struttin' in like you own the joint, size up the homeys- don't want to get punk'd for goin' in half-cocked. At all costs, keep your distance from screamin' crumb-snatchers, gals standin' round gossipin' in fancy threads, and swelled-up gangsta types hangin' wit dey homeboys- they prob'ly talkin' smack on the side, even if it is a church function.

Look for the lady who's busy settin' up the groceries, hangin' the table covers jus' right, tryin' to get somebody's attention and a little help. Wastin' her time, cuz she be doin' it all, regardless. Get my drift?

This lady be your mark.

Maintain a no-grab position, kinda on the sly, but so's she'll notice you. Cuz b'lieve me this lady don't miss nuttin'!

Tilt your head a mite, give her the goo-goo eye and a melodic note for her ears only. Sometimes it's worth it to show her your scars-invite the moms in her makeup to rise to the occasion. Word- she can't help it. Gal's born to be jus' what she is- an earth angel.

Once I hear her deep sigh, "The Lord had his scars, too, kitty cat," I know I'm in. She's balancin' bowls of grub, but givin' me the time of day.

With a true Christian remark like dat un, chances are ridin' high- cuz she's also the one who takes care of every little livin' thing- that she'll study on your predicament, figure you're starvin', and bow to God's wishes regardin' all His creatures.

She'll give a scant glance at the table wonders, check to make sure nobody's watchin' (though I do believe she'd go on and do whatever anyway and fight to the death any rude objections to her Christian duty) and a phat chicken leg will underhandedly sail your way. That's dope!

Now, be polite and do your Christian part to this good woman- cuz you may pass this way again- thank her with a serene wink, murmured meow, and skedaddle wit da quickness, goods in mouth.

"Go on with you, you little beggar, and God go with you," you'll most likely hear her pray in her send-off.

Don't be a hog and return for more. Don't work like dat- caretakers gotta make sure ever'body gets a little sumpin' sumpin'.

Gets trickier when the event isn't outside.

Only time my puttin'-it-on sorta failed me was one bad-boy cold night- not a tasty critter to be found. But I lucked out. Shindig goin' down in a church basement. Followed my nose, smellin' the goods long afore I arrived at the godly gates.

Studyin' on my entry, and more important on my exit, I slinked through a cracked-up vent and continued on in.

Fish-fry in the underground! Smell got my juices flowin', guts agrumblin'. Made damn sure I'd not be cornered and trapped. Checked out the quiet varmints hidin' and waitin' in the wings for leftover scraps of any size.

Best consider you ain't the only hungry critter on the make, 'specially on a night like that un. And hey, if the fish ain't flyin' your way, a mouse or two'll do ya. Curl up next to the heat-maker and chow down.

This partic'lar night, a huge grease-shiny homeboy was mindin' the kitchen. Cuttin' up, breadin' up, fryin' up and platin' up. The sizzle and scent almost made me jump out of character and steal me a piece a fish. In a church, mind you!

Not my first choice- the beggin' bidness, but baby it was COLD outside. I'd been on the road agin for a length a time. Dumpster-divin' with slim pickin's, dodgin' icy fallout, and I'm here to tell you Let it Snow ain't my theme song.

With my rear end prepped and hunkered in a safe retreat zone, hankerin' for warm fish, I struck a blues chord. Had to kick up the volume cuz dude's deaf with his melon head tucked under the fryer hood. The noisy fan was whiskin' fish scent out into the night air and grease be poppin' off as the fish hit the hot oil in the basket goin' down. But I can do volume.

Finally, a head swivel, unwelcomin' eye, but a glib, "Yo, we work for our food round here, ya feelin' me?" Big as he was, I figured he didn't work much. But ya gotta work wit what ya got.

A smart cat like me don't need directions twice. In three shakes of a mouse tail, I accosted the trade-off. One dispatched mouse at his fat feet and a blues sonata kicker for an appetizer.

"Now, that's what I'm talkin' 'bout! Knew them little buggers," I'm keepin' it clean, folks, "was hidin'. Saw the evidence up in this here kitchen. Too smart to fall for my mouse traps, though. Tell you what, you stick with me through the winter and I'll pay you for huntin'. Got us a deal?"

He give me a funny pop-eye look, battered fish hangin' from humongous fingers, waitin' for my decision.

Well, the fish was phat- couldn't compare to Hook's, but I was starvin'. Hook's was long in my arrears, and mouse appetizer, let alone mouse main entrée, ain't cuttin' it for long.

Tunes weren't hittin' my idea of a mark that night, either. Once the chowin' was done, the churchers cleaned up, lumbered upstairs, and got to singin'. Thought somebody was gonna fall through the floor onto me and the cook's heads any minute- the way the entire ceilin' reverberated. Buckin' up and down like Bad Sign on Saturday night.

Some of the ladies had power enough to hit a sweet string of notes, but preacher man wasn't cool with my tryin' to direct the proceedin's. Let alone cravin' my share of solos- hey, a cat of my musical 'sperience can't idly stand by! So, after a single warm night I hit the road, Jack- goin' with God in my rearview mirror and a full belly.

Thanks for the memories, but right now there is a fried chicken limb callin' my name.

From a secluded vantage point in a distant tree, I cadge a suitable gander at the festivities poppin' off down in the church's backyard.

No bologna, or pizza, but there's chicken afryin' in a vast barrel, and a side of ham half as big as Yogi lyin' longside all sorts

175

of other goods on a cloth-covered table. Folks bustlin' about, kids runnin', balls aflyin' with the crack of bats, a dude strummin' on a guitar singin' 'bout gimme that old time religion. Wit his pickin' skills he should get a load of whiskey drinkin' blues, but I reckon that ain't religious. One Step at a Time or Hard Lesson to Learn'd work cuz I'm bettin' religion ain't all that easy if ya do it up right.

Hel..heck wit religion, gimme some eats for the love of ol' Albert King!

And there she is! The caretaker. This lady works way too much- ain't no bigger than a cast-off broomstick. But she moves wit da quickness- kinda like the clacker/crappers. She's hoistin' grub from out of sidelined boxes to several long tables. Callin' for help that don't pay no never minds. Straightenin' the cloth flappin' as she sets some kinda confection (folks call it cake- not my bag) on it.

A gutsy breeze sweeps the end cloth flapper up-n-up, wrappin' up the ham. S'okay, I'll have it to go…

Wit stealth, I flow to ground, tuck into shadows, avoid the fracas, and creep as close as safety allows. She sets a pie down, scans her territory, and hand behind her, stretches and massages her achin' back.

Makin' my move, I swiftly sidle to her and stretch up on my hind legs, paw pawin' the air.

"Meowwww?" I keep it on the down-low. Don't want to attract the wrong kind of charity.

"Well, hello there! My, aren't you a beauty."

Darned if a tear doesn't sidle from her warm gaze and roll to her quiverin' lips. She swipes at her cheek.

"You remind me of an old friend," she sniffles and takes a cloth from her pocket, wipes her nose.

I sense friend's gone to the spirit in the sky and she's been too long on her own. Lonely days. Worse- lonely nights.

She diligently picks amidst the plated chicken which is drivin' my tasters to dribble stage, I'm past fittin' on eatin'.

"Here you go, my friend. Eat in good health and may God be with you always."

My eyes are bulgin'- she hands me an entire breast- a big un!

"If you are in the neighborhood again, please stop and look for me." The lady now wears an almost smile, watchin' me rollin' phat.

Hallelujah, she doesn't presume to pet me; simply pours on wordy goodness and fond looks. "My name is Christina, and you'll always be welcome."

My thanks are on point, "*Meeeeowwwwwww.*" I gently accept the unexpected bonus- no snatch and grab lack of manners towards this angel. I give her a long slow wink and head for a safe place to indulge.

What was it CatSkill said- Sky's learnin' a new language? Well, if it's mind-speak I'm gonna tell her this dear kind lady needs a new friend, or two. And wit da quickness.

In the cool, cool, cool of the evenin', I'm high on my roost, doin' my extra-diligent wash-up: paws clean-up first in order to swab pristine paws on cheeks, ears. Swivel my head, lick all surfaces, mind my undersides, tail...

Oooooeee, I'm stuffed and yawnin'. What did CatSkill want me to do? Oh, yeah- mind gazin'. I'm too tired to even star gaze. Reckon I'll procrastinate. Got time before the Top Cat comes callin' for our blues session.

Threads all sparkin' clean. Curl up with the scent of sweet grass ticklin' Mr. Sandman. And I'm out for the count in z-land.

29

Am I blue? Can't seem to wrap hook, line or sinker on it. Kinda similar to the stickin' in my craw when I snap at the kit.

Been movin' on reg'lar-like since leavin' the hood. Prowlin', fightin', gettin' my mac on wit da queens. Singin' my mojo, huntin' up grub.

Peerin' inside a body's head ain't part of always on the lookout, scopin' possibilities, bein' prepared for whatever's cruisin' my way- messed-up, phat or fly.

Yeah, I do it my way…

Don't think CatSkill will be on point with this mess of cat-a-ponderin'. Sh…shoot!

Daddy left home for I's born. Wasn't named Sue, thank you. I did grow up fast and hard. I'm fearless, feisty, TOO-pretty, a high-steppin' singer. One step ahead of the honkies, two steps ahead of the rest. Got lives to fill up my shoes in the best of the blisterin', low-down, speak-to-me blues.

Don't reckon that'll cut it with CatSkill, either.

I'm a loner. No, that ain't 'xactly right. I'm cool wit company. Amenable females for one. Quiet, shy kits for another- I mean, hey, if you're gonna brag it's best to have a listener. Same with singin', or maybe not. Got a feelin' that lady diva at Bad Sign didn't need no audience to sing the blues in the night.

CatSkill says blues gotta tell the story from your heart, more'n just rattlin' off notes. Janis Joplin tellin' it like it is from deep inside a her when she belts out Piece of My Heart.

Can I troll out my heart?

What rouses my ol' inside drummer? Hoodbillies aimin' to hurt my charges- the kit and Sky, for sure. That part of the blues, I get. I'm on the battle scene like ol' Speedy Gonzales (Jose and I'd watch that lil skedaddler some Saturdays).

What else strikes me? What...hurts me?

I'm set recallin' the lady diva at Bad Sign. The one the ol' scarred gangsta hid in the corner to watch. The lady sent chills up my fur, made my tail stand attention. The way the place rocked, she must a stirred many a soul, 'specially the one hidden in the shadowed corner. My night vision caught the glisten in his eyes, his fingers stuck on his empty glass.

I can dig it- that's singin' from the heart, singin' your story, the victories and the...upsets.

Upsets. Homeboy. He listened up, seemed to be a friend, brought my fave grub and I sang for him. Friends- a two-way street. Me and my homey cut heads without a lick a jealous- jist for the fun of it. But m'man's gone now. Outta da picture.

Well, I tried friends once and what did it get me? Dumped a far cry from Hook's- no fresh fish in sight, catch your own and good luck! No bologna sandwiches, or pepperoni pizza to share, either.

Homeboy was a fine guitarist. Smoked them strings. So what? He didn't help a brotha out when a brotha got kicked to the curb. Don't need him. Don't need anyone...

There's an itch I can't scratch. But, hey CatSkill, I'm...tryin'.

Gotta stretch my legs. Ain't so bad movin' on. Had some kicks on Route 66. Hard times were larnin' times- blues times.

Met Jose and his spicy grub and cedar shavin's. Til he headed on the highway hisself. And I...moved on, too. Again. What's a cat to do?

Ain't into makin' up to some human to be curled up wit and locked up in some house. Save that for the ghost cats. Those cats don't mind the same ol' same ol' scenery. I wanna go where I wanna go. When I wanna go.

Fact is, I ain't bustin' to turn me loose from this here crib. Why? Reckon it's like CatSkill said- Sky knew everythin' I need is right here. 'Cept a phat song list of my makin'.

So, what am I goin' to do 'bout it? I'm entertainin' y'all with the story of my pimp daddy days, tryin' to keep the language suitable for all ages. Too much thinkin' goin' down, need a break. A roll in the cedar shavin' pile, take care of bidness, and I climb to my crib. Maybe dreamin' won't be a killjoy.

"Good morning!" Finally, rescue from the night's endless mind-meanderin'. And groceries for the ever hunger grillin' my guts.

From my roost, I get a load of Sky. Cheerful, rested, her old self, movin' to feed all the noisy hungry critters. Yet I can sense a lingerin' of sad deep in her heart. Hmmm, sad to the bone.

Wait til she sees the elder. The ghost woman winks at me, smiles at Yogi paddin' to her side, and Boo and Shiloh and Dessert have eyes and ears pricked the elder's way, too. Can't be too long now.

But what the…

For the love of S.R.V., she puts up with those three hooligan ghost cats in her crib! How can she be oblivious to her grand asittin' here in/on a hay bale with all kinds of love on her puss?

'Take a real look around, Sky,' I trill, but apparently, she's not down wit the mind-speak lingo yet. I get a glance and a smile and a salute wit a can of grub. Better than nuttin', but save me, B. B.!

And what's perched like a fuzzy parrot on her shoulders?

'Strut, look at me!'

'I ain't blind,' I smartly quip, and immediately a remorse-kick twists my gut. I kinda name this quirky twinge I have concernin' the kit as mis-placed impatience tinged wit a I'm-helpless-to-help-the-kit-be-unafraid.

'Whass up, Catch, sides yoself?' I glide partway down my beam to a suitable turnaround superb vault to ground, checkin' the attitude in my query.

Yogi and Boo eagerly gather to hear Catch's story. The elder sits in/on her hay bale, Shiloh's head restin' through her shoulder.

The skank pussy-footers and clacker/crappers could not care less, but who gives a rat's a...butt 'bout dem non-players?

The re-born kit leaps off Sky's shoulder after bussin' her puss along Sky's jaw. Who'd a believed the kit'd have it in her after all the creepy-crawlin'? CatSkill works miracles, s'all I can figure.

"Thank you, Catch. You want to hang out with your friends awhile? Have some breakfast and later we'll go see your brother," Sky smiles.

'Brother?' Yogi, Boo and I chime like supreme back-up singers.

'My brother...I thought he was...dead. He got trapped and I couldn't...save him and he cried and cried and cried and

I…couldn't do…anything. I was so afraid they'd find me and kill me, too.'

That certainly explains a lot. Poor kit- what might a tiny kitten do to put the fear of God in hurtful ***? Watchin' your bro bein' taken, maybe killed…and nuttin' you can do 'bout it!

Say what? I picture the scared kit hidin', tremblin', and my brain kicks up a notch.

Did my homey feel…anythin' when I didn't come to practice? The window sill minus my hefty, blues-lovin' self…no one to share a sandwich wit. Did he care, but couldn't do a damn thang cuz he didn't know where to look for me? Save my soul, New Orleans- I feel an upswell comin', a string of…unrecognizable notes. Hold on, hold on…til later, I kick myself.

This is Catch's parade.

'He's alive! CatSkill took me to see him! His name is Cap and he's living with a friend in a house he loves and everything's all right and we're going to see each other and play like we used to before and Sky loves me and I…I'm not afraid anymore!'

'I catch your drift, Catch.' Kit's got more to spew than all the ol' G's perched on stools at the barbershop on Friday afternoon!

Yogi lovingly eyes the elder and nuzzles Catch. And the kit- standin' on all fours- rubs her entire body 'longside Yogi. Then friskin' Boo dances in for his turn. Surprises keep it comin' when the kit hops over Boo and lays into the elder's lap for a moment, gazes up at her with love and gratitude. To Sky it prob'ly looks like the kit is kissin' Shiloh!

Sky's grand's still sumpin' special. She kisses the top of Catch's head and fondly pets all along her back which arches up into her invisible-like hand; she strokes the length of the kit's tail, too. The tail is straight-up approvin' and forms a reg'lar music note at the very end!

Good on you, ghost Grand! Reckon a bein's qualities remain once a body's got to the see-through stage. Certainly did wit Fat Frank, Cahoots and King. Whole lotta ghostin' goin' on in dat house!

I'll have to perch front row window seat and watch the ghost elder play wit dem ghost cats. Wonder if she'll use some of the toys she made for Catch. Betcha I'll still hear the ring of her voice warnin' Fat Frank to "Lay Off!", and Cahoots and King to "Get Down!" while stuff flies off the fridge and outta cabinets and slips/topples from the table. Betcha the whole show goes down like clockwork. And no way, Jose, Sky gonna miss seein' her Grand in dat action! Wonder if Catch will play 'long- I'm bettin' ghost grand'll see to it.

A follow-up shock stops my ramblin' wit da quickness. Kit's comin' my way, expectin' to…

'Strut…I—'

'I ain't a touchy-feely kinda G, Catch.' My gut's puckerin'. But the kit's lime-lights lock on mine despite my cautionaries. She keeps advancin', tail happy-high. A completely reborn kit. And hang it if the music note symbol in the curl of her tail ain't akeepin' heartbeat time- metronome style!

'Afraid?' she dares to dare me wit a confounded question!

'Hell no! Go 'head,' I brace my entirety. Ain't bein' run off by no kit! All four feet's claws dig in, prepared.

Since M'Moms cradled and suckled me I ain't felt nothin' as sweet as this tiny kit rubbin' agin the bulk of my side. Big as I am compared to the kit, and worldly as I think I am, I can't resist what's brewin' deep in my innards. I lean into her- wantin' more!

184

Catch begins to purr.   Rock-n-roll heaven!   Sub-consciously, I nose her flag-pole tail, 'specially the curl-note of its tip, and darned if she doesn't stroll my other side with her purr-serenade in full bloom!

Can't resist…here it comes…added to my blues repertoire is a bass-lovin' purr that startles the whole show! Who says it ain't all about da bass?

"Strut, how lovely," Sky murmurs, enchanted, a trickle runs on her cheek. Tears are a'glistenin' in the elder's eyes, too. The rest of the barn has gone quiet. Floored 'em all.

I feel like callin' out, 'Set 'em up, bartender,' which was the standard cry at Bad Sign when the tunes was rollin' phat and the hoopla 'preciation got out-a-hand.

I'm sittin' right outside the barn. Thinkin'.

Was movin' on got me here. To a crib full a critters and singer Sky. Grub and cedar shavin's that never end. Gotta admit I'm one lucky puss.

Maybe here is where it's at. For keeps. Maybe this is how it's supposed to roll. Reckon family and friends annoy each other now and agin. No problemo. I gots feet if the irksome crosses the line. And I can practice…new feelin's, sensations, in my songs.

The anger and…pain of missin' my homey might stick 'round. Hey, I can't control the whole world! Shame, but facin' facts is part of life.

My homeboy on guitar, eyes squinched shut, concentratin' while his guitar gently weeps. Teasin', flirtin', lovin' on that old axe. Pianissimo whispers slowly soar, crescendo to near violent heights as his guitar strings do the impossible. Talk 'bout exultin'!

185

Memories. Yeah, they can't take that away from me. No way, Jose.

Where are you, Homey? You still kickin'? Hope you're cool, wherever you are.

Ok, Strut, you can do it. Turn up, heart of my heart. Do it for my guitar man. Listen up, Homey, this one's for you.

The ticker's a twingin'…and it's fly on, little wing!

"*AaaaaaAAAAARRRRROWWWrrrrrrraaaaaaaaaa*!" The flex of artistic vocal muscles sears the night. I do believe an owl's echoin' the gist of my song. Tree frogs close up shop and re-open with a vengeance. Hood hound howls. Good time Charlie ain't alone-ever'body's got the blues!

Notes ride the scale- boastin' of my fightin' and lovin' prowess. Missin' my homey softens for a bar or three. Suddenly rage rises- some hoodbillies think they can mess with my…family-they got another thing comin'!! And I'm gonna sing it all out!

Studyin' on my awakenin' wakes an expanded range of octaves and the reverb is so far off the hook…

'Strut, that's enough. It's getting late,' Yogi hints, paddin' to my side.

"*RRRRROWWWWWWrrrrroWWWW*!" I spin the last turn around just to watch him. Yogi plods outside in resignation.

See, he knows me. Nicely cuttin' into a bro's mojo is his warnin'. The early-to-bed set don't 'preciate the music of the night and I am the phantom of this here opera- waitin' for the midnight hour to shine, let it shine, let it shine.

Guess I am kinda like dat ol' boll weevil the ol' geezer wid the banjo sang 'bout at a Sunday church-goers shindig I chanced across. BBQ and a song. Boll weevil trillin', yearnin'- lookin' for a home, lookin' for a home.

And a phat song list!

'Yeah, yeah. Do you know far, far away?' Exasperated, Yogi wanders back inside and paws hay, fluffin' up his bed.

Hmmm...far, far away? Ha!

'You be trippin', smart a...aleck dog!'

'Take your show out of hearing. Practice elsewhere. And I'm not kidding!'

I might just do that. Too bad Catch's tucked up inside the house; the kit could use a little music boot camp. Betcha I can talk her into goin' out some now, and betcha Sky'll let her, too. Chick can dig Catch be safe wit dis here cat. One of my peeps.

Wait til CatSkill gets wind of me, cuz I b'lieve I'm livin' large, flyin' high, freebird! I'm really feelin' it!

There's a blue moon struttin' tonight. Some little honey could be jonesin' for a concert, or I could track down the hood hound and cut heads, or hope Sparky is out for a last call takin'-care-of-bidness and boxin' match.

I gots options!

30

"Yo, my main music man, come with us."

Since the night of retribution (like that word) comin' down, scar-face Garrett makes extra nice with me.

No doubt CatSkill apprised him of my rockin' the Casbah while outtin' da hoods. You can lay odds dem dudes was toredown right proppa!

Betcha Garrett gave Sky all kinds of hell…heck 'bout traipsin' off into trouble on her own. I've heard him mindin' her to be safe and I've watched her almost listen. Sky's one sista gonna take care of bidness and hang the consequences.

Yeah, she shoulda called him though- mighta saved her a bump on the head. But CatSkill and I tag-teamed and I'm not sure if brotha Garrett deserved to have all the fun!

All smiles and shi…stuff, poor strummer brings his guitar out to the barn to entice me. Long on chutzpah, but short on the skills breakin' down nat'ral to my homey. Garrett digs into some simple old time rock'n roll stuff. I play along for a minuto. Wish he knew mind-speak I'd make him hip to blues. Ok pipes, but mighty borin' after a number or three.

'Cept for one git down, rockin' tune 'bout a bird dog after his chick. (Talkin' 'bout 2-legged chicks not clacker/crapper chicks- try 'n keep up peoples!) Dog be playin' where shouldn't be aplayin', ya feel me? Daddy Cool, here, go ol' school on dat dog and ain't nuttin' be straighter den dat un when I'se gits tru wit 'im. Won't need no boots, either. Word. Don't believe me, aks da boneyard hoodbilly.

"What do you say, Strut, coming?"

Dude's trippin'- none of that runnin' for a snack, not this cat! I seen these coupla days a week ridin' horses, escortin' the pussyfooters with Yogi and Boo keepin' 'em from hasslin' bunnies and birds. Sky and Garrett (fillin' in for Sky's Grand, who, beknownst to us critters, whisks along in company with her smilin' ghost beau) toss treats for the hide-in-the-woodwork-when-trouble-comes-callin' cats.

Sky sing-songs, "Milk, Dark, Bitter, Semi! Come on, Hershey gang."

And hang it, if they don't pad along, catchin' tidbits on the fly. Domestic wannabe felines, yuck!

Not this cat. I wanta snack on the squeak, or a handout on a plate as befits my propers.

Today, I study on the cleanliness of my claws, unobtrusively spyin', actin' like I don't give a sh...poop.

Sky vaults onto Dessert- chick's definitely got cat in her- and scar-face, Garrett, (in another form he and me'd go at it for her attention) leaps wit da agility atop the big-head, Shiloh. The pussyfooters are idlin'- millin' and mewlin' unfit for a musical ear. Exhibitin' some smarts by stayin' outta stompin' range of the horses' hooves. 'Bout the only intelligence I've witnessed in 'em.

Catch, Yogi and Boo give me guilt-trip eyes.

The change in the kit is old blues versus car-wranglin' rap- flat-out amazin'. I'm happy for the tyke. Nobody should hunker in constant fear- t'ain't livin'. No way, Jose.

'Wouldn't hurt you to admit you care. Wouldn't kill you to participate,' Yogi saunters into my personal space and softly woofs.

'C'mon, Strut, it'll be fun!' Catch, on all fours in the sun- no more belly-to-the-ground sneakin' in the shadows- meows a note wit potentiality, while Boo dances, yippin' without a key. Per his norm.

Garrett gives Shiloh his head and the parade begins. There they go, troopin' on out. The clacker/crappers ain't invited- they gotta cluck and wait and lay eggs til the end of the...festivities.

Sky hesitates and...whoa, hold your horses! She's inside my head! Mind-speakin' just like CatSkill intimated. Fast learner- where did she get the lessons?

'From a very wise cat named, D.C. You'd like him, Strut. He's very independent and he's taught me a lot. I wish you would go with us- like a family. I'm working on a surprise for you and..." She abruptly shuts it.

Hmmm. What's up wit dat? A surprise? For me?

'Please come.' Mind-speak, again.

Right now, a clacker/crapper feather'd upend my a...butt. I stare, stupefied, and I don't use that word in the same sentence with my name on a reg'lar basis- get my drift? 'Cept it seems to be happenin' a mite too often lately!

She kindly gives me a moment to ponder.

Resignedly, she brushes Dessert's sides with her legs. There they go- one big happy family. Happy as the brothas when the eagles fly and the creak of Bad Sign's door indicates openin' time.

What's pummelin' at my heart? It's crankin' as I watch them plod through the mud. Happy. Together. An invisible link is pullin', yankin' an invisible...chain. Kinda git a gist of what a dawg must feel, bein' scooted 'long by his person.

Well, hel...heck! I vault forward, race to catch up, veer round the horses, scatter the pusses.

'Look, Strut, I'm leading,' Catch sings.

Sings? The kit is definitely demonstratin' potentialities!

'Don't be all uppity, Catch,' I hiss, and immediately I'm snared with a sense of...regret?

This here's another of those moments- feelin' feelin's. Whole 'nother ball game. Catch simply stops and eyes me, waitin' it out. Is dat compassion? Certainamento no hard feelin's simmerin' in da kit, but dam...darn, there's a quirk diggin' in my gut.

'It's ok, Strut, you lead. I'm glad you're here.'

Glad I'm here? 'Cept for Sky, dat's a first. Whoooeeee.

'No, together. Side by side,' and I chill-out to maintain pace with the kit til we're out of sight of the barn and the snacks start flyin'.

I might git the hang of this 'we are family' stuff- just not all at once. After watchin' the pusses and Boo- Catch stays beside me laughin' at the antics and Yogi remains on scout duty- I decide to bounce.

'Catch your act on the fly, Catch. Got bidness to tend to.'

'What kind of business?'

I prepare for the roll out the barrel questions.

'Aks me no questions, I'll tell y'all no lies.' No unnerstandin' in the kit's gaze; she simply cocks her little head wit those too-big-for-her-face peepers shinin' bright. 'Private bidness,' I qualify.

'Will you let me go with you some time?'

This polite query snatches me off guard. The kit finally wants to hang wit the cool cat? In the past haven't I thought it'd be the best thang goin' for the tyke? Was thinkin' the very same just the other night.

'I'll get back to you.' I'm mullin' it over now that's it out in the open. Will the kit cramp my style? Don't have to take her all the time. Be the chance to get her away from the domestics and larn her a thang or two 'bout the wide world. And the lingo to go long wit it. And maybe some music lessons, too.

'Please,' Catch's plea warbles. Hmmm, built-in reverb.

'We'll see. Gotta bounce. Peace out.'

I snatch a hopper off a long stem and swat it in the kit's direction. Distraction- best thing for a kit bent on... I need a break. Too much poppin' off inside my head.

Pick up my reg'lar recon trail. Eyes open for trouble with a capital T. Aware is prepared. And my range goes way beyond Yogi's.

No more scent or sign of hoodbillies. Wonder what the dragon did wit 'em? Have to ask CatSkill what 'xactly is a dragon at our up'n comin' jam session. And get the low down on the whereabouts of the thugs. Maybe they got offed as befits their idiocy.

Gotta tell Sky 'bout the comin' shindig. We gonna be jammin'. Word. I'll mind-speak, tell her to put a song list together, includin' some blues for the love of Cab scattin'!

It's an up a lazy river kinda mornin'. Maybe I'll swing round see if Jose is back and makin' any more shavin's- not that I need any, Sky provides plenty. Could invite him to the jam session- he's a good player. I don't know- it's a bit of a jaunt... He...hang fire, do I sound like a laze-about or what? On the flip, he's probl'y got other company by now. Hmmm...

Quiet. Too quiet. Wit nuttin' to put to rights it's tops for a day-dreamin' boy. Climb a tree and hang out like dat Cheshire cat Sky read to us about. See what comes along. Quiet. Cat-nappin' quiet.

Or it was.

What is poppin'? Way off in the distance. What's croonin' to spit bars? Ain't no boogie woogie bugle boy. But close…

Am I dreamin' a little dream?

Shrillin' notes. Startin' in easy slow and low, soarin' high, lingerin' like the sustain on my homey's guitar!

Whatcha know, Joe? A nightingale does sing in…

But lambastin' the sound of heaven is the pulin' ramblin's of that bone-head goofball, Sparky. Can't his keeper, David, keep his over-grown wicket-wack dog in check?

Best see what's goin' down on my turf. Wit da quickness!

31

Great balls of fire! What has slobfest Sparky treed now? His clacker/crapper hulaballooin' and boundin' round the ol' oak tree has sumpin' sumpin' up in the blue yonder undeterred and flat out layin' it down.

Ain't no square note beltin', just a voice fixin' to send a cat to blues heaven. Mama mia, my blue heaven!

"*rrrRRRrrrRRRrrrRRRRAAAAAAA!*"

Take me to the river and dunk my puss! I been saved. Found my religion. I'm a believer! Gotta git a load of…the new talent in town.

I bolt house-afire mode, puffed up like a pimp daddy on eagle's fly night with all the honey babes drippin' on every inch of his new phat ensemble.

I'm fittin on dispatchin' the hoppin' bopper dawg gawkin', growlin' and grinnin' at the substantial tree trunk better than all the Saturday night players hittin' it at one time- talk about Saturday night's all right for fightin'!

'I need a hero,' diva's singin' in her tree tower, and I'm all that and more.

Wack a dawg. Wack, bam, wack…lose count of my punches battin' dog nose. And never mind the snot slingin' on my boxin' paws and ears and he…heck, it's everywhere!

Lame brain dog thinks it's all play. Ain't I tough enough?

Bite down hard on his ear. Earn an ear-splittin' yelp, finally. Gotcha, hoo yeah! Dat's da dog sound I been aimin' for.

Sparky's got weight, but nary a cat skill one.

Whine, he's got aplenty.

"Arr, Arr, Arr, Arr," he tells it like it is, but dumbo don't retreat. Told you the dog's a 'bubble off plumb'- one of Jose's fave curses. Least a ways Jose always said it like a curse.

Sparky just sits, slime droolin'. Long limbs spread akimbo like mounds of Hook's fish and fries drippin' off a plate. Hmmm, the thought of food... Back to bidness!

Dog's pantin' an askew bass drum rhythm. Lets me duke it out wit his nose til I figure he's conceded. No fun pullin' punches when the off side up and quits with a blank, hang dog expression.

Suddenly, he plops- a sunk balloon, little Jack Horner style. Woe begone, tongue hangin' out like a mis-placed inside out snake.

High above the turf war, the diva-in-the-makin' is swayin' to her own music, "aaaaaAAAAaaaaarrrrr," on a limb commensurate (like that word?) with her miniscule size. Her claws dug in, baby blues are bulgin' wit an 'I'm in deep' scare.

Finally, Sparky's homeboy, David, huffs and puffs into view, "Sp...Spark...y, h...here boyyy." He stops at the stand-down, doubles over, tryin' to catch his breath. Worthless lead dangles in hand.

Dog casts a 'don't mean no harm' pitiful pair of big eyes at his homey. With the gall of dumber than dumb, he attempts to swipe my puss in lieu of 'I'm sorry'! Gets a triple dose of wack-a-dawg for his nerve.

Da...dang it, if he don't sit and raise his big head up so high I end up pummelin' a broad, impervious (sound like an educated cat, eh?) dog chest! I'm 'bout to go ol' gangsta on his a...butt!

"Sparky, heel," dog-savior, David, clips the line on to his Houdini's collar. Po boy needs a lesson in walkin' the dog. I got a few pointers I might relay- whap, whap, whap- dog be followin' right proper.

Won't find a cat kow-towin' on the end of a line! I should say not!

"You ok, Strut?"

'Seriously?' I triple glare.

"Need some help?" David tilts his head to see where the concert is poppin' off.

'Do I look like I need help? I got dis.'

David chuckles, pets Sparky's head. "You da man, Strut! But hey, call me if you need a back-up. Sparky and I will wait over there while you claim your little honey." He points to a shady stretch up the road, closer to Sky's house.

As he turns to go, it hits me- he understands! David's got mind-speak, too!

Ch ch changes. Good ones. Celebrate!

Now, if he'd larn the dang dog... Nah, no fun in that prospect.

'Yo, baby cakes, you can come down. I run off the dawg.' In record time, I might add. Give my ruffled coat a lick and a promise. Hang the taste of dog snot!

"meowwwwwwwwWWWWWW?"

I cock my wanderin' eyes at a vision I ain't never seen the like of! Hang it, if dere ain't a cloud up in dat tree!

'Lady, come down,' I trill and receive an echo vocal response, but the chick ain't movin'.

'C'mon, ain't got all day, sheesh!' My way of encouragin' the one milkin' it. 'Ain't no enabler waitin' on da likes of youse!'

'I c...can't. I'm afraid,' she wails fit to try the most hardened ol' G struttin'.

Now, you prob'ly got the impression I'm completely insensitive, but...I been larnin' a thang or more, see.

Breeze turns hostile and her thin life line's fixin' to dump her if she don't move it, for the love of Elvis! There's a G could sing anythin' he put his pipes to. Wit some cat moves throwed in, for good measure.

'It's simple, just take one step at a time. Tack onto the bigger limb- it's safer.' I'm wastin' my breath. Baby girl don't unnerstan the physicality of comin' down from goin' up- can you believe it?

"*MEEOWWWWRRRRR*," crescendos down on me.

'Gonna make me go all Tarzan on your a...butt,' I snort, and a Sparky spit-ball flies off an ear. Dang dawg surely got his dibs in- the snotty kind. Well, clean-up gotsta wait.

So how do I know 'bout Tarzan? One walkabout in my early illustrious past, music was nowhere to be found. I'm talkin' real tunes. Not that cryin' in yer beer whine, gratin' hip hop, rap, or anythin' else that makes a box on wheels jump, jive and wail.

Heard this long, strident, reverberatin' ululation escalatin' from a weedy crib.

Wit da thought of possibilities giggin' my a...butt, I leapt up to an open window to glean a better see. Dude holdin' a bottle of sody pop, sittin' on the lay-back, watchin' a noisy box with one bad (bad = good here, folks, try to keep up) singer swingin' from tree to tree, vine exchangin' from one hand to 'nother.

Imagine, cat skills in a human! First time I ever encountered such. I figured to join in the sing- baby food for this cat.

"AAaaaAAAAAAAAA, aaAAaaaaa,AAAAAAAAAaaaa!"

Sody pop pop most overturned his chair, bustin' up like a po-po found hoodbilly. Did spill the fizzy stuff. A bit flew my way, landed in open mouth. YUCK! Sticky, sweet goop. What humans eat beggars my brain. Didn't stop my solo, though.

Dude must a thought ol' Tarzan hisself come swingin' into his crib!

Stuck around a day or two. Pops was cool 'cept no reason to kick it. Called me Tarzan, but grub wasn't up to par, and other than Tarzan flicks, no musicality to warrant a cat of my talent's continued presence. I bounced.

'Slow your roll! Hold on, I'm comin'.' I spy the most efficient ascent, what with all the bustlin' branches conspirin' agin me.

'Hurry!' she cries.

'Take a chill pill, little Betty.'

Ah, I spy a likely shot and stake my game plan.

'My name's B...Blue, because of my eyes. Hurrrrrrryyyy!' She's clutched on like Mama wit da check in hand.

Sweet Home Chicago! I get a real good gander at... Wheel of fortune, shine on me! Jeepers creepers, where'd ya get them peepers?!!

I'm up the substantial tree trunk to cash my ticket. Take a breather on a branch under the kit, scout a proper projector angle.

Heights don't confront me none, but da correct strategy is da thang. Get as close as possible. Hanged leaves whistlin' Dixie on twistin' the night away branches are impairin' my plot.

'I'm 'bout to get physical, stay loose.'

'Wh...?'

With one mighty leap (Tarzan, eat your heart out) I propel from my hefty branch to another, rocket-off again and catch Blue's nape in my mouth on the fly while hurtlin' to a safer launch pad for the final descent.

The kit's mighty young and seems weightless, hangs still as I crap shoot descend. Don't bother stoppin' in a handy fork. Gotta git to ground and check out my winnin' number.

Safe on green land, I gently release Blue and scrutinize the kitten. All in one piece- thank my Tarzan stars!

The white angel pierces me with a set of off-the hook marbles- I feel the earth move under...

At last! Beauty and diva skills in the same phat package!

'You are magnificent! Thank you, thank you, thank you,' she sidles into me and rubs her whiskery jaws against mine. Talk about a... What a feelin'!

She begins to purr, pianissimo, starts to cleanin' the dog snot off me...

'Hold on, little sister!' I regain some sense of...sumpin'.

"You're beautiful, big and strong, my black and orange hero!'

Ah, the sweet nothin's in my ear. Ain't nuttin' makes my world go 'round like a well-deserved compliment or five. 'Cept if'n you add a pepperoni pizza to the mix. Or a chunk of Hook's fish...

But I need to get the upper hand, take charge, and right quick!

'Name's Strut,' I back up a step, pose catwalk style to beef up my masculinity.

'Strut?' She moves into my space. Again.

'Yeah, got a song named after me- Stray Cat Strut.' Facts is facts and I ain't shy 'bout speakin' the truth. Word.

'There's a song about you?'

Are those baby blues growin'?

'What you think gonna happen, lil darlin'? You be talkin' to da man.'

'Ooooooh, I know! I want to sing your song,' she trembles with excitement, stirrin' mine even more. And I betcha y'all thought I'se beyond dat, huh?

'Baby cakes, I'll teach you,' I manage under the right proper overwhelm of adoration pourin' down on me.

CatSkill's words ring inside my head. 'Strut, you've been fighting a natural affection for others, but guess what? Caring won out. You didn't stop to quibble, rushed in to help Catch and Sky. Heart-brain connection enhances life. Compassion, empathy leads to love. All this will enliven your singing. It's the other side of learning the blues. Think on it.'

'How'd you get yourself in this shi...poop fest?' I return to the vision.

'Oh,' immediate dejection. She sinks to her haunches, tucks a plume of a tail close about her and her eyes mistily fall to the ground.

Somebody put the hurtin' on lil sister! I feel like startin' a major sh...poop storm. Just let me find the SOB!

Instead, I lick a sap spot on her shoulder. 'C'mon, spill. It'll make it better to tell it right out. I promise.' I reckon Catch has taught me...consideration, and how to apply it.

My heart contracts mindin' Blue's blues.

'This morning everything was normal. Todd gave me my breakfast while Lana fed our new baby. I love to watch the baby sleep and I want to comfort her when she cries. I climb into the baby bed to be close and purr. The baby smiles at me when I do.

They only brought her home a few days ago.'

I nod as her voice trails off. Sadness magnified. I know what's up. Ain't no dumb cat here.

'Go on,' I nudge her tiny soft shoulder.

'They don't want me anywhere near the baby! Lana screamed at me. I was only trying to take care of her. After my breakfast, Todd put me in my carrier. I heard him ask her if they were doing the right thing. That I was just a baby, too. I meowed to be let out. I didn't want to go...away.'

'So, the pieces of shi...' Save me from humans. 'He dropped you off?'

'He opened my carrier right over there, never said a word and hurried away. I started to follow when suddenly this huge dog is running to me. I had no trouble climbing this tree,' her tiny puss swivels to spy the height of the safety zone.

'I climb the curtains at...home when I'm startled by visitors or loud noises.'

A lengthy silence, and I'm 'bout tremblin' with rage listenin' to the kit livin' her ol' life, but I gotta keep cool for the sake of little sister.

From such a small young kit comes a heart-rendin' lament, 'What'll I do? Why don't they want me...anymore?'

201

32

'Am I blue?' she cries/croons.

In unfamiliar and- I gotta confess- ultra-awkward territory, I make a move on her sobbin' puss. Heart-stricken blue eyes swim in pain.

Oooh, yeah, I'd like to get my stickers on dem hurt-deliverin' fools. Give 'em sumpin' to really make 'em scream and scream and scream!

Me, I took all the shi…poop in stride growin' up, learnin' the blues. Never felt Blue's or Catch's predicaments. Ain't nuttin' scarin' me. My hurts were relegated to war wounds. Never cogitated on the psychology of shi…poop. Sh…stuff happens. No time to sit around waitin' for the next train to roll over a body. Movin' on up, out, or wherever.

But it's for damned sure ain't nobody gonna hurt on my watch, 'cept wannabe bad asses cruisin' for comeuppance!

I lap her tears tils she quiets, steadies.

'Listen up, I'm the real thang and I ain't gonna pour a little honey on it, sugar, sugar. Some humans are the dumbest dumb shi…as…butts ever born. Not fit to…' I gotta keep it clean for her young ears, but real.

Ain't I tough enough to set little sista on Easy Street? You betcha a mess of blues I am!

'Forget about 'em! They wouldn't know the right of love if a truck full of angels dumped it on 'em. See, love carries through sad, bad, between rock and hard places. Love don't fail a body, ya feelin' me?'

I reckon I'm paraphrasin' the advice CatSkill offered, cuz I for damn sure don't recognize no reg'lar lingo comin' outta my mouth!

She rubs her soggy cheeks against me, tucks into my chest. Ain't zactly what I meant to impart, but I ain't 'spressin' no belly-achin'. Kit's got enough to deal with.

'I been through hard times, Lucille. Learned every minute of livin'. Always knew I got the world on a string.'

'I...I don't have a...home,' she mistily peers up at me, her paws kneadin' the ground in despair.

'The best thing those deadbeats did in their entire lives is set you out on my turf. See, my peeps got real love. None of that summer wind shi...poop.' No brag, if'n it's the truth, right? Word.

'What's shipoop?'

Tears are endin', replaced by curiosity, and shades of Catch- questions! Here I go again.

'I think I understand what you are saying, but you do talk different.' Her little head cocks left and right, checkin' out all my goods.

'You'll get used to it. Spice up your vocab. Be good for your singin'.' I deftly ignore the cursin' query- gotta watch my mouth.

Return to my fave subject. 'Wait til you hear me sing. I'll larn ya a thing or two and we'll duet- sing together,' I clarify. By the look on her puss my rico suave smooth talk slips home.

I feel like tellin' her we'll live a little la vida loca, too. But too much info at once ain't kickin' it.

'Sing- I like the sound of that. But where am I to go?'

'C'mon a my house, Blue,' I nudge her in the correct direction. I'm fixin' to show her zactly how extensive my territory is along the way.

'That's Sky's home.' I stop and let her get a gander. 'She rescues critters, sings to 'em to keep 'em calm- quite a vocal talent, but needs new material. Too much borin' strangers in the night and moon river tunes. I'm fixin' to help her out of her rut.' Cuz that's the kind of cat I am.

'You live inside?' Blue studies the house with interest. Prob'ly thinkin' 'bout curtains and house stuff. Yuck!

'Hell no! House is full of ghosts and constant racket. Can't figure why ghost cats don't catnap. The other ghosts are quieter. Now, Catch sleeps inside with Sky, but she's often at the barn. You'll really like Catch- kit's only a little older than you.'

'You think she'll…like me?'

'Are your eyes blue?' I ask by way of 'are you serious?'

'What are ghosts?' she continues the quiz.

'Tell you what we'll do- school and all questions later. Want you to see the lay of the land before we eat. Bet you're gettin' hungry?' I peer down at the little tyke. Not fat, but not missin' any groceries, either.

'What's school? Yes, I am beginning to feel hungry. What will we have to eat? At home…oh…' she balks and her head drops.

Patience, Strut.

'Gonna be all right, now. You'll get plenty to eat, sister. School is questions and answers. I'll apprise you of everythin' you want to know and what you need to know, just not all at one time, deal? C'mon, try to keep up.' I buss her shoulder. Movin' is improvin'- heard that somewhere.

'Okay,' she sighs a mite lighter than a second ago.

'Let's take a short jaunt into these here woods. Supper time's close—'

'Oooh, all these to climb?'

'Yeah, but be sure I'm wit you. No wanderin' off on your own, got it? And I'm dead serious on that score.'

Blue matches me step for step, seein's I check my stride. Don't want her to be afraid of anything. ANYTHING. Been down that road with Catch. Blue's curiosity is got her spyin' up, down, all around- like a kit should be doin' while we amicably stalk the trail the horses use when Sky and Garrett ride out.

The breeze has ebbed to a whisper in the tops of the woods. It's cooled a bit, perhaps a shower later. I'm weather-wise as well as readin' the need-to-knows of the moment. Fixin' on teachin' Catch and Blue my weather skills, among other life-enhancin' abilities.

'In days to come we'll visit the pond, see the hoppers. Couple of the brothas got a nice, deep rhythm you'll 'preciate.'

'What's a pond? What are hoppers? So many new things to see and learn about. I can't wait. We will sing with whatever they are?'

'You betcha. Got trillin' toads and burpin' bull frogs, tree frogs, crickets in the fall, birds- all kinds of music-makers. And at night we'll band a trio with hooters. You are gonna have the time of your life. Word.'

'Word?'

'Means d...' Gotta watch my big mouth. 'Means you betcha, or oh yeah.'

'Word. I like it!' She winks at me- sendin' all sorts a thoughts apoundin' inside. Feels like Mr. Drummer man come to set in my chest. Strong beat, Krupa rhythm.

Choo, choo, chaboogie, I gotta tiger by the tail. Just jonesin' to rock on. And we'll have all the time in the world. Together.

I'm aware sunlight's headin' for its crib and my gut's fixin' on a protest growl. Suddenly, I hear a minor scuffle in a stalk of weeds. Blue surprises me by her immediate, true-to-cat response. Ears hone, eyes focus, tail swipes, her little butt wriggles...

Oh, for those lookin'-for-some-tush nights! 'Ceptin' she's a mite too young. Big brotha, that'll be my role. Always. Remember, Strut, ya got 'sponsibilities now. And missin' some of the goods which come in handy when playin' the romantic field. No neverminds- don't gotta make kits to have kits.

I watch her perfect pounce, but the varmints round here (the ones left) are pretty quick 'bout goin' to ground. I cadge a glimpse of chipmunk tail as the tiny speedy critter ducks into a cat-proof hidey hole just shy of Blue's takedown.

'Wow, that was fun!' Little sista practically pops the dancin' queen number. Obviously, she's recovered her aplomb- nothin' like a hunt to cheer a kit up. Previous home with deadbeats won't confront her none. We'll be busier than a one-legged as...butt kickin' contest. Lookin' forward to it.

'Sky'll be on the way to the barn with grub. Let's head, Blue.' I guide her in an about-face toward home. Home...?

'What's a barn?' she breaks into my momentary reverie.

'Home for horses, chickens- I call 'em clacker/crappers and you'll see why, dogs, cats. My crib's on the top floor. Got me a penthouse suite, like the boy from New York city.'

Before she starts rattlin' off what are penthouses, horses, chickens, etc., I redirect her attention, 'Try this set a notes for me--
'

"RRROWWWRRRRRerrrRRRRR!" I let fly.

'That's easy,' she ain't boastin', either. A perfect echo of yours truly hits the air. I got me my own diva!

Satisfied with creatin' a proper entrance, I nudge her through the barn door.

Oh, the night has a thousand eyes and they're all turned our way!

"Why, Strut, you have a new friend!" Sky is busily openin' cans, dishin' up the goods. Got way more manners than the others oglin' me and my gal.

'My rescue. Her name's Blue,' I tout. 'Ain't she sweet?'

"Well done, Strut. Hello, Blue." Readin' my mind-speak- thank that other cat- Sky smiles a warm, sincere welcome. "Aren't you a beauty in your dazzling white coat and sparkling blue eyes!"

My head lofts high and I puff up like the mac daddy I am- right proud of myself.

'Save us, there's two of them,' Yogi scratches behind an ear and rolls his eyes. 'Good luck getting any sleep around here.'

'She knows my name!' Blue is soundly amazed.

'That's cuz Sky really knows how to talk to critters!' Knowin' questions are gonna tumble, I tell her I'll give her the rundown later. Her tummy is gearin' up for a concert and mine is comin' in on the beat.

Catch is totally enthralled with the newcomer- more questions fixin' to spew, and Boo is scamperin' a mite too close, so I check him wit an O G glare. Blue surveys it all with natural-born curiosity. No sign of fear at all, at all. Hallelujah, I just love her so!

The milksop queen of the pussyfooters ventures out and dares to hiss. Her entourage slinks behind her.

'Get back, skank. Keep your hands off my baby.' My ears flatten, tail wrings, and I prepare to launch. But my warnin' snarl seems to suffice. 'Can't touch dis, she's mine!'

Sky and Yogi have manners dictation in hand. Yogi upends the snob and Sky murmurs, "Manners, Semi, manners. All are welcome here. You know this."

Blue stands close, but firm. No inkling of retreat. My gal knows I got her back.

'That's my dawgg, Yogi. He's the best; you can always depend on him, and Sky, too.' I pass out the props, show her what an upstandin' G her rescuer is.

'Why, thanks, Strut.' Surprise registers on the lead guardian's face; he seems to regard me in a new light. 'Pleased to meet you, little Blue, and welcome.'

Catch bounds from Sky's shoulder and cuddles into Blue. Best of friends in the blink of an eye. Two crumb-snatchers. As top cat, I've got my work cut out for me! Gotta raise 'em up right- my kinda right.

"Here you are, Blue, hope you enjoy being part of our family." Sky places Blue's dish first. I watch for any takers, but all's cool.

'Grub's on, let's eat,' and I snatch at the night's chicken-a-la-cat directly after Blue starts lappin'.

Interruptin' the quiz-r-us Blue and Catch volley back and forth- some without a snowball's chance of an answer they're so excited- Sky volunteers a story.

"Tonight, I'm going to tell you about a cat—"

'Can't we have a concert instead?' I harrumph.

'Patience, Strut, patience.' Wit her starry-eyes aglow, I'm wonderin' what Sky's hidin' up her sleeve. Hmmmm...

I reckon I can wait. Jam time'll be comin' round the mountain soon. I knead a sofa of hay into play and settle in for the haul. Blue might like story time. I know she'll like what comes after.

"Should I tell of Old Possum's Practical Cats?"

'Not those outta space cats,' I put in my 2-cents' worth. Seriously, what right-minded cat would allow bein' called Jellylorum or Jennyanydots? Or Asparagus? Save me! Mungojerrie is a possibility. And where the dev...dickens does a possum come off talkin' 'bout cats?

"I hear you, Strut. I've another idea. A new story."

Huh, sumpin' new, but not musical. I knead my pallet again, keepin' my eyes on my gal.

The youngsters sit at Sky's knee and the tale begins. Their eyes and ears are agog. Betcha Blue never had a bedtime story before.

"I recently heard this tale of a cat burglar," Sky begins.

A cat burglar?

"This isn't about a human thief, but a true cat, cat burglar," Sky surveys her audience, waits it out, tweaks curiosity. At least, cat curiosity.

Yogi yawns and Boo cocks his head as if 'what about a dog story?' Instead of interest, he twirls round and settles.

I'm game, ya got me. Humans imitatin' cats and makin' off wit da goods- I seen plenty of. Don't need no hood for such goin's on. But sumpin' wrong wit a feline forager havin' pack rat tendencies. And this is supposed to be a true story.

Cat got a head problem makin' off with the darndest stuff-most anything carry-able. Human glad rag pieces, human blings-too weird for words.

Figure if I was gonna steal sumpin'- what would I take? Guitar picks, drumsticks, a mic? A waste o' my time. 'Cept...maybe a mic. If hooked-up to an amp, might be truly phat! But get real, the only thing I'd be hoofin' it wit would be grub. That I'd carry on the inside. Better to bounce wit all paws free, let alone my fangs.

Why weight yo'self down, Bro? Cat can't head out on the highway that-away. Born to be cat wild don't encompass baggage. No cat and carry cat here- not on your blues butt! Word. (Meanin'- oh, yeah- for y'all still learnin' the ropes.)

Weight. 'Sponsibilities. Me, with Catch and Blue? Nah, I ain't feelin' no weight. I'm walkin' on sunshine.

Story's toast. Snacks been snatched like Friday's eagles (payday, case y'all laggin') and Yogi's monitorin' call, 'Lights out, early to bed, early to rise.'

Dog ain't got a midnight prowl anywhere in his bod, but he's got his own 'sponsibilities.

Catch's fillin' Blue in on sumpin'. 'I bet Strut's done more than any cat you ever heard of, except maybe—'

'Maybe who?' Blue is quick on the draw.

'Catch, let's save the surprise,' I hint. Blue and CatSkill and me and Sky singin'- gonna be a hot time in the ol' barn.

"Good night, all. Catch, you and Blue coming?" Sky lingers in the doorway.

'I'm tellin' Blue about chasing the chips tonight with the ghost cats, Fat Frank, Cahoots and King and...I might make it to the top of the refrigerator and--'

"Catch!" Sky's eyes are twinkling, but I gather she'd rather Catch didn't attempt to fly tonight.

'Come on, Blue,' Catch invites, full of hope.

Blue studies Catch and Sky waiting together. Yogi eyes the light bulb above. If he had a watch, he'd be eyein' it. I 'spect he'll out the light if Sky happens to forget.

I'm intent on a possible spot on my paw. What's the verdict comin' down? Will she stay or will she go now? Does it matter? Sumpin' inside me indicates, yes, it does. A whole lot.

'No thanks, Catch. I've lived inside, I want to try outside. I'll see you in the morning and hear about your game with the ghost cats. You can introduce them to me some other time, ok?'

That's my girl!

'You are the man, Strut,' Sky's words are for me only in a special mind-speak. 'Well done. Later, please fill me in on Blue's rescue particulars. And bless you. I might just have a job for you now and then.'

'Hold yer horses, woman, I got a job right here!'

She sweetly laughs and winks at me, lifts Catch who promptly curls around her neck, and strokes the kit idlin' on her shoulder, turns and heads home.

Blue's up the beam to my penthouse suite like a shootin' star. I kinda wonder if this kit'll be hittin' a downer thinkin' 'bout her last night in her old crib. Can I dig out a rock-n-roll lullaby? Shi…shoot, I ain't heard o' such before. Might have to make it up on the fly, but no, Blue saunters to my bedroll, starts adjustin'.

'Hold it! Cry me a river, lil darlin'! Don't be comin' up in a homey's crib and disturbin' his bidness, baby cakes.' I show her how to play it- my way.

'Are you my homey, Strut?'

'Da…dang straight. Word.'

'What's a homey?' My kit yawns, showin' all the teethy goods.

'Homey's the one's got your back, count on it,' I wink at her tired puss.

She kneads a flake of hay I've shuffled to her- right next to mine- curls up, presses into my hind quarters.

'Thank you, Strut. For everything. G'night.'

The purrin' starts up immediately. And zing go the strings of my heart!

While sleep claims my rescue kit, I mull over the daily school agenda. Thoughts scroll through my head: gotta tell her not to chase the clacker/crappers, and for the love of B.B. King- watch yer paws wit dem noisy birds, gotta make sure'n warn 'bout the neighborin' striped stinker, gotta have eyes in the back of my head, gotta make sure no kit climbs up more'n she can climb down, teach 'em to swim, stay away from stranger dogs or humans. Keep 'em larnin', but safe. Whew!

Gotta tell Sky 'bout those sorry sorries droppin' off Blue and my Tarzan rescue. Can't forget to tell Sky 'bout the church lady givin' me a chunk a'chicken and how she really really needs a friend, gotta show Blue the shavin's and show her rollin' in the deep keeps out the itchers…

Gotta get a nap!

33

"What are you up to, Wife?" Riordan CatSkill wonders to himself as he puts the finishing touches on the massive wood pile he's contrived- chopping and stacking for the past two hours. Not that cold affects his shamanic status or his wife's. Temperature control, to a point, ranked among their many shamanic gifts. His all-too-human father-in-law though, would certainly appreciate the warmth of lighted logs.

Handsome, the black stallion his wife, Bonnie, rescued from an affronted rancher who thoroughly disagreed with and disputed the stud's opinions, bobs his head up and down repeatedly.

"Yeah, I know Mr. High Horse, your supper's on the way. Try a little patience for a change." Riordan shucks his long mane out of his gold eyes and strolls to the feed quarters inside the barn to prepare the various meals.

A flock of chickens clucking at his heels, as well as the dogs, Sticker and Stalker, and That's Amore in her feline tux attire closely follow.

"Pied Piper, eat your heart out," Riordan chuckles at his groupie entourage.

Little Joe, the black and white paint, and Hoss, the draft cross, neigh their respective orders from another paddock located a safe distance from the stallion, who now deigns to prance and roar- quite out-classing the others.

"I hear you. Too bad for me my dinner order is being ignored." CatSkill refers to his and his wife's preternatural access to each other's minds. Except when one of them wishes to surprise the other. In which case, mind-mum's the word.

Being extremely talented shamans, they not only have ultimate-in-healing capabilities, but by virtue of spirit-guided communication enjoy the ultimate freedom of shape-shifting into many guises. Their favorite animal to don is that of their spirit-guide, the mountain lion. Many are the competitive races the pair have engaged in as cougars.

With a glance at the parting sun, pats and scratches to the willing during hay dispersal, chicken food strewn, full dog bowls set in place, and a "C'mon, That's Amore," he saunters, full-throttle, to the log cabin. Bonnie's closed-to-him mind is tickling his cougar curiosity to the hilt.

Carefully stepping over the racing, cavorting, tumbling, begging-for-affection house kittens: Super, Cali, Fragi, Lis, Tic, Expe, Alidocious, he winks at the proud mother, That's Amore. She vaults atop a plush recliner back, Sphinx-like sinks into comfort- all the better to enjoy her brood's proceedings.

Spying the recently rescued contingent from Xavier's Clinic, who congenially sit high atop shelves eyeing Riordan's every move with limelight love, he high-fives their adoration with his own. Once these kitties receive their due consideration, they glide down like liquefied gems to be coddled, too.

"Wife?"

"Riordan, hurry, shower, change clothes, we're going out," Bonnie quickly apprises him.

"Ah, to Irma's for designer salads?" Bonnie is artistically adept at taking advantage of Irma's extensive salad bar offerings.

"For starters. Dad and Grandfather have poker night, and Grace is making enchiladas for them." She tiptoes up and kisses his shades-of-Kirk Douglas dimpled jaw. And grins as his Virginian-style (reminiscent of James Drury who played The Virginian in the old cowboy series) brows rise in response.

"Something else is in the air," he intimates, arms enclosing her and pulling her tightly to his chest for a more thorough passion play.

"You'll see," Bonnie enigmatically replies. "Instead of taking extra time and guessing--"

"I'll savor the thought of a Porterhouse Steak, or two. Chopping wood builds hunger."

"Hurry, hungry man! I'll feed this lot and be ready to go in a gif. Don't want to be late!"

Outside Irma's Steakhouse, in the tourist-friendly historical town of Cody, Wyoming, a stream of incomparable blues' notes wends its way round passers-by, ineluctably luring them inside, rather like a spell in a fairy tale.

"Live entertainment tonight," Riordan hums along with the trilling.

"You'll see," Bonnie simply smiles and gigs his imperturbable ribs.

"I get the feeling I'm really going to enjoy tonight," his gold eyes gleam into her merry, Celtic-green ones.

"I wonder if I should have invited Dr. Gunne," Bonnie murmurs.

"As much as he's coming around to music, I'm glad you refrained. Call this date night, shades of our first date, and three's a crowd. Especially in his case." Riordan less-than-subtly refers to Dr. Gunne's annoying and ceaseless penchant for his wife's attention.

Reliving their first date and the battle before it ended involving the dispatch of local bullies, Bonnie snuggles under Riordan's arm, inhales the scent of his stalwart chest and thrills to his answering rumbling purr.

"I guess he'd say no, anyway. He's reluctant to leave his new pirate rescue kittens. Riordan, do you know he reads pirate stories to them? TREASURE ISLAND for one, and Long John Silver actually limps around for snacks!"

"Cat lover in the making. Just as long as he's not drooling over my Kitten."

Bonnie's chime of laughter is cut short by Riordan's leaning down and delivering a heart-stopping kiss.

Until the interruptive hostess clears her throat, "A hummmm."

With a, "This way, please," she guides the pair to a table for two, center stage view, hands out menus, and delivers the night's specials.

The beefy-shouldered, muscular guitarist, finishing his sound-check licks, is caught in the spotlight of the CatSkills' friendly gaze. Amiably nodding at them, he addresses the audience in an incongruous mellow tone.

"Thank you, folks, for coming out tonight. Name's Rom. My bass man's Randy and Jimmy's on drums. First number, as always, is dedicated to a friend of mine. We've...lost touch, unfortunately." The blues man's short-shrift grimace is not lost on Riordan or Bonnie.

"Cool Cat's a survivor. Here's to you, buddy." The opening walk-down of Stray Cat Strut brings in the band. And the ensuing story is related with all the verve and energy of the original version by Brian Setzer and his Stray Cats.

There is a follow-up mixture of blues highs interspersed with many originals equally as worthy. The bass player vocalizes several numbers, but Rom is the main singer. Storytelling emotionally set to music at its finest.

Bonnie glances at Riordan, the music lover. He taps his foot and sings/hums along with evident enthusiasm.

"Not many guitarists can pull off numbers with such talent and yet keep a sound level conducive to conversation," Riordan admires.

"And?" Bonnie prompts.

Riordan's dimples and his Virginian-worthy, expressive brows liven his face- as if that were possible!

"He's the one Strut tried to hide from me, but I saw the picture preying in his head. Looks like Rom isn't the only one affected by the mishap-interrupted friendship."

At show's end Jimmy and Randy case their instruments and drift off after shaking hands with Rom.

Riordan rises, makes his way to the guitarist, introduces himself and invites the lingering-on-stage Rom to join them at their table.

"My Wife, Bonnie," he grins, avidly on tenterhooks for what's coming.

"Pleased to meet you, Bonnie," Rom offers his hand, warmth in his deep brown eyes.

"You demonstrate the dynamics in your playing that most can only dream of, Rom." Riordan draws up another chair for his guest, presents him with a menu and flags a waitress.

"Thank you. A life of living the blues put to music," Rom shyly admits.

"Please, let us buy your dinner," Bonnie congenially states rather than asks. "We waited, hoping we might eat together."

"Most kind of you. Cheeseburger, baked potato and salad bar," Rom smiles, star-perfect, at the no-nonsense waitress which brings a reciprocating smile to her face.

She retrieves the menus after jotting down the CatSkills' orders. "Be right back with your drinks."

"Rom, will you tell us about--"

"You look like you and your guitar grew up together," Riordan completes his wife's query, peering past his guest at the nicked-up, but obviously well-loved, electric Gretsch guitar. Missing more red-gold paint than not, the instrument holds pride-of-place in its guitar stand.

"That's Paycheck. My father was a blues man before blues hit prime popularity. He did a week's work baling hay to acquire enough funds to buy that guitar- and it was a used one way back then.

Said it was the only guitar he'd ever picked up and right off the bat felt like it was part of him. Had a singular sound to it, especially after he made a few modifications with the pick-ups, and put on elevens- the strings."

"You sure make it talk," Riordan compliments Rom.

"Should've heard my daddy. Man alive!" Rom shakes his head in remembrance, and his eyes turn lustrous. "He told me he named the guitar Paycheck because when money was tight, he could usually turn up a gig or two. Play all night and work all day. No quit in him."

"Sounds like your father and you were very close," Riordan acknowledges.

"Yes, until the day the tax collectors came to auction off our farm. Times got too hard for words back in the day. Three years of 'unfriendly' weather did us in. No one to turn to. Bankers could not care less. Mellencamp sang it in his hit, Rain on the Scarecrow.

Daddy used to say, 't'aint' nothin' but the blues, son. Jist sing 'em outta sight, s'all you can do sometimes.'" Rom's deep dark eyes mist, but the big man simply blinks them half-clear and continues, voice fraught with emotion.

"Dad worked himself to death trying. Used his playing and singing to shore up his spirits. My older brother hied off at 15, sent us a few dollars when he could. My mother passed, probably from exhaustion, when I was born.

Just Dad and me met the joshing-among-themselves, good-old boys...robber bankers..." Quite obviously, Rom is having a difficult time maintaining polite terms.

"Daddy had his ancient shotgun in hand- only gun we possessed, so I carried a pitchfork."

Rom hesitates, sips his root beer. Revealing intimate details of his past is new to him, but something in the young couple's manner inveigles into his reticence.

The three accept their food from the returning waitress and slowly begin to eat, pausing at intervals to talk.

Bonnie lightly touches his thickly muscled forearm, channeling a soothing spate of energy which easily comes at her call. Waiting a moment for its effect to sink in, she supportively urges, "Please go on."

Rom's partially eaten burger rests on his plate, and his eyes travel far away into the past.

"Arguments flew. The greedy are hearing-impaired, though. Daddy was never one to curse, but a few damns made the go-rounds. The sheriff tried to take the old shotgun. In the struggle, Daddy suddenly dropped. I…I thought the sheriff killed him! I jabbed all five tines of that pitchfork into his gut and dug in for more. Took four men to pull a 14-year-old boy away."

"Your father died of a heart attack," Bonnie states. Being in tune with the spirits allows answers to her slightest query- part of a shaman's role amid native peoples, and certainly an inherent aspect of her shamanism, as well as Riordan's.

"Yes, but I didn't know it then." A deep sigh wrings from Rom's soul. "The sheriff ended up in hospital and I went to a reform school. Finished growing up somebody you didn't want to mess with. Got the bulk to back me up.

Jasper, a kind neighbor, had slipped into our…home and freed the guitar from the auction. I'm able to continue playing Daddy's music and my own compositions along with the other stuff I've been tickled into over the years. Right proud and blessed to feel Daddy with me through his guitar."

"Your talent speaks life, the blues…your hands," Bonnie drew attention to the rough-calloused, huge hands resting in prayer-mode on the table.

"I don't put up with… You know," Rom pointedly studies Riordan, who merely nods, empathetically. The true and resolute-of-heart easily recognize each other.

"Got some of the same, my friend," Riordan admits, winking at his wife. In his long history, Riordan has never suffered fools, gladly or otherwise.

"The best blues musicians put the heart of their story into their playing. All those ups, downs…feelings. Hitting the notes doesn't count if you aren't…feeling it, making it all part of you- my theory, anyhow," Rom equably offers.

"I'll never forget every nuance of that nightmare. Seeing blazing heat create a mirage-like surround on our dried-up farm. The tornadic dust kicked up by the swaggering…bankers and their minion sheriff as they high-tailed it to our demise. Their coughing, hacking, sweating. My tongue swelling, eyes stinging. Smell of dry, despair…death- all branding me for the remainder of my time…here. The end of life with my Daddy on our own farm." Rom clears his throat, glances around at Paycheck- the Gretsch guitar stand-in for family.

"The use of every sense, living memories…all come alive…in my music. It's easier to play and sing than talk. Original blues have roots in the old plantation workers. Slaves brought their singular call and response chants with them. Native peoples, the Indians, had similar music talk. And the tars on the old sailing ships had their chanties. Would improvise on the fly. Aided them through hard times, work times. And celebrated good times, too. Pour out your heart to music, let your feelings out instead of grudging inside causing issues."

Rom picked up the last of his burger, dipped a fry. "T.S. Eliot said: 'Music heard so deeply that it is not heard at all, but you are the music while the music lasts.'" Rom shrugged his massive shoulders. "I read a lot. Self-education is the best education."

"We're in total agreement on that score, Rom. One's learning shouldn't be another's covert agenda. And that's a beautiful sentiment by Eliot. All you've expressed is in the advice I've been telling a friend of mine," Riordan agrees.

"Blues player?"

"Singer. I think he's beginning to catch my drift."

Rom senses a mysterious allusion in this revelation, but he hasn't a chance to pursue it because Bonnie abruptly changes the subject, after a slight silent caution to her husband.

"So, you are alone? No other family? Your brother?"

223

"Lost touch. Heard Ceasar passed years ago. He never married, no children. Our line is…gone. Alone… Yes, it's better that way. Don't own a thing except Paycheck and my truck. And I don't consider Paycheck a possession." Rom politely eyes Bonnie and Riordan, assessing their response to this rather strange statement. He is gratified to sense their complete in-sync mentality.

There is a brief interval when the waitress comes to refill drinks and ask for dessert selections. All are on board with banana cream pie.

"Tell us more," Bonnie encourages after a quiet tasting of her pie, and according Riordan and Rom the same pleasure.

"I travel, stop when I feel like it. Play some, move on. I've played solo gigs, and filled in with other musicians at times. It seems there's a secret hotline with players, kind of like the hobos of old," Rom shrugs. "No ties, either. I remain…an outsider. A free bird, I guess you might say."

Bonnie changes course and Riordan is quite content to watch his intuitive, lovely wife in action- tacking better than any sail captain ever could.

"Interesting name, Rom."

"My mama was of the Romany people." He doesn't stop to gauge their comprehension, decides to clarify just in case. "The Travelers, or Gypsies as they're usually known. She was left in our town, orphaned, or maybe there were simply too many to try and support. Anyway, Daddy chose, no that's not right- they chose each other.

My name is Roman- Mama liked the history of Rome, for some reason- Rand. But I prefer Rom," Rom finishes his pie with a satisfied grin and tummy tap. "Full up, and thanks for the company and dinner." He starts to rise.

"Well, Rom," Riordan's eyes sink into Bonnie's as in 'I got this part, Wife.' "I have a proposition for you."

Bonnie slides a first-class Delta airline ticket toward Rom, accompanied with a thick envelope.

Surprise tweaks Rom's face. "What's this?"

"Inside is $1000, in hopes to convince you—"

"To come to a jam session this coming Wednesday in Summer, Ohio," Riordan completes his wife's sentence as they are often wont to do.

Puzzled, Rom sinks back into his chair, thumbing the ticket, eyeing the envelope. "$1000 is too much. Summer, Ohio, eh? Never been there." Unlike others who might have 1000 questions, Rom equably entertains the idea in silence.

"I personally guarantee this will be a most memorable jam session," Riordan touts.

"My husband loves music with a passion—"

"Only exceeded by my love for you, Wife," Riordan winks.

"You play, Bonnie?"

"No, but Riordan loves to sing and I love to listen. You will get a kick out of the other jammers," Bonnie mysteriously chuckles.

Riordan refuses $500 worth of bills which Rom attempts to return. "You're worth every cent, my friend."

"Please come," Bonnie's gaze gleams, trance-like, upon Rom.

Riordan simply relaxes into his wood-back chair, savoring his wife administering the coup de grace- for no one can possibly resist Bonnie when she pours on her full-throttle, glorious Celtic-green-eyed shamanic energy.

The big guitar player's eyes water; he doesn't try to hide his emotion, "Shoot, why not? I'm not getting any younger. Never flown before…"

"Bonnie, your surprises are—"

"Amazing?"

"Beyond description," he pulls her into an all-encompassing embrace.

"Shall we run home as—" she teases.

"Cougars, our favorite," Riordan acknowledges the inherent challenge from his fast-as-the-dickens runner wife.

No sooner do the words pass his lips and Bonnie, under cover of a dark alley, shape-shifts and races off.

"Why am I always giving you a head start, Road Runner?" Riordan laughs aloud recalling their first race and her high school nickname, and promptly follows suit (no pun intended).

Bonnie leaps 12 feet in the air, clearing a security fence with athletic gusto- a prime mountain lion specimen in action.

Admiration vying with competitiveness, Riordan's huge paws eat up the distance between them; his lengthy tail maintains balance on sudden turns as he endeavors to outmaneuver his wife. Ultimately though, he curtails his 40-foot bounds and with the greatest pleasure eyes her saucy tail as it flicks his whiskers. 'Silly question,' he trills.

34

Summertime, but the livin' sure ain't easy. More like overly invigoratin'. Got my paws full.

Now, I ain't no lazy bones or belly-acher, but since I stepped up to the plate in the role of teacher/mentor/savior regardin' the two kits' discovery of the whole wide world, it's all in my hands. Get the picture- ya feelin' me?

It's put me in, Coach, full time. Ain't none of that hidin' under the boardwalk shi…poop. We be goin' at it 24/7.

Every day is an ode to joy, rockin' blues. Kits into every little thang, mind you- and not necessarily together in any way, shape or form. One up a tree, the other investigatin' a burrow in the ground or slippin' into some other potentially dangerous curiosity. I now fully unnerstand why it's the mama takes care of the kits, cuz no male is oriented in this particular way- save me, Blues Brothers!

With the advent of my music phenom protege, Blue, Catch is up'n pipin' a few notes wit potentiality. Quite a workout for her previously unused pipes. Catch ain't no mo a rainbow in the dark.

I'm rethinkin' the stage prospects. What with Blue, my diva duet partner, and Catch soundin' off in the background, our show might be road worthy in a cat's eye (no need to bring pigs into it). This top cat is more than encouragin' the novices. I'm a believer, and a conductor, and a vocal instructor, and what-all in between.

We're out on safari today. Early, after the grub's been dished and dispensed wit. What a day for a daydreamin' boy. I'm…

'LOOK!!' Blue exclaims octaves over confab level, nose pointin' one way and tail another, poised to skeddadle.

'Hold that tiger!' I put my hefty paw atop her excited head to stay her for a moment.

'Where I lived there were no big open spaces. Small rooms, and I wasn't allowed outside. Had curtains to climb, but LOOK! All the trees!' Blue happily ascends the register again, peers up at me, no apparent regrets for her past life.

A hot child in the city, I surmise. My tail twitches as her vocals climb up, up and away. High C ain't no problemo- gloria! I throw in a few bars to mesh with hers. What we need is a guitar player. Garrett is okay with rhythm, but his song list leaves much to be desired- no blues, just old-time rock n' roll. Kinda hard to get my mojo goin' on singin' wit his limited program, 'ceptin' for dat bird dog song. Now, my old homey could kick it my way and he'd get a kick in the head hearin' Blue n'me cuttin' heads on vocals. But dat ain't happenin'- more's da pity.

'This is country livin', darlin'. Green acres is THE life! Y'all weren't born free the way your homey was. I'll teach you my version of I Will Survive. Git you hip to the smarts this hood-born cat's picked up,' I inform Catch and Blue. 'Cept they're split in different directions, again! Stuck in the middle of nobody listenin'- Catch to the right of me and Blue to the...

'Blue, where you at?' Can't see the kit- bad sign.

I hear a muffled splat that spurs my head 'round worse'n an exorcist shindig on speed. Save the bass player, she's fallen in the pond!

I'm off- shades of the blazin' fast licks in Too Hot to Handle, see a light-colored, bobbin' kit head in amidst swayin' cat tails and fleein' hoppers and flyin' bugs. Unafraid of any ol' thang, includin' water, I dive in- with a Splish SPLASH commensurate with my stature.

Ain't no dog kin paddle better than this here top cat. Pushin' aside cat tails and thick goop, I grab the gaspin' kit (gotta give out swimmin' lessons, too, put it on the list) and drag her a...butt to the bank. Drop her without ceremony on dry grass in the warm sun.

Covered in slime, she coughs a coupla times. 'Just what the,' keep it clean, even if she did give me a heart skip, 'blue bayou you think you're doin'?'

Sodden like a rat caught in a sewer flood, she scans my puss, calc'latin' up how angry I might be. Hacks a bit to gain time. I see there ain't no slime in her spit- a good thang. Scuzzy coat sticks to her little bod. Even her whiskers are plastered towards her tail. Her wet head looks so tiny, makes her eyes pop.

Good golly, Miss Molly, if I ain't gittin' an inklin' of why dogs are put on a leash!

'I...saw...a...hopper. It was staring at me, big eyes...made a funny sound..."rrrriiibbbbttt" and I...I... "aaaAAAARRRR," look at my coat!!!'

'Those kinds of hoppers, frogs, belong in the pond and kits belong on land. No frog kissin'—'

'What's kissin'?' Blue interrupts me wit her big blues poppin'.

Poo yeah, I'm beginin' to see the light- what a lotta work kits are! But I...love 'em. So, I'll try and 'splain. 'Kissin' is what Sky and Garrett do when they think we ain't lookin'. Got their mouths real close—'

'I thought they were sharing food,' Catch, boppin' up from a leaf pile, is flabbergasted. Sits stunned.

'Nah, they're biting each other,' Blue scrunches up her puss.

'You're both wrong. You know when you rub your jaws against—'

'Well, they're doing it all wrong,' Blue exclaims, appalled.

'I guess we need to show them,' Catch nods to Blue and shakes/releases a necklace of leaf bits.

I swear I can't get a word in edgewise, cuz Blue is fallin' to pieces over her coat condition after the small confab respite over kissin'.

"Waaaaaaaaaaaaaaaaa…"

'Hey, listen up!!' I holler. 'Blue, you gotta larn to ask afore you leap, you little-- Oh, for the love of Cab scattin'! Yer all right, hu…hush, clean yoself up. You don't see me whinin' do you? And look at the state of my prestigious, pimpin' threads!'

I lay out a few choice words to purge my exasperation, "RRROWWWRRRR…ro…RR!" Dang me, if I don't catch a catch in my throat!

'Pears grunge vocals ain't strictly the domain of those who smoke stinkin' sticks. I'll warrant that hoarse sound comes from screamin' at kits! Bet that teeterin', hell-on-heels-diva, whose act I caught on the sly one prowlin' night, yelled at kits all day and sang raspy blues come the night! Blues in the night, fo' sho. Good thang, I've strengthened my voice wit years of practice. Now, if I survive these two kits with my sense of sanity intact…

Lookin' like sumpin' drug out from under a brush pile, Catch hotfoots it our way, worriedly checks on the slime-fest status of Blue. Content I 'complished the rescue in time and Blue will live, Catch sets up beside the soaker. Got us a three-way groomin' session goin' down- shades of the barber shop blues in the hood.

I's always believin' it's a man's world, but I can see clearly how playin' mom, dad and big bro to two female kits is one monumental dope ride!

Catch, wit da least perturbed coat of the three of us, comes clean with a hard-earned reveal, 'I was born out here. I used to be scared to death of everything, til Yogi, Strut, Sky and CatSkill helped me.' The ex-scaredy kit, licks the goop from inside Blue's ears.

'Who's CatSkill?' Blue reciprocates- swipin' leaf litter from Catch. What a sight! Gives me the gee willikers inside.

'You'll see,' I covertly warn Catch to hold the beans. Jam night's comin' up soon and I can't wait to introduce my top-notch, supreme partner Blue, and the all-new back-up, Catch. Yeah, Strut and his Supremes- a catchy moniker! Ain't talkin' no smack here, word.

Somethin' else draws Blue's attention- imagine that! And she sprints away, trackin'…

'Yo, Blue, lay off! Yogi ain't into bunny bashin', snake slayin' or bird battin'.' She slides to a stop, swerves and greedily ogles the baby bunny duckin' into its den.

Wonder what the guard dog thinks of pond critters- fair game? Gotta step up my game, watchin' these kits. For the first time in this here cat's life, I got a important job!

Yogi knows better than to step into my paws- try and keep up with dis lot ain't a dog's world. Stayin' in the cool barn where it's fair quiet wid the clacker/crappers outside peckin' bugs, or goin' out on patrol for exercise and guard duty is his ride. Dog's probably cadgin' a nap bout now- smart dawg! And Boo, the nick-nack-paddy-whack terrier, is no doubt curled up close-by.

Word- Blue's cat skills are out wit da quickness. Cats are cool, naturally takin' to the wild, but for the love of a…I need a snack!

Catch is hot on her tail. Didn't take long to come out from hidin' under the woodwork once CatSkill worked his magic.

Disappearin' little crumb-snatchers! I shout after 'em, for all the good it does.

'Catch, you know the rules. Best play big sis, or get a whuppin'.' Not that I'd lay a wrong paw on either kit. However, I do grab their attention- for a whole second.

Together these kits are on the fine edge of ain't misbehavin'- take it from a master of the genre!

'There's plenty of bugs to play racket-ball wit. And Sky provides toys for catch and soccer- like the ghost cats in the house slip slidin' away poker chips,' I fasten down the big bro hat. Maybe I should let the ghost cats babysit once in a while- I can't be raisin' kits 24/7- I need some 'me' time!

I seen the invisibles have at it inside the house. Catch now fills in- an off-the-bench, 4-handed player. Can you believe Catch ain't afraid of the ghost cats, Fat Frank, King and Cahoots? And dem players ain't shy 'bout showin' Catch the inside dope, either. What a wang dang doodle! Yeah, I got options- Blue will...

'Blue, don't you do it!' Flirtin' with disaster, for the love of...I gotta git.

No sense a'tall, mud-for-brains, Sparky, lets the kits slug his nose. He rolls over and seems to think he's the cat's meow, lettin' 'em climb over his belly, grab-as...butt his tail and ears, munch on his muzzle, chew and bat his whiskers. That dog don't hunt. Not sure what his breedin's good for. Make one heck of a feast for a junkyard cur, though. The big dingbat even takes the kits for rides, like mother possums, for the love of a pepperoni pizza! Pizza, I gotta ask Sky 'bout pizza...

Seein' the kits balance atop the b-ball tall knucklehead's back while he prances like a proud circus dog is sweet! Most likely I could sell tickets.

Yogi and Boo are both cool with the kits and put up with certain liberties, but they're nowhere near as much fun as Sparky, who has dibs on dipstick like nobody's bidness.

'BLUE!'

The kit wriggles her little bass end, front low to the ground, tail swipin' dirt- prime hunt mode. Voila- she's off! Catch knows better and echoes me callin' her to stop, to no avail.

What'd ya expect- a cat, a kit at that, to listen and obey? Don't bet on it!

C Nova, Garrett's rescue dog, seemingly an amiable hound, ain't Sparky. He don't put up with the unmannerly, of any sort. And he's got a ululatin' drawl to turn your ears blue when he gets to bayin'.

Silently, C Nova stands fast, four legs planted, ready to take on the flyin' kit-comer full blast. By the look in his eye dog's got sumpin' in mind; he's got enough age to play fair, but does he have the patience?

Where's Garrett? He's usually… Ah, I spy him sneakin' round the corner with Sky linked in his arms. Does he think he's Mack the Knife? It's up to this top cat. Again!

'What's going to happen, Strut?' Catch cautiously sidles close, watchin' in alarm.

'Dog gonna be sorry he's ever born if he harms one hair…'

With the skill of a top bouncer tendin' a rowdy drunk at any well-run bar, C Nova's nose tackles Blue mid-leap, upends her, sticks his muzzle into her belly and…

"*Ar, ar, ar, ar, ar, ar, ar,*" he whiffles through cat hair, his tail swingin' in time to his own drummer.

And Blue's response?

Gabriel, blow your horn and ring my bell! Dude sayin' it's all about the bass is trippin'! Blue's hittin' notes so far off da hook ain't no fish in sight. The chick's chortlin' a high-pitched Indian love call chuckle like no tomorrow!

And I thought I'se the bomb!

35

The songfest fades out and C Nova nuzzles Blue upright and howls her in my direction with the customary 'found the prey' hullabaloo of his hound ancestors. Hmmm, what wit his bayin' and howlin', I'll be doggone if this hound just might fit into our jam. I'll be soundin' him out on the matter. Directly.

'Best put a lid on her, Strut. Sparky, Yogi, Boo and I aren't your everyday dogs,' C Nova warns. A glint of humor sparkles in his big hound eyes and his long ears swat to and fro as he shakes his head in forbearance. 'I think your voice has met its match.'

'Got it.' I clamp on Blue's nape and cart her away like the kit she is. Under a suitable chastisement tree cuz the shavin's shed is too far off, I deliver vital info.

'I say, listen to me, Blue, listen up! You better think! Don't EVER do that to dogs you ain't perfectly on the level with! You hear me?' I rattle her chain, layin down my deepest, under the boardwalk growl. My worldly experience makes me shudder knowin' what mighta been.

"Meowwwww," she contritely stares up.

Ah, them there eyes be the undoin' of this ol' school marm!

'Let's go play in the creek,' I suggest. I mean how much trouble can one get into in a creek that's two inches deep?

'I'll show you how to catch fish- minnows.'

'What's a creek?'

'Fish come in creeks, not just on plates?' Catch is astonished.

Ring the bell, school's in session.

It's live entertainment seein' the difference in the two kits. Catch cautiously maintains contact with flat rocks at all times, and awkwardly swipes at the tiny swimmers.

Blue is all in- a true water cat. Course she scares off the fish and as they swim for safety, she turns over--

'STOP!' Darn if I didn't forget to warn about the pinchers!

Too late, one of the *** has latched onto her paw. She frantically hops, singin' in the rain of her splish splashin', and the crawdad swings like England do til I crunch his a...butt into the great bug beyond.

'Hurts,' she mews, holdin' up the injured toes.

'Stick your foot into this tiny pool; the cool water will take away the sting. Sorry, I forgot to mention those darn things,' I find myself apologizin'. What a road I've traveled, from king of the road to...this, and...I'm cool wid it, ya feel me?

'S'okay, Strut. You can't remember everything. And it doesn't hurt anymore,' she puts me at ease, standin' in the slowly meanderin' creek water. Her eyes focus on the water striders and she bats at 'em.

'So, what I should have told you is,' and I glance over at Catch, 'don't grab anything you find when you turn over a rock,' I preach after the barn door is closed.

Man alive, I'd go for a Hook's fish handout 'bout now. And a cat nap! Mindin' kits feels like fastin' for a week- I'm 'bout to swallow my tongue. And after a hefty meal, kits usually collapse in sleep. I know I do.

I git to musin' on my kit days. How did me and my bro not drive Moms to drink? If she was inclined, the free juice certainly trickled through Bad Sign's rickety ol' floor boards. The later it got, the heavier the flow. Raisin' kits- what a trial in patience, and every other sensibility.

A smatterin' more of tryin' to catch minnows and tired-out, we head on home.

"Story time, tonight," Sky happily asserts after we eagerly down our grub.

"Rahhhhhhhh," I break-in. 'Need some tunes poppin' off in dis--' I can't wait for CatSkill to come jammin'.

"We'll get to music, Strut. Bear with me a little longer, my friend. Blue might like to hear a story before snack time and bedtime."

'Then tell her 'bout the orange-colored cat,' I harrumph.

"Perfect!"

I motion Catch and Blue on each side of me, Blue wonderin' whass up 'bout a cat she ain't met.

The others perch on various stall walls, shelves, hay bales, leavin' space for Sky to do her thang.

"In old Ireland- a very green land far, far away, lived a piper man—"

'What's a piper man, Strut?' Blue leans in.

'Listen and larn, little sista.'

"I'll show you, Blue, hold on."

This is the best part and we audience know it. Shiloh and Dessert poke their long noses over the stall doors. Yogi, Boo, and the pussy-footers expectantly hone in on every move Sky makes.

It's like the tic toc of a metronome- didn't know this here phat cat had high school music edgeecation, did ya?- all the heads swingin' right and left with each of Sky's high-prancin' steps as she imitates that ol' piper man.

Hang it, if she ain't got a pocket pianee- Mississippi sax- she's blowin' into, creatin' her own dance tunes! This wasn't part of the original story- too cool for school! Sky's branchin' out on the musicality scale- playin' a sweet swell of notes and keepin' the beat wit her feet!

We gots us a dancin' queen!

"Now this piper man was extra special entertainment for the villagers because his best friend was an orange-colored cat who liked to dance along as he whistled on his pipe- if you can imagine," Sky gives me the eye.

I can take a hint. Moms never raised no fool- not that there was much raisin', more like feed yer a...butt and then, hit the road, Jack!

'Skip the 'magination, Sky. Let's dance.' I can swing wit da best of 'em. Talk 'bout puttin' on da ritz!

Roll me over, Beethoven! Afore I can claim da stage there goes Blue up on her hind legs dancin' to Sky's tin-sandwich trillin'. Looky there!

'I can do that,' Catch pipes up. She tries to follow Blue's lead, but can't quite catch the tempo, falls, rolls in the hay and dirt. One of the pussy-footers rudely snickers til I knock her upside the head.

'You think yer the cat's pajamas, you do it,' I glare, but snot- nose in the air, Semi retreats.

Catch never-minds. She's up and at it again- finally finds the rhythm. 'That-a-way, Catch- you go girl!'

Oh, what a night, oh what a sight! Blue and Catch and Sky.

Hell, I'll show 'em the straight dope. I got a few fancy steps to toss into the mix and I leap on my hind legs on the count of one, which earns me props from all and sundry. Even the horses are muzzle-noddin' and neighin'!

Next thing ya know, Yogi and Boo- the original break-dancer- are woofin' and wrigglin'. We's all slidin' some moves, cuttin' the rug!

'Express yoself,' I cheer and bop higher and higher. Ain't no b-ball homeys (basketball players case y'all still catchin' on) got a thang on me.

'Workout!' I shout. Better yet, I kick it up a vocal notch when Sky momentarily pauses for breath from blowin' her mouth harp, "*ArrArrArrAAAAAAAAAAAA!*"

Up in my penthouse suite, me and Blue. I'm thinkin' over the events of the day. Devil or angel?

Don't make no snam snifference. This baby girl's all mine. No somebody stole my gal goin' down round here, ever. Word.

She stretches in her sleep, tucks in tighter. By the light of the silvery moon, we spoon. Too close for comfort? Nah, I'm cool.

Hey, Mr. Moonlight, save a moondance for me. Maybe tomorrow I'll go walkin' after midnight.

'Night, Blue,' I dulcet purr. My little sleepy time gal, Blue, is long lost to Mr. Sandman. Gotta git my own self some zzz's.

36

'What should we do today?' I give my students options. Too late, baby. Double trouble- I realize I should be makin' da calls. All da calls, for the love of SRV!

'I want to swing from the grape vine,' Blue blurts.

'I'd like to play in the creek again, especially now we know more about what to look out for,' Catch shyly offers.

'Let's go to the woods,' Blue is fixin' to bounce. Talk about stardust twinklin' in her eyes.

'Hold up,' I stifle her progress with a hefty paw atop her overly-energetic puss. 'I suggest we do both.'

'Climb first? Catch?'

'Fine by me.' Would Catch ever argue?

'Ok.' I release over-active who bounds off like a red rubber ball.

'C'mon, Catch,' she tosses to her rear.

'I'm coming.' But instead of hot pursuit, she pin-points me with expressive insight on parade. 'You nailed it, Strut.'

Caught off guard, which is happenin' all too frequently for the likes of this here cat, I forget about Blue and ogle Catch. The kit is speakin' my lingo, for the love of a bass note and a bologna sandwich!

'What'd you say?'

'What I say- you nailed it, being a big brother. Thanks,' she purrs and proceeds to astound me further with, 'Race ya, homey!'

'Oooyeah, I'm feelin' ya, little sista,' I comeback. And rather than the race is on- easy as pickin' a blue note to win against Catch- I keep pace, proud as…well, as a big bro should be. Who'd a thunk it?

I apprise both kits of my Tarzan skills (even though Blue has already witnessed me in rescue mode) and watch Blue tempt fate by ignorin' all my born-of-experience advice.

'Blue, keep it cool, or you'll be sittin' bench-side singin' put me in, coach. This is your final warnin'- don't want to be pickin' you up dead!'

Catch has scads more sense and chooses the thickest vines to climb, explore and make the safest swings from. No worries there.

'Blue, hey! HEY, WHAT'D I SAY?'

Blue, like a body freed from in the jailhouse now, is intent on tryin' out for that darin' young man on the flyin' trapeze. Sinkin' her claws into a thin tendril, she's sailin', on the fly. She flies all right. Jump, jive and wail, for the love of… Clap, snap!

Thin lizzy line breaks. The wannabe flyin' squirrel sails space-bound, scramblin' frantically, no safe landin' reachin' out lendin' a you got a friend hand.

'Save me, B.B…' The rhyme dies sudden death as does my risin' Tarzan ululatin' as I fixate on her trajectory. Strut dandy to the rescue. Liquid quickness, I pour up the oak; perfectly balanced, I speed out onto the likeliest branch, wait for her free fallin' to come within range, and just in time, perched on my hind legs, claws dug in for anchor, stretch out and sink my fangs…

"*MEOWWWWW!*"

'Serves your a…butt right. I told you to back it off. Just because you landed on your feet flyin' off the curtains in your old life don't mean you'll make it way up in dis here wild blue yonder-ya feelin' me? This ain't let's go fly a kite class.' My bass vocals lay it on the line.

Her head swivels to try and soothe the bruise a'comin, but can't reach dat pinch.

'Been a whole lotta hurt more if I hadn't caught you're a…butt,' I snort. 'Cats kin only land feet first a certain distance and I don't see no parachute on yer a…butt! Whatsha tryin' out for, cat of constant sorrow?'

Catch, eyes a'poppin' below, doles out my props, 'Nice catch, Strut!'

'You hearin' me, little missy?' We're side by side on the savior branch. I'm plumb over-irritated with Blue's lack of respectful response and eye contact. Nonchalant Kit's groomin'- for the love of a roast beef sandwich! Wish I had one 'bout now…

I figure I jist might bring it on home to the kit and nudge her rear end off the branch. Let her land in that soupy mud puddle that's just hankerin' fer a splish splash.

My ticker is slowly coolin' it after the trials and tribulations of kit-savin', but I'm still ticked. Y'know, I b'lieve I'll do just that. Chick's got mass game, but is mighty shy in the listenin' up department. I'm madly calculatin' distance from limb to puddle, depth and width of puddle. Target it just right…

The comeuppance paw shoots out. Thwhap! Startled blue eyes bust open like early fourth of July shindigs.

Watch that kit rollin' and tumblin' on down! Legs akimbo, pawin' air. Splash! Yucky water rains up, but don't confront me none. Catch ducks away wit da quickness- safe and dry.

'Cept Blue's response ain't zactly what I'm lookin' and listenin' for.

'Can we do it again?' She shakes off her full-body, squishy mud mask and starts climbin' the hanged tree trunk! A mixed blessin', indeed! 'I wanna do it again!'

'No,' I hammer, 'it's creek time. Git some of dat mud outta yer coat.' Un-freakin'-believable! Descendin' with dignity and a chuckle in my heart, I cadge another wor...concern.

In evictin' Blue, I've a whiff of her up-comin' maturity. I'll be singin' keep your hands off my baby, while I dispatch every Tom, Dick and Harry Casanova darin' to come callin'.

Hmmm, seems CatSkill handled Catch's growin' up, I'll ask him. Course it might be fun to accompany Blue and Sky to the rescue clinic and wreak a little- hell, a LOT- of Strut havoc. Maybe they missed me the day I'm gone?

Nah, don't want to harass Sky, or scare the kit. The easiest route is my shamanic, blues-lovin' friend. CatSkill, it is.

Creek-bound and here we go again!

'Blue, you're cruisin'- ain't you learned no damn lessons a'tall?' She's splashin' like a water born mer-cat- mud dissolvin' in her wake. All's just for the fun of it in her world. Game for anythin'.

'Is that one of those—'

'Yeah, pincher. Can't you see those things on the end of its front feet, Catch? Best remember the other day, Blue. Blue?' But she's bent on...misery and mayhem. Memories definitely ain't her theme song. Wouldn't ya think a kit'd recall past larnin' hurts?

My head swivels from pouncin' kit to tentative kit. Catch is playin' it safe from rock to rock- no worries there. Blue is a whole nuther ball game. Medicine time comin' round the mountain, and there ain't no spoonful of sugar to make it better. She's tossin' one mother of a crawdad she's dislodged from its peace.

The big bugger splashes into the creek, scuttles in the current with Blue in hot pursuit. This here pincher's got smarts, though. It's backed into a rocky crevice and its snappers are a'snappin'.

Catch, beside me atop a ledge of rock eyein' millin' minnows, fears the inevitable. I hear it in her tremblin', 'Strut, Blue's gonna get in trouble.'

'And what else is new?' I harrumph. At least I don't have to wor...think about Catch bein' swept downstream. I'm intent on Blue, for all the good it'll do. Amazin' grace, save the...

'BLUE!!!' I roar.

"Mew, mew, MEWWWWWWWW!"

Divin', dousin', and swimmin' in the deepest section of the stream- what'd I expect- to rescue trouble; I big-bop the pincher til it releases Blue's nose.

'You got my vote, bud,' I magnanimously eye the still-livin' critter driftin' with the current, victorious, searchin' for a new hidey-hole. Can't blame a homey for protectin' hisself. I ain't no come to papa enabler, no sir.

'Never larn, never larn! You'd be a sittin' duck if it weren't for me. Now, git yer a...butt up the bank. No caterwaulin'- s'all your own fault. Ever hear curiosity killed the cat? Gotta have your hearin' checked, for the love of a cool lick!'

Catch is commiseratin' wit Blue, leaves me time to tend to sticky squishy paws. I'm pickin' at reluctant flotsam stuck between two hind toes, falsely b'lievin' the kits are safely takin' care of business tendin' to their own selves.

Til Catch starts hollerin' for all she's worth.

Cry me a river! What in a wonderful world is Blue itchin' after now?

'Don't do it, Blue! Strut, *help!!*'

Save my soul New Orleans, I recognize that striped tail- a stink sprayer. Fast as you, I'm on it. Jim Dandy to the rescue. Again.

'Blue, stop in the name of... You STOP this instant or I'll drop you off wit a junkyard dog havin' you're as...butt for lunch!!'

She don't stop, but slows enough for me to knock her off a raisin' tail shoot-out and roll her as...butt to a sunny side of the street. Shake, rattle and roll- that was a close one!

I rant til my ticker ticks normal, explain the horror of the fallout when mixin' it up wit a stink sprayer. Nobody wit a lick a sense dares that little striped-tail cat, certainly not yours truly.

'Sorry, Strut, too many interesting things I've never seen.' I almost cringe, she seems so contrite. 'You wouldn't really drop me off, would you?'

'Hell no, but you best git to askin' for you cotton to anymore trouble. Ya feel me?'

'Ok,' she sidles close. 'Sure does stink,' she wrinkles her tiny puss, watchin' the stinker waddle off in the distance.

'Woulda been a whole lot worse if you'd got hit.' Save me, we're safe. For the moment.

One fiasco too many- I'm down for a little quiet time and I know right where the phat combo of sunbeam and shade waits to catnap in.

'C'mon, Catch,' I call to where the shy kit hunkers in the creek, out of range of stink-spray. Though the warnin' odor lingers all round.

'Is Blue okay?' Catch trots over.

'She'll live unscathed due to my timely deliverance,' I pat myself on the back.

'Wash up, kits, nap time.' I survey their ablutions (like that word?) and in no time the two tuckered kits are curled into me, purrin'. I spy my charges with a deep sense of well-earned tranquility. Just who says y'all can't get no…satisfaction?

Now in case y'all be frettin' on how this here cat came by his stink sprayer smarts. It's like dis, see: I'se roostin' Cheshire cat style (another one of Sky's stories) up in da crook of a big ol' tree watchin' an interestin' critter, all dark wit a stripe long its back, nosin' sumpin about in da grass. I be thinkin', grub for me? But smart cats roll by watchin' and larnin', 'stead of makin' a mother of mistakes.

'Bout dat time along moseys some dog on a very, very long line wit a person way, way back not payin' no neverminds to his dog- too busy talkin' into his hand. I tell ya most dawgs ain't got a lick a sense and most humans ain't got none either.

Well, dawg sees a critter, thinks he's got a playmate wit a toy and poo yeah it's on! Gives a happy woof and shucks right into the critter, pullin' stupid human holdin' a hand to its ear along for da joy ride.

'Cept ain't no joy ride goin' down, no way, Jose! Critter about faces, thrusts up its tail and the stench of the ages shoots out right in the face of the ol' dawg. Good thang I'se hangin' high, but I still gagged on the stench.

Dog ain't got a clue what happened, 'cept his eyes be stingin' and his nose ain't sniffin' steak, word. Singin' da blues wit a high-pitched tone dawg races to its human who's screechin' "*NO, NO, NO,*" to da wind. Dawg wants to share da misery, see?

He's jumpin' on his person who ain't talkin' to his hand no mo, but is cursin' worse dan all da players losin' bets after da eagles fly. Stink sprayer ambles off peaceable, knows he's da cock a da walk.

I can spot all sorts a stinkerds. In a story one night (*SOUL SEARCH*) Sky told us 'bout stinkerds workin' on a ship. This poor kit, Damned Cat, got shanghaied by 'em and tossed into the dark bottom of the ship to eat rats. Pretty darn sweet comin' of age tale! I coulda showed dat poor kit a thang or two, but Damned Cat made out, found a rescuer like Sky and got a new name to boot- Capable. Now dat I've put y'alls minds at ease...

Me and my kits be asnooze wit da quickness.

37

For the love of a... What time is it? Guts are gripin' worse'n a guitar overdue for re-stringin'. Or an amp with blown tubes.

'C'mon, sleepy time gals! Grub's poppin' off an I ain't talkin' 'bout no midnight special.'

Blue and Catch rise slower'n molasses in a freeze- whatever molasses is. I give it the ol' one, two, arch my caboose and brush up on my sartorial splendor waitin' for the kits to finish engagin' in all the stretchin' our superior species uses to sustain suppleness.

The kits decide the race is on. Me, I'm too dignified for that shi...stuff.

Bullsh...! Look out, big daddy's rollin' in! I bluster by 'em- a tornado on the loose. I may be older, but I'm the goods, baby- ya feel me?

Near the home plate goal, I slide into third- put me in, coach. Decide to blow my own horn and make an entrance.

"rrrrRRRRRrrrrRRRRR!"

Blue is right on cue- no fake diva wannabe singer here- got da real McCoy.

My gal's hittin' high heaven notes, complimentin' my under the boardwalk blue notes with her shades of Aretha soulful hurrahs.

'Go, go, go little queenie,' I cheer her on.

Rock me baby, what the...? Like dousin' fightin' dogs wit cold water, we instantaneous shut up our call and response fracas to get a load of...

'Strut, what is that?' Catch asks, peerin' up at me, starstruck. Blue is put-a-spell-on spellbound, too. And me? Dreamin'?

"RRRREEERRRRrrrrRRRREEEEEEERRRRRRRRRRRR R!"

HOLY SH...SWEET HOME CHICAGO! I know that sustain. I know that riff. Sweetest stream of notes ever blues born and way too hot to handle!

'Strut?' Catch re-quests while Blue, a true hootchie cootchie lady, steps up and rattles the air with her high-pitched response.

'Hey, wait a sec, that's my line!'

'Catch, hold onto your hat, cuz you're 'bout to hear heaven without the tears.'

Light my fire, what am I standin' here for?

Barn door's wide open. Can't see from right off, but...

"RRRRRah, rrrrrah, rrrah rah."

It's my walk down, my cue to come in, unlike the diva singer who ain't got a key, I'm hot on it!

"RRRRRahhh, rrrrrahh, rrrah, rah," I sound off; Blue backs me up wit enthusiasm to equal a hail Mary pass.

Nobody does tight right like my...

Gripin' guts forgotten, one paw in the entry, I savor sound better'n any grub I ever ate.

"*arrrrr, Arrrrr, ARRRR, ARRRRRR,*" guitar lays down the vibe and we duke it out. Cuttin' heads. Like in the ol' days. No player-hatin', just pure love of the blues.

Can it really be? Why…?

I puff up like the head clacker/crapper wit his mac on full blast and strut inside.

THERE…there's my HOMEY!

One last call and response. The big player's eyes are water fixin' to topple over the edge. So's Garrett's. It's rainin' men, hallelujah!!

MY HOMEY! And his ol', beat-round-the-world-blisterin' axe in his huge skilled hands. The ol' scrapper is handed off to…CatSkill! Top Cat's standin' next to the angel. Both smilin' like cats in fish bliss, skip that cream stuff.

"Cool Cat! It is you, my friend?" No hood talk ever come out of his mouth. One educated player.

Home boy crumples to his knees, tremblin' hand stretchin' to me.

Hell yeah, it's me. I will survive, I get along. Simultaneously, I'm stuck in place yet feel a string strugglin' to cannon me forward.

"Cool Cat," huge hands swipe at his wet puss. "I looked for you, buddy. I looked for weeks, took every road out of that hell-hole after catching up with the road-rash, shanghai, good-for-nothing. He couldn't remember what route he drove out… Saw you gave him one fond remembrance he'll never forget…" He's trippin' on words, emotional-like.

Home boy tried to find me? Me! He…he did…does care!

I ain't too proud to beg. I let that tug propel me- shoot the hoop- and I'm in his hands, in his arms, snuggled into his gushin' peepers- jeepers, creepers!

I come a long way from 'don't touch dis'.

'You bet I had that J.C. spoutin' hound dog seein' double vision wit my 16-bar that's life givin' him what-for. No happy days for his a...butt. Word.'

"I know, Cool Cat. He won't be sneaking off with any more cats, either."

He's softly strokin' my coat. I'm bussin' his puss. I feel plops of tears. Til a sudden realization- Homey gets my drift? Flash, bam, alakazam- I'm on the bright side of the road! Who could ask for anything more?

"Cool Cat, I think I always understood you, friend. Being a traveling man, I didn't think you'd be cool with giving up your lifestyle to be cooped up in a van for hours on end. I would have invited you..."

Ain't got to sing is you is or is you ain't my homey. Word.

Rain drops are fallin' on my head, less they're mine fallin' on my feet? From somewhere deep inside me I dig out an unfamiliar tune and purr loudly in his ear, lap his saturated face while he gently makes over me.

"Thank you, thank you," he whispers aside to CatSkill- who else? No secrets from a shaman of his caliber.

'Thank you, CatSkill,' I trill and buss my boy upside his head, over and over. I'm on the top of the world, never ever felt this good.

"You're very welcome, my good friends. Signed, sealed, delivered, eh, Strut?"

'You da man, CatSkill, you da man,' and I return my attention fully to my homey.

I feel another gentle, insistent paw or two pattin' my back. Brings me to…a sensibility of sorts.

"I see you've got a little honey, or two." Homey eyes my kits with a smile big as all get out.

'Yes sir, thems my babies. Blue- she's sweet child of mine, and my friend, Catch. Both kits are my pride and joy,' I boast.

"And very talented; I heard your duet with Blue. We'll play Sweet Child of Mine and some other great tunes- like we used to, Cool Cat. Or should I call you Strut?"

'Call me whatever you want- just don't call me late to grub or practice! Now my homey, Catch, is gettin' into the whole music scene. I'm larnin' her good,' I wink at Catch. Won't do to let Catch feel left out. 'She's showin' pos'bilities, too. If I'm lyin' I'm dyin'.'

Both kits, Catch a little on the shy side, man up to my homeboy. I have to disengage Blue from around his neck. She's playin' wit da beads swingin' in his hair, claws tanglin', for the love of a… Hey, I wonder if he brought a pizza!

"Pizza next time, I promise," Homey steps up.

Next time, Good Golly, Miss Molly, I'm jonesin' on the sound of that! Havin' my homey mind-speakin' is da shi…is da BOMB!

"I think we now have the makings of a jam group fit to rock the roof off. My Wife, Bonnie, hasn't heard your like before, Strut, and I'm pleased to see you've acquired back-up singers."

"Hello, Strut, Catch, and Blue," the angel who aided Sky on that comeuppance night- when CatSkill and I tag-teamed sendin' the hood billies to bluesdom for real- sing-songs greetings.

252

"I can't wait to hear you jam. Riordan's been on needles and pins in anticipation. He loves to sing!"

CatSkill sings, for real? Well, let's get dis party started!

'All I gotta say is, if the barn's rockin', don't bother knockin', jist come on in!'

"Ready, Cool Cat?" My homey's lookin' for the signal to count it off.

'Born to be wild 'n ready, M'man, you know me!'

'Groupies ready?' Garrett releases his hold on Sky and adjusts his guitar strap, fingers his pick.

'No groupies, my back-up singers- Strut and his Supremes,' I correct him. Takes me a loaded sec to realize scar-face Garrett unnerstands zactly what dis here cat's talkin' 'bout! He's got dat shi…poop-eatin' grin plastered on his puss. Too cool for school! Mind-speak is gittin' learned- 'bout time humans get together.

How lucky can one cat be? Ain't it a kick in the head?

I pour my heart into my homeboy's dark, no longer water-drownin' eyes. All my past hurtin' is total wipe out. All cuz of CatSkill, my main man. Best watch myself or I'll be cry baby.

CatSkill's angel smiles mysteriously up at him as he nods my way at my seein' clearly now. Sky claps happily, winks at me. Darned if Singer Sky hadn't known all along 'bout me! And so did Catch. The way Yogi's tuned in I believe he had my number, too.

Didn't bluff nobody but myself… Lonely, hurtin' days all gone, at last.

'Just count us off,' I challenge before the sweet emotion gets us all sidetracked.

"You ready, Sky?" Homey lifts his chin at Sky, receives a cue, adjusts his pick-ups and…

"Told you I had a surprise." Sky's biggest smile is for…me!

Homeboy leads off with a lightnin' riff that mellows, slows, sustains.

"Ain't got the… ain't got nothin' but the blues."

La, listen to dat nat'ral croonin'!

Sing to me, baby girl! I knew she had it in her; talk 'bout mellifluous tone, natural vibrato, vocal range, depth of feelin'- wow, can she draw out a note! Etta, eat your heart out- got some comp'tition here, Lady Blue.

Sky and I duet fit to bring down the house, and Blue and Catch softly sing it on home with Garrett diggin' on rhythm and my homey layin' it full-throttle on his ol' guitar. Wrapped up in each other, CatSkill and Bonnie sway to the blues beat.

Boo dances and yips at opportune moments- hittin' it right on the beat. Yogi wags his plume tail in applause. Shiloh and Dessert nod their big heads and wander outside with farewell whinnies. Too bluesy for yas?

"Hey, what's up, homehorses?" CatSkill salutes the tail end of the equine contingent. "Where's the song list, Rom, Strut?"

"Strut, I told you Riordan can't resist," she snuggles into her shaman man.

"I'd like to sing a number," Garrett shrugs, shyly. "I could fill in on some older tunes- like Everly Brothers songs."

'Stead of curlin' my puss on his idea of material, I dither, 'How 'bout later? Do dat bird dog number? It's a jam session and we all play star. No player haters, here.' I know he gets the memo, cuz he nods with a silly grin- really sets off the ol' scar. Whew, the house is loaded wit gangstas!

'All right, Top Cat, let's see what ya got,' I challenge CatSkill.

And he joyfully joins in on my theme song. I walk him down wit my homey and hit da highlights. Ooooh yeah, listen to dat cat go! CatSkill's got mojo in dem vocals- surprise, surprise!

Stray Cat Strut- dat's me- no Tennessee bird walk goin' down! And I throw in a little pimp daddy strut on my way downtown. Oh, happy day!

Durin' lead time my homey and I cut heads, cuz we got it like dat. Just like old times, but way, way better. We stay, kinda linger on, seems no one wants to quit.

But soon after, I sense my Supremes tirin', so I cue m'man, CatSkill, my homey, Garrett and Sky and we end on a sweet note.

As our due, we stars savor the whistles and clappin'. He...heck we're whoopin' it up, too. Even the clacker/crappers join in- a true barn jamboree, though the pussyfooters are right scarce.

Sittin' next to my homey, I give Sky a mighty slow wink of approval and gratitude before gittin' down to bidness, 'Treat time?'

Oh, what a night!

The best sound in the whole world- my new band. Homey on his gangsta guitar, Sky and I duet, Blue and I duet, Homey and me cuttin' heads, CatSkill layin' it on, and the rest comin' in in timely fashion. I got the world on a string.

'Tell it like it is,' I croon to my fellow jammers, 'cuz we are family!'

Guess my homeboy been lookin' for a home, too- like that ol' boll weevil asingin'.

With Sky and Garrett hitchin' up, Homey's offered Garrett's and C Nova's barn apartment close by.

"It's time I decide where to sink some roots," I hear him tell Garrett. "I thank you for the opportunity to…return to the land, play and sing my songs, and especially, hang out with my best friend, Cool Cat Strut."

Me, I aint' walkin' after midnight lookin' for a rumble, lookin' for some tush, or any ol' thang. Nah, I got 'sponsibilities. Gotta raise up Blue and Catch to keep it real and cool. And I got…friends, family! Even makin' inroads wit da pussyfooters, 'magine dat!

Used to believe the boll weevil gotta be trippin'. The dumbest thing- livin' and singin' 'bout lookin' for a home. He…heck, the whole da…darn world's my home, but I'm singin' it a might different today:

When the winds and rain come rattlin'

You won't find this cat skedaddlin'.

Be singin' blues easy and loose

From the top of my phat warm roost.

Cuz I been struttin', been struttin' my way home-

Took me some long roads, took me some close calls

Struttin' my way home!

Struttin' home!

I'm straight up and flyin' right. What a wonderful world, eh Satchmo?

Strut's eclectic song list born of his numerous adventures. Surprise, surprise- not all blues. Check your list- did you find them all?

1- Insensitive, Anything You Can Do I Can Do Better, I Hear You Knockin', Johnny B. Good, One Step At A Time, King Of The Road, Cathy's Clown, Ol' Black Magic, Got My Mojo Workin', Sweet Emotion, Rock-n-Roll Heaven, Rip It Up, Me And The Devil, Tell It Like It Is, Takin' Care Of Business, Give Me One Reason To Stay Here, Brickhouse, Pride & Joy

2- Born Under A Bad Sign, Further On Up The Road, Bridge Over Troubled Waters, Tell It Like It Is, Cotton Fields Back Home, Boom Boom, Dust In The Wind, Good Vibrations, Born To Be Wild, That's Life, Lookin' For Love, Ooh Child, Whiskey Blues, I Put A Spell On You, Rock Around The Clock, Bring It On Home, Hit The Road Jack, One For My Baby And One More For The Road, Birth Of The Blues, Learnin' The Blues, The Gambler, Respect, Walkin' After Midnight, Bare Necessities, Bad Moon Risin', Crossroad Blues, Got My Mojo Workin', This Magic Moment, 13 Women, Blue Moon, Piece Of My Heart, One Step At A Time, Call Me The Breeze, Poor Side Of Town, Young Blood, Heart And Soul, Jump Jive And Wail, Bad Boys, Nobody's Baby

3- Zat You, Anticipation, Hey Good Lookin', Jesse's Girl, Walk Like A Man, Come Together, How Long How Long,

4- Turn On The Love Light, Keep Your Hands To Yourself, Respect, Black Magic Woman, Hell On Heels, Takin' Care Of Business, Hellzapoppin',

Think, Bring It On Home, Dust My Broom, Get Ready, Stray Cat Strut, Come A Little Bit Closer, My Way

5- See Ya Later Alligator, Born To Be Wild, Ain't I Tough Enough, It Ain't Me Babe, The Gambler, Don't Mess Around With Jim, Bad To The Bone, War, Save My Soul New Orleans, Hellhound On My Trail, I Can't Help Myself, Sweet Nothin's, Go Away Little Girl, Get Back Jack Do It Again, Blue Moon, I Hear Ya Knockin', Yackety Yak, Bright Lights Big City, Boogie Chillen, Sweet Child Of Mine,

6- Got Me Runnin', Blues In The Night, She Thinks My Tractor's Sexy, Friends In Low Places, I'm Walkin', Hit Me With Your Best Shot, Welcome To The Blues

7- Down On The Corner, Old-Fashioned Love Song, Slow Ride, Satisfaction, I Will Survive, Highway To Hell, Won't You Come Home Bill Bailey, Who's Sorry Now, Sunny Side Of The Street

8- Dirty Work, Rock & Roll Heaven, Welcome To The Blues, Kentucky Rain, Feelings, Pappa Was A Rollin' Stone, One Step At A Time, Nobody Knows You When You're Down And Out,

9- Tumblin' Dice, Still Of The Night, Hellzapoppin', Singin' The Blues, Come To Papa, Lookin' For A Home, Just One Of Those Things,

10- Rockabye Baby, Silhouette, Sound Of Silence, New York New York, Feelin' All Right, Smooth, Wayward Wind, House Of The Rising Sun, War, I Put A Spell On You, My Blue Heaven, On The Road Again

11- Shake Your Booty, Walk On, Freebird, Mind Your Own Business, Minnie The Moocher, Daydreamin' Boy, Guitar Man, Peaceful Easy Feeling, Light My Fire, Crazy, Feelings, Gotta Sing Gotta Dance, Smooth, Got My Mojo Workin', Workout, Evil Ways, Long Tall Woman In A Black Dress, Just In

Time, Malaguena, Tomorrow, La Bamba, Jumpin' Jack Flash, Johnny B. Good, Turn On Your Love Light, Every Day, I've Got The Blues, Hitchin' A Ride, Something's Got A Hold On Me, Thrill Is Gone, All Right Now, Just One Of Those Things

12- I Ain't Got Nobody, Footloose, Tomorrow, Don't Worry Bout Nothing, That's Life, Further On Up The Road, Wang Dang Doodle, Twist And Shout, Fly Me To The Moon, If The House Is Rockin', Spooky, Mack The Knife, Lay It On The Line,

13- See Ya Later Alligator, That's Life, Slip Slidin' Away, I Need A Hero, Bad Bad Leroy Brown, One More For The Road, Hey Bartender, Slow Ride, Takin' Care Of Business, Still Of The Night, Steppin' Out, Further On Up The Road, Thrill Is Gone, Blues In The Night, Boogie Shoes

14- When The Blues Come Knockin', High Steppin' Daddy, Takin' Care Of Business, Mack The Knife, Lady Sings The Blues, You Got Another Thing Comin', Stuck In The Middle With You, Down So Long Down Don't Bother Me, Keep on Moving, You Got Me Runnin', Hit The Road Jack, Moon River, Dreamin', Fools Rush In, Beat Me Daddy 8 To The Bar, You Put A Spell On Me, I fought The Law

15- Crazy, In The Jailhouse Now, Birth Of The Blues, Sugar Sugar, St. James Infirmary, Got A Hold On Me, Get Back, Nobody Knows You When You're Down And Out, Til We Meet Again, Got My Mojo Workin', Turn Me Loose, War, Bring It On Home, I Got You Babe, Jailhouse Rock, Freebird, Jump Jive And Wail, Wang Dang Doodle, Come Fly With Me, Shake Rattle And Roll, Sailing, Shame Shame, Over The Rainbow, England Swings, I Can See Clearly Now, Rip It Up And Ball Tonight, Chain Of Fools, Matchbox, Highway To Hell, Rico Suave, Get Ready, How Come You Do Me Like You Do

16- Bicycle Built For Two, Strangers In The Night, I'm A Believer, House Is Rockin', Respect, Hit The Road Jack, Dizzy, Up On The Roof, Walkin' After Midnight, That's Life, Smooth, Roof Is On Fire, Crossroads, Ramblin', Summer Wind, You Don't Own Me

17- Pretty Woman, Hey Good Lookin' Watcha Got Cookin', Shake Rattle And Roll, Move It On Over, Sound Of Silence, Walk Like A Man, My Blue Heaven, Yellow Brick Road, Follow Your Leader, Get Ready, Slip Slidin' Away, Pave Paradise, Bright Lights, Them There Eyes, Should I Stay Or Should I Go Now

18- Cryin' In The Rain, Wayward Wind, Give Me One Reason, Sweet Home Chicago, I Don't Ever Want To Feel That Way Again, I Don't Want To Talk About It, Memories, Venus, Tears In Heaven, Sugar Sugar, Burnin' Love, Route 66, Jim Dandy, Learnin' The Blues, Down Don't Bother Me, I'm Walkin', Saturday Night's Alright

19- Lookin' For Love, Tush, Keep Me Hangin' On, Further On Up The Road, Doin' What Comes Naturally, Yackety Yak, Sweet Child Of Mine, Moon River, Sailin', My Man's An Undertaker, Goody Goody, Under My Skin, Stormy Monday, Shame Shame, I Got It Bad And That Ain't Good, Respect, Don't Worry Bout Nothin' Cuz Nothin' Gonna Be Alright, On The Road Again, The Wanderer

20- Comin' Round The Mountain, Told You So, Homeward Bound, Look On The Bright Side Of Life, Ramblin' On My Mind, Ramble On, Respect, Hound Dog, Bad To The Bone, Little Wing, Young Blood, Boot Scootin' Boogie, Lookin' For Love In All The Wrong Places, You Gonna Miss Me The Day That I'm Gone, Dreamin', Light My Fire, Wang Dang Doodle

21- Tell 'Em I'll Be There, Freaks Come Out At Night, Mr. Grinch, Fa Who Dor Ay, Born To Be Wild, Please Come Home For Christmas, Blue Moon, Rock Around The Clock, You Got Another Thing Comin', Under My Thumb, Satisfaction, Starry Starry Night, Got My Mojo Workin', Silent Night, In The Mood, Something's Got A Hold On Me, Santa Baby, Here You Go Again, Sound Of Silence, Blow The Man Down, Whole Lotta Shakin' Goin' On, This Magic Moment

22- The Stroll, Sound Of Silence, At Last, I Get Around, Little Less Talk And A Lot More Action, Penny Whistle Peddler, Moon River, Strangers In The Night, Choo Choo Cha-Boogie, Bring It On Home, Yesterday, Every Day, Put A Spell On You, Drift Away, Hootchie Cootchie Man, Further On Up The Road, Raindrops Keep Fallin' On My Head, Don't Worry Bout Nothin' Cuz Nothin' Gonna Be Alright, Stormy Monday, What's Goin' On, Call Me The Breeze, Spirit In The Sky

23- Here Comes Santa Claus, Boom Boom Out Go The Lights, Steppin' Out, Rock All Our Blues Away, Born To Be Wild, I Could Have Danced All Night

24- Who Let The Dogs Out, Every Breath You Take, Because The Night, I Need A Hero, Hellzapoppin', Saturday's All Right For Fightin', Boy From New York City, Stormy Weather, You Really Got Me, You Got Another Thing Comin', Day Dreamin' Boy, Cry Baby, Hallelujah, Highway To Hell, Dancin' In The Dark, Sway

25- I'm Still Standin', Good Vibrations, My Girl, In The Arms Of An Angel, Dreamin', He Ain't Heavy, You Got Another Thing Comin', Wang Dang Doodle, Say It Isn't So, The Roof Is On Fire, Jailhouse Rock, Fascination, High Steppin' Daddy, Boy Named Sue, 2

Out Of 3 Ain't Bad, Tumblin' Dice, Let It Roll, Rock-n-Roll Hootchicoo, A Mess Of Blues

26- Party's Over, My Man's An Undertaker, Shame Shame, Good Golly Miss Molly, Lucille, Oh What A Night, Anticipation, Knockin' On Heaven's Door, Jump Jive And Wail, Take It Easy, My Way

27- You'll Never Get Me Out Of Your Mind, Stormy Monday, Lady Sings The Blues, Mind Your Own Business, I Know A Little, Feelings, See Ya Later Alligator

28- Spirit In The Sky, Somewhere Over The Rainbow, Earth Angel, Baby It's Cold Outside, On The Road Again, Let It Snow, Hit The Road Jack, Thanks For The Memories, Give Me That Old Time Religion, Mr. Sandman, Spirit In The Sky, Lonely Days, In The Cool Cool Of The Evening, Hard Lesson To Learn, One Step At A Time

29- Am I Blue, My Way, Boy Named Sue, Blues In The Night, Tell It Like It Is, Piece Of My Heart, My Man's Gone Now, Just For The Fun Of It, Get Your Kicks On Rt. 66, Head Out On The Highway, Turn Me Loose, Takin' Care Of Business, Save My Soul New Orleans, Hold On, Keep It Comin', Rock-n-Roll Heaven, All About The Blues, All About The Bass, While My Guitar Gently Weeps, Memories They Can't Take That Away From Me, Guitar Man, Little Wing, Good Time Charlie's Got The Blues, You Got Another Thing Comin', Music Of The Night, Midnight Hour, Let It Shine, Lookin' For A Home, Freebird, Blue Moon

30- Toredown, Rockin' The Casbah, Old Time Rock And Roll, Bird Dog, Daddy Cool, Boots Are Made For Walkin', Happy Together, Side By Side, We Are Family, Roll Out The Barrel, Trouble, Up A Lazy River, Day Dreamin', Dream A Little Dream,

Whatcha Know Joe, A Nightingale Sings In Berkeley Square

31- Great Balls Of Fire, Mama Mia, My Blue Heaven, Take Me To The River, I'm A Believer, Saturday Night's Alright For Fightin', I Need A Hero, Tough Enough, Tell It Like It Is, Walkin' The Dog, Sway, Changes, Celebrate, Wandrin' Eyes, Lady Come Down, My Way, Insensitive, One Step At A Time, Jump Jive And Wail, Hold On, Sweet Home Chicago, Wheel Of Fortune, Jeepers Creepers, Dixie, Twistin' The Night Away, Physical, I Feel The Earth Move, At Last, What A Feelin', Little Sister, Sweet Nothin's, Stray Cat Strut, Little Darlin', Your Song, Learning The Blues, What'll I Do, Why Don't You Want Me,

32- Am I Blue, Learning The Blues, Movin' On Up, Real Thing, Sugar Sugar, Ain't I Tough Enough, Easy Street, Mess Of Blues, Lucille, You Picked A Fine Time To Leave Me Lucille, I Got The Blues, World On A String, Summer Wind, Here I Go Again, Rico Suave, Smooth, La Vida Loca, C'mon A My House, Strangers In The Night, Moon River, All Right Now, Choo Choo Cha Boogie, I Gotta Tiger By The Tail, Tush, Dancin' Queen, Boy From New York City, The Night Has A 1000 Eyes, Me And My Gal, Ain't She Sweet, Hallelujah I Just Love Her So, Get Back, Can't Touch This, Keep Your Hands Off My Baby, Comin' Round The Mountain, Will I Stay Or Will I Go Now, Born To Be Wild, Walkin' On Sunshine, My Girl, Shooting Star, Rock-n-Roll Lullaby, Cry Me A River, Lil Darlin', My Way, Rollin' In The Deep

33- Stray Cat Strut, Rain On The Scarecrow, T'ain't Nothin' But The Blues, Freebird

34- Summertime, Lazy Bones, He's Got The Whole World, Put Me In Coach, Under The Boardwalk, Everyday, Ode To Joy, Together, Workout, Rainbow In The Dark, I'm A Believer, Day Dreamin' Boy,

Hold That Tiger, Hot Child In The City, Up Up And Away, Gloria, Old Time Rock-n-Roll, Kick In The Head, Green Acres, Born Free, I Will Survive, Stuck In The Middle With You, Too Hot To Handle, Splish Splash, Blue Bayou, Good Golly Miss Molly, Frog Kissin', I'm Beginning To See The Light, Hush Hush, Dang Me, I Fall To Pieces, Hell On Heels, Blues In The Night, It's A Man's World, Ain't Misbehavin', Slip Slidin' Away, Wang Dang Doodle, Flirtin' With Disaster, Mack The Knife, Gabriel Blow Your Horn, Ring My Bell, All About The Bass, Indian Love Call, Tomorrow

35- Doggone, Think, Under The Boardwalk, Them There Eyes, Singin' In The Rain, Splish Splash, England Swings, King Of The Road, Pennywhistle Peddler, Dancin' Queen, Hit The Road Jack, Puttin' On The Ritz, Roll Over Beethoven, Young Blood, Oh What A Night, Puttin' On The Ritz, Express Yourself, Workout, Devil Or Angel, Somebody Stole My Gal, By The Light Of The Silvery Moon, Too Close For Comfort, Moondance, Walkin' After Midnight, Too Late, Mr. Sandman, Sleepy Time Gal

36- Double Trouble, Stardust, Red Rubber Ball, I'm Lonely, What'd I Say, Little Sister, The Race Is On, Put Me In Coach, Daring Young Man On The Flying Trapeze, Sailing, Jump Jive And Wail, Clap Snap, You Got A Friend, Jim Dandy To The Rescue, Free Falling, Just In Time, Wild Blue Yonder, Let's Go Fly A Kite, Bring It On Home, Man Of Constant Sorrow, Splish Splash, Lay It On The Line, Rollin' And Tumblin', Keep Your Hands Off My Baby, Come To Papa, Just For The Fun Of It, Comin' Round The Mountain, Spoonful Of Sugar, Memories, Amazing Grace, Beautiful Ohio, Takin' Care Of Business, Cry Me A River, Wonderful World, Save My Soul New Orleans, Fast As You, Stop In The Name Of Love,

Sunny Side Of The Street, Shake Rattle And Roll, Satisfaction

37- Sleepy Time Gal, Midnight Special, Put Me In Coach, Sweet Home Chicago, Too Hot To Handle, My Gal, Hootchie Cootchie Man, Tears In Heaven, Light My Fire, It's Rainin' Men, Straighten Up And Fly Right, What A Wonderful World, Ooh Baby, Under The Boardwalk, Rock Me Baby, Dreamin', Put A Spell On You, I Will Survive, Ain't Too Proud To Beg, Jeepers Creepers, Hound Dog, Double Vision, That's Life, Happy Days, Pennywhistle Peddler, Flash Bam Alacazam, Bright Side Of The Road, Who Could Ask For Anything More, Travelin' Man, Is You Is Or Is You Ain't My Baby, Raindrops Are Fallin' On My Head, Top Of The World, Sweet Child Of Mine, Pride And Joy, Good Golly Miss Molly, Needles And Pins, Anticipation, If The House Is Rockin', Born To Be Wild, Get Together, Ain't That A Kick In The Head, Wipeout, Cry Baby, My Way, I Can See Clearly Now, Sweet Emotion, Ain't Got Nothin' But The Blues, Sway, Stay, Oh What A Night, Got The World On A String, Tell It Like It Is, We Are Family, Lookin' For A Honey, Walkin' After Midnight, Tush, Lookin' For A Home, Struttin' My Way Home, Straighten Up And Fly Right, What A Wonderful World

Many thanks to

My husband, Ronnie, for helping with slang terms.

Tery Metcalf, for most things musical and colorful adjectives.

The lovely musicians I still get to jam with: Victoria Grindle, Jimmy Grindle, Randy Vaughn, Mikey Lenehan, Tery Metcalf, Kitchicoo and Firefly- my purrin' kitties.

Pam Crouch, for sharing the story of her cat, Lucky, enthroned on the roof and being serenaded by his many amorous feline fans below.

To the muses that fascinate my life and all those who enjoy my stories- Many thanks for spending your time with me.

Correspondents welcome at: lisaannettepowell@gmail.com

Thanks for liking and sharing my CatSkill Trilogy Facebook page where all stories are celebrated.

www.ingramcontent.com/pod-product-compliance
Lightning Source LLC
Chambersburg PA
CBHW072211170626
46813CB00003B/887